Katharine's Remarkable Road Trip

Gail Ward Olmsted

Black Rose Writing | Texas

The author grants the final approval for this literary material.

First printing

This is a work of fiction. Names, characters, businesses, places, events, and incidents are
either the products of the author's imagination or used in a fictitious manner. Any
resemblance to actual persons, living or dead, or actual events is purely coincidental.

ISBN: 978-1-68513-432-7
PUBLISHED BY BLACK ROSE WRITING
www.blackrosewriting.com

Printed in the United States of America
Suggested Retail Price (SRP) $20.95

Katharine's Remarkable Road Trip is printed in Sabon Next

*As a planet-friendly publisher, Black Rose Writing does its best to eliminate unnecessary waste to
reduce paper usage and energy costs, while never compromising the reading experience. As a result,
the final word count vs. page count may not meet common expectations.

To my husband, Deane,
for a lifetime of love on *our* remarkable road trip!

Praise for
Katharine's Remarkable Road Trip

"Kate makes me want to take a road trip. She's lovable and charming, and her voice...SO GOOD."
~ **Kerry Chaput, award-winning author of the *Defying the Crown* series**

"They say the best authors reveal character not by describing it to the reader, but by revealing it through the protagonist's actions. I dare you to find anyone better at this art than Olmsted."
~ **Cam Torrens, bestselling author of *Stable* and *False Summit***

"Olmsted was able to integrate the details of Katharine's vivid life, but more importantly, she was able to capture the essence of the person which made Katharine special, and that was her kind and compassionate heart."
~ **The Historical Fiction Company**

"The characters are diverse and well developed, the memories are vivid, and Olmsted's flawless descriptions of early 20th century America will put you in Kate's shoes for the entire journey. It's a feel good story you won't want to end."
~ **Gary Gerlacher, author of *Last Patient of the Night* and *Faulty Bloodline***

"If you love genuine characters and the commentary that's shared, as well as more than a few surprises, be sure to pick up *Katherine's Remarkable Road Trip*, and join her on the ride of a lifetime."
~ **Mary Ann Noe, author of *Water the Color of Slate***

"This excellent novel reminds us that there are so many women in history whose stories need to be told. Because Katharine's life was so remarkable, it isn't too far-fetched to imagine that she did indeed have a remarkable road trip like this toward the end of her life."
~ **Diane Nagatomo, author of *The Butterfly Cafe***

"A wonderful novel, the author immerses the reader in Katharine's life and those of her secondary characters in this most engaging work of historical fiction."
~ **Sublime Book Review**

To my husband, Deane,
for a lifetime of love on *our* remarkable road trip!

BIOGRAPHICAL NOTE

Katharine Prescott Wormeley, Civil War volunteer nurse, hospital administrator, educator, author, translator, and philanthropist, was born on January 14, 1830, in Ipswich, Suffolk, England. Her parents were Admiral Ralph Randall Wormeley and Caroline Wormeley, née Preble. Her father had been born in Virginia, but after the untimely death of his mother, he was sent to live in England, where he later entered the navy and became a British subject. Her mother was the daughter of Ebenezer Preble, a wealthy East India merchant from Boston, and his third wife, Elizabeth.

Katharine (Kate) was the third of four children and grew up on the eastern coast of England in a home filled with laughter and friends. Steeped in maritime history, the nearby waterfront was always bustling, in sharp contrast to the rolling hills and pastoral countryside that could be found inland. She attended schools in both London and Paris, where she studied the classics, learned to read and speak French fluently and to play the piano, preparing her for the anticipated future of most well-bred girls of her generation, that of wife to a professional man—a banker or solicitor. But marriage and a family were *not* the path that young Kate envisioned for herself.

Although a respected officer in the British Navy, Admiral Wormeley's vocal support of Liberal causes caused him to fall out of favor with his Tory friends. An early retirement appeared to be the most sensible choice. The family relocated to the United States when Kate was eighteen and settled in Newport, Rhode Island. A few years later, her older brother, James, contracted tuberculosis and died, and in 1852 her father suffered a fatal stroke. Firstborn Eliza married Randolph Latimer of Baltimore, and together they lived a rich and cultured life of privilege with their three children. She was renowned as a translator and an author of multiple volumes of European history. The youngest, Ariana, was a gifted writer as well, and after marrying Daniel Curtis, a prominent banker and patron of the arts, she lived in Boston with her husband and their two sons before moving permanently to Venice.

As the unmarried daughter, it was Kate's responsibility to look after her mother. The two women enjoyed hosting guests or taking off on an excursion at a moment's notice, and soon became involved in a number of philanthropic and charitable causes in their adopted hometown.

At the outbreak of the Civil War, Kate formed a local Women's Aid Society and, after securing a government contract, was able to employ local women, primarily the wives and daughters of soldiers, to produce some fifty thousand flannel shirts during the winter of 1861- 62. Soon after, she joined the hospital transport service of the recently created United States Sanitary Commission (USSC). She served as a volunteer nurse on hospital ships during the Peninsular Campaign, caring for sick and wounded Union soldiers. After returning home, she accepted the position of Lady Superintendent at the Lovell General Hospital in Portsmouth Grove, Rhode Island, where she was in charge of daily operations for the 700-bed facility.

After the war, she once more focused on volunteer efforts and in 1879 started the Newport Charity Organization Society and served on the board for the next fifteen years. Seeking an opportunity to enable young women to learn trades and become more employable, Kate founded the Newport Industrial School for Girls, offering classes in cooking, sewing, dressmaking, and household work. She funded the entire budget herself for three years until the school was taken over by the city of Newport.

Dividing her time between Newport and her newly acquired home in Jackson, New Hampshire, and scaling down on her volunteer efforts, Kate devoted herself to translating into English the literary works of French authors, including Honore de Balzac,

Alexandre Dumas, and Moliere. An accomplished French scholar, she became a highly sought after translator based on her keen understanding of French culture.

Following a fall on the steps of her home in New Hampshire, Kate contracted pneumonia and died on August 4, 1908. Her cremated remains were buried in Newport beside the grave of her father.

Her own published works include: *The Other Side of War* (1889) and *A Memoire of Honore de Balzac* (1892). She is included in *History's Women: The Unsung Heroines; History of American Women: Civil War Women; Who's Who in America 1908-09; Notable American Women, A Biographical Dictionary: 1607-1950* and *A Woman of the 19th Century: Leading American Women in All Walks of* Life and figures prominently in *With Courage and Delicacy: Civil War on the Peninsula.*

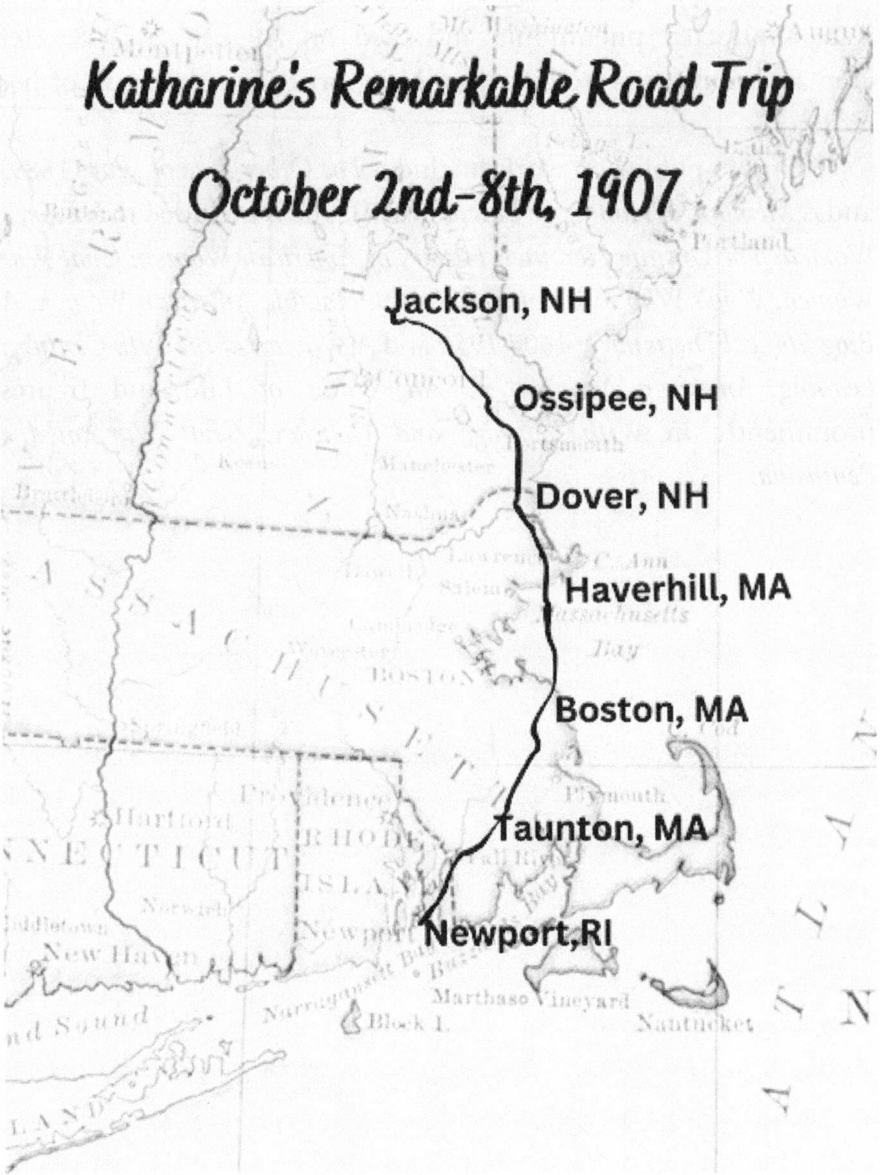

Katharine's Remarkable Road Trip

October 2nd-8th, 1907

Jackson, NH

Ossipee, NH

Dover, NH

Haverhill, MA

Boston, MA

Taunton, MA

Newport, RI

Katharine's Remarkable Road Trip

"It's not the destination; it's the journey."
–Ralph Waldo Emerson (1803-1882)

CHAPTER 1

Newport, Rhode Island
Wednesday, October 2, 1907

I held the telephone's mouthpiece as far from my ear as I was able, but my sister's shrill voice could still be heard. I did not want to believe that Mr. Alexander Graham Bell had invented the telephone for the sole purpose of my younger sister screeching at me from two hundred miles away. Clearly, he'd had far loftier goals in mind. It was definitely time to assert myself back into the conversation since tuning her out for the past several minutes had not produced the desired effect of a change in the topic of discussion or, even better, blessed silence.

"Ariana, you know that I have made the trip between my two homes on dozens of occasions, yes?" Before she could respond, I continued. "And you know that I have crossed the Atlantic more times than I can count. And that I served on a medical ship during the Civil War and ran a hospital and founded a school?" I waited for verbal confirmation, assuming that she was nodding.

"Yes, but . . ." she finally conceded.

"If you know all those things, then why exactly do you feel I am incapable of making the drive from here in Newport up to New Hampshire?"

"Because you're all alone, and I love you and I worry about you," came her slightly muffled reply.

I let out a long sigh. I knew she loved me and that she worried about me and, yes, I was most definitely alone. That fact was indisputable. For most of my seventy-seven years, I had been alone. I tried to adopt a gentler tone.

"A, it's going to be fine. You'll see. My car is brand new, and Jasper down at the garage just checked it out for me. Gave it a clean bill of health. There is absolutely nothing for you to worry about."

"But on your own? All that way? You're getting up there in years, you know." I chuckled at that, as my sister was only four years my junior. "You had a doctor's appointment last week, didn't you? What does your doctor say about this folly of yours?"

Oh my. I hated to lie to my own sister, but sometimes a small fib really was in order. "Yes, dear. I saw Doc Hopkins last week. He said that I was as healthy as a horse." My breath caught in my throat as I recalled his actual words to me. The word "healthy" had never been mentioned. Not once. But there was no time to think about that now. I needed to hurry this along if I was going to make it to Taunton in nearby Massachusetts, my scheduled stop for the evening. A close friend of mine had lived there for years after her marriage. Sarah had passed a couple of years back, but I had remained in contact with her husband, Edward, who had invited me for dinner and an overnight on my way to New Hampshire.

"Edward Talbot has suggested that he might like to travel the rest of the way with me," I lied, this time without any hesitation, as this was a prevarication on a much smaller scale as well as of much less importance. "So I'll probably be on my own just for today. There is nothing to worry about," I repeated with a touch of finality. "I need to get going." I cut her off before she could respond. "And, of course, I'll call you tonight from Edward's," I promised. "I love you, and please don't worry. Give my love to Daniel. Goodbye for now." I hung up the phone, feeling relieved to have checked off the call from my to-do list. As much as I appreciated her sisterly concern, it irked me just how much effort she expended worrying about little old me. Hadn't I proven time and again that I was quite capable and could take care of myself? Indeed, I had!

I unplugged the icebox and made certain that the doors were locked securely and then paused to look around my home. It was located in the center of Newport, the sparkling oceanfront city where I had lived for nearly sixty years. Red Beech Cottage was meant to be my forever home; until recently, I could not have imagined ever giving it up. But I had bought and sold two homes up in Jackson, New Hampshire, beginning sixteen years ago on a whim. The first was too drafty and not large enough to entertain my guests properly. The second home was larger and closer to the center of town, but the lot was small, and the water supply to the home proved to be woefully inadequate. Twelve years ago, I built a third home on a lovely one-acre plot on Thorn Hill Road and had it properly winterized. I named it Brookmead, and I had spent a good amount of time there ever since. John Riordan, a gentleman friend of mine back then, had referred to me as Goldilocks when we were alone. "This one is too small. This one is too dry. But this one is just right," he would whisper in my ear. I laughed aloud at the memory. Good old John. I vaguely recalled hearing he had remarried and moved out west somewhere. Colorado, maybe?

I planned to live at Brookmead for the next several months and, possibly, for the rest of my life. If Doc Hopkins's prediction was accurate, it would appear that I was likely to enjoy only a couple more trips around the sun. His words had left me reeling, certain that his reasoning was flawed or that he was underestimating my determination, my will to live. But in the past week, I had started to come to terms with my mortality. I was certainly not going to simply give up, but in reflecting on the past seventy-seven years, I realized it had been a good run, and my list of goals and things I needed to do in whatever time I had left was manageable. At the very top was a heart-to-heart conversation with S. I wanted to clear the air and set things right between us. My confession was long overdue and something I planned to accomplish toward the end of my trip.

It had been a hot and very humid summer this close to the ocean, and the promise of crisp and clean mountain air was most appealing, as was snow, real heaps of snow, that would blanket the woods surrounding my cozy home. Not like the insipid stuff we usually received down here—a thin coating of flakes that quickly melted or turned to gray sludge on the very same day. The *Farmers' Almanac* indicated it would be a snowy winter, and I looked forward to it. I planned to host friends for casual Sunday suppers, take long bracing walks, read the stacks of books I had been acquiring in front of a roaring fire, and, following my doctor's orders, get plenty of rest. It was quiet up north, and I relished the idea of escaping from the hectic life I lived here, my daily schedule packed with committee meetings and luncheons for the various charities and civic groups of which I was a member.

I had traveled to New Hampshire with friends in the past, most frequently by train, but this solo trip in my new car felt like the best course of action at this moment. I chuckled at the ridiculous idea that I had planted in Ariana's head about Edward Talbot traveling with me. The very thought! He would insist on doing all the driving and smoking those foul cigars of his and, based on Sarah's account of trips she had taken with him, would need to stop for frequent bathroom breaks. A five- or six-day journey would turn into a two-week odyssey if Edward had anything to say about it! No, this was a trip I had envisioned taking on my own for some time. If not now, then when?

I shook my head to rid my brain of my doctor's grim pronouncement as I gathered up the last of my things and made my way to the garage, where my newly purchased vehicle was freshly washed, waxed, and ready to go. I vowed I would be very careful, and at the first sign of a problem, I would . . . Well, I honestly hadn't thought that far, and there was no sense borrowing trouble. I would be fine, just fine. I had to be. "My chariot awaits," I murmured to myself. I went through the quick series of steps to get it started and, after cranking the engine, was rewarded with a robust growl from under the hood. I patted the steering wheel appreciatively, and seconds later I was off! This trip was mine and mine alone to navigate, and I planned to treasure every single moment.

Why, who knew what sort of exciting adventures I might discover along the way?

CHAPTER 2

I set out through the busy streets of the bustling city I loved, determined not to become maudlin reflecting on all that I was leaving behind. I would maintain close relationships with a handful of dear friends; of that I was certain. Most were in good health and certainly had the wherewithal to come and visit me as they pleased, and I would welcome them with open arms. As far as my neighbors and the women I knew through the various charitable organizations I was a part of, well, that's what writing letters was for. I hoped I would correspond regularly with several of them, if for no other reason than to stay abreast of the latest comings and goings in this little corner of the world. I knew that not all of these relationships would survive the distance, but I was looking forward to a fresh start, and certain sacrifices would naturally have to be made.

I drove toward the newly rebuilt Stone Bridge in order to cross the Sakonnet River into Tiverton, leaving the island of Newport. Despite its name, the bridge was constructed of steel and had been completed earlier this year. I had driven over the original wooden bridge, which it had replaced, literally hundreds of times and was grateful for the much-improved driving conditions. Traffic was light, and I crossed without incident, letting go of the breath I had been holding once I was back on solid ground. Driving over water never failed to unnerve me. Imagine that; I was not only a British Navy brat, but had served on a hospital ship during the war for goodness' sake.

Once I was off-island, the roadways were relatively clear as it was the middle of the day, and I imagined most locals were at work or enjoying their lunch at home. The sun was shining, and it was a lovely early fall day. I knew that the seasonal foliage would be even more spectacular as I drove farther north. I had promised my housekeeper that I would take her for a drive around the area to see the fabulous fall colors that had first drawn me to the White Mountain region many years ago. Hilma Pitman was a no-nonsense, quite capable sort of woman living on the Jackson property with her husband, Arba, who took care of the grounds. They were a wonderful couple, and I counted them as friends.

Despite all the assurances I had given to my sister, as well as to friends and neighbors in both Rhode Island and New Hampshire, I was *not* 100 percent confident in my skills at driving or navigating a journey like this alone. The 270-mile trek might prove to be a bit more daunting than I had let on, given road conditions, changes in the weather, and potential car trouble. I had been warned by my doctor to watch for signs of fatigue as well as any shortness of breath and had given myself an extra couple of days to allow for briefer stretches of driving each day. Although I planned to stay on the main roads, keep my travel to daylight hours only, and had an itinerary planned with overnight stops along the way, anything could happen, and I hoped I would have the good fortune to arrive safe and sound, on my own, and in just less than a week.

At least for today, I was making good time and felt confident that I would turn up at the Talbot home by 5:00 p.m. as promised. If I was any later, I could guarantee that Edward would become grumpy, impatiently waiting for me in order that he might indulge in a pre-dinner glass or two of sherry. It was unlikely that he would start without me, despite the fact that he apparently spent most every evening on his own, rambling about in that huge house on the hill since Sarah had passed. What a dear and treasured friend was Sarah Andrews Talbot. I had met her soon after moving to America with my family in 1848. I knew not a soul in this strange new land, but quickly found a best friend for life when I met Sarah, quite literally the girl next door. It may have been just a lucky coincidence, but I believe it was fate that of all the homes in town, my family had purchased the one closest to Sidney and Diana Andrews and their eighteen-year-old daughter. We became inseparable, despite the efforts of my pesty younger sister, who enjoyed spying on us and interrupting our conversations.

I smiled, thinking of my spirited sister Ariana. She had grown from an uninvited tagalong to a trusted confidante and friend. For many years, our relationship had been comprised of writing letters, interspersed with her annual visits to Newport and New York City. She and her husband were currently staying with their son at his home in New York for another week or two. Our relationship was still a close one, but her recent obsession with this trip I was on made me somewhat relieved that she would be going back home soon. Being in her beloved Italy would provide a much-needed distraction from worrying about her misguided spinster of a sister, living all alone in the frozen tundra of the north.

Despite my unmarried state, or possibly because of it, I have experienced true love and passion of the romantic sort a number of times during my lifetime. I've had affairs of the heart, as well as those that were physically consummated. I never told my family, but I once even halfheartedly entertained a proposal of marriage for nearly two days before respectfully declining. The men that I am referring to were all lovely in their way. Some were dear friends, others more casual acquaintances. To look at me today, you would see a gray-haired, plainly dressed, and slightly stooped older woman, but in my heyday I was quite attractive, fashionable, and lively. As a matter of fact, the well-known landscape architect Mr. Frederick Law Olmsted once introduced me as his "most fetching friend." Imagine that!

Despite these close friends and paramours, I have stayed the course with my original plan of remaining single. I much prefer the term "single" to "unmarried"; I believe it sounds more deliberate, like it was something I chose as opposed to how I just happened to end up. Would I have enjoyed the companionship of a loyal and loving husband to accompany me on a journey like the one I had just embarked upon? Well, yes, perhaps I might, but honestly? If I had ever married, the experiences I've had, the love I've known, and the work that has sustained me would likely not have occurred. My life would certainly have progressed in an entirely different direction, perhaps even one that included children. That might have been fulfilling, but those are the regrets that I must not dwell on, especially not on a lovely day such as this. For today, I was relatively healthy, possessed of sound mind and spirit, and financially secure. I felt confident that I would leave this earth in a state better than I had found it, and there's nothing better than that. I certainly knew that I had much to be grateful for in my life, but I admit to occasionally falling victim to the what-ifs. Eliza had passed away a few years ago, and with Ariana and her husband living in Italy, I was the last Wormeley living here in the States. The only one. *Stop dwelling on the losses,* I scolded myself. *Just enjoy this most beautiful of days.*

I stopped to stretch my legs, pulling onto a section of grass along the side of the road, somewhere just outside of Fall River. I had been noticing with a touch of alarm that my legs tended to cramp up if I sat still too long. That had never been a problem for me in my prime, as I had rarely been at rest and had always thrown myself into whatever project or passion I was pursuing. As a young girl, I had been constantly in motion, running through the fields surrounding our home with my siblings, climbing trees, or swimming in the pond on our property. Ariana and I taught ourselves to skate when it froze, causing our mother to worry constantly and beg us to stay close to the shore. I admit that we rarely heeded her advice and on more than one occasion found it necessary to return to the house and sneak up to our rooms, our clothes dripping and our teeth chattering when the thin ice near the stream that fed our pond had given way. Eliza could always be counted on to bring us towels and dry clothes, and sweets had been an effective bribe to keep James from squealing on us.

There was no doubt in my mind that the relatively sedentary life of a writer/translator was a key contributor to the aches and pains I had been experiencing of late, although some of the blame should rightly be attributed to my advancing years on this earth. At least until the heavy snows that were part and parcel to life in northern New England from early December until well into April arrived, I would need to keep to my goal of taking at least two long walks every day, beginning as soon as I arrived in New Hampshire. I pictured my cozy home and the dozens of nearby paths and winding trails I still had yet to explore. Many offered views of the breathtaking mountains, as well as the most rugged and challenging terrain in the region. Naturally, there were loads of easier routes for the less adventurous souls, like me. I could picture the tall spruce and stately fir trees that were so glorious, with or without a coating of snow. *I'm coming*, I silently messaged my beloved White Mountains, home to some of the highest peaks in New England. *I'm on my way.*

After a last stretch, I reluctantly returned to my car and continued the drive, now less focused on the lovely scenery and more on the time of day. I estimated that as long as I encountered no issues to delay me, and I spent more time focused on the road and less on my fond memories of the distant past, I should arrive in Taunton in plenty of time to freshen up before joining Edward for a pre-dinner glass of sherry. *Heaven forbid I keep my host waiting!*

CHAPTER 3

I entered the outskirts of the city of Taunton at 4:30 p.m., just as it was getting dark outside and the streetlights began to glow. I recalled that Taunton had earned the moniker of "Silver City" for producing high-quality silver items for over a hundred years. Years ago, I had purchased a silver tray as a housewarming gift for newlyweds Sarah and Edward from Reed & Barton, a most prestigious silver maker right here in town. Sarah had been so excited about their new home and starting a family. I could picture her oh so clearly, flitting about and making sure that her guests had whatever they needed: a mug of hot tea, an extra pillow, or a soft-as-down woolen throw to ward off a chill. A lovelier and kinder woman you would never expect to meet. A sudden wave of nostalgia brought unbidden tears to my eyes. This visit might prove to be more of a challenge than I was prepared for.

Less than fifteen minutes later, I drove up the hill and turned into the driveway of 23 Prescott Avenue. I had arrived, on time, at my destination. My host for the evening, Edward Talbot, hurried down the walkway to greet me. He had lost some weight, I noted, but still carried himself with his characteristic erect posture and long-legged gait. His hair, which appeared to have been freshly cut, was snow white in contrast to his salt-and-pepper beard and mustache.

"You're a sight for sore eyes, Edward," I called out as he approached, a wide grin stretched across his face.

"Katie, it's so good to see you. You're looking well, old girl." Edward's voice boomed in my ear as he took my arm and led me up the stairs to the wide, well-appointed front porch. I would have happily found respite on one of the overstuffed settees or lounge chairs, but he clearly had other ideas. "Please leave your luggage. One of the girls will deliver it to your room." I allowed him to move me along until we were inside, when I stopped to admire the beauty of the home.

The high ceilings and large stained-glass windows were classic features of Victorian homes and nicely complemented the marbletiled hallway and the floral-patterned wallpaper. The overall effect was warm and inviting.

"Just as lovely as I remember," I told Edward, who nodded as he surveyed his home.

"It's been too long, dear one. Far too long since you've graced us with your presence. Why, I don't believe you have been here since, well . . ." He stopped and shook his head. *Since the funeral of our beloved Sarah in the spring of 1905* was left unsaid.

"Yes, much too long, my friend." I squeezed his hand. When Sarah was alive, she and I had taken turns, alternately meeting at one or the other of our homes and, more recently, traveling up to Brookmead together. Rarely had more than a month or two passed without us visiting for a couple of days, sometimes as much as a week. We were like two peas in a pod; everyone always said so.

"I like what you've done with the place," I said with a chuckle, which he joined me in, as it was quite apparent that nothing of importance had been changed in the opulent home for years.

"Hard to improve upon perfection," Edward agreed. Standing in this spotless, gleaming home made me realize just how grubby I must appear after an afternoon of driving. A young maid who had been standing nearby came over to help me off with my coat, gloves, and hat, promising me their return first thing in the morning. I figured it would take her quite some time to beat the dirt out of my coat with a broom.

"I would appreciate the opportunity to wash up after my trip," I said. "I feel as if I am positively coated with dust and dirt."

"Of course, of course. Right over there," he said, pointing to the far side of the entrance hall. I made my way into the large lavatory and availed myself of the modern pull toilet, the warm water, and one of the Turkish towels displayed in a wicker basket. After patting my face dry, I took in the still familiar scent of my dear friend Sarah. Sweet, warm, and fresh: she had always smelled of sandalwood— and frequently of peppermints.

Once more grateful for my decision to spend the night in the home that still resonated with Sarah's vibrant personality, I hurried back to find Edward, noting with a mixture of both joy and grief just how much the home that she had decorated to reflect her unique sense of style had remained virtually the same. I was grateful to Edward for his decision, conscious or not, to allow it to stay untouched. I poked my head in the drawing room, not in the least bit surprised to find Edward sitting in one of the two high-backed Victorian-style chairs flanking the fireplace. Although it was still early in the fall, the crackling fire was quite effective in warming up the drafty room with its soaring ceiling and north-facing wall of windows.

"There you are, my pet," he called out. "Jolly good that you finally decided to join me. Come, come. I've poured us each a lovely glass of sherry to stimulate our appetites for what I assure you will be a good and proper nosh up. Milly has collected your overnight bag from your car and brought it up to your room. Please sit and relax, won't you? You must be positively knackered."

I groaned silently, having nearly forgotten my host's penchant for using, often incorrectly, terms and phrases that only a born and bred Englishman might use, and only sparingly at that. I had previously thought this particular affectation was something he brought out only in my presence, as I was British by birth. But a mutual friend had once shared that she also found this habit of his particularly loathsome. "Everyone knows he's from Hoboken," she'd said with a touch of cheek. I smiled appreciatively in Edward's direction and sank down into the overstuffed chair facing him.

"Such a warm welcome, Edward. I have been looking forward to seeing you since we first made our plans last month," I said before stifling a yawn. It had been a long day, and if I spent too much time sitting so close to the fire, I would likely nod off before dinner. If I found myself getting drowsy, I decided I would give myself a good old pinch in order to remain upright.

"Come and have a drink with me, won't you?" He focused his gaze on the brimming purplish-red glass of sparkling sherry waiting for me on the spindly oak table to my left. To be hospitable, I took the glass and raised it in his direction.

"What shall we drink to, do you suppose?" I asked. "Our health? A prosperous 1908 or the successful dropping of that seven-hundred-pound ball from the top of the New York Times Building scheduled for this New Year's Eve?"

"All the above," quipped Edward before downing half of his drink in a single movement. "And you heard it from me first, but that ball drop will be a flash in the pan. One and done, of that I'm certain." I found the whole idea to be quite intriguing but kept that thought to myself. I sipped at my drink before returning it to the table. Combined with fatigue and the warmth of the fire, I knew that even half a glass would have me horizontal in the blink of an eye. "So tell me, Katie, why on God's green earth are you abandoning the sparkling town of Newport for the frozen tundra of the north? I must admit that Sarah and I could never determine just what caused you to build not one, but two homes up there." He shook his head, demonstrating his amazement.

It's actually three homes, and please do not deign to tell me what my best friend of over fifty years thought of me and the decisions I made. I took another small sip of sherry to buy myself a bit of time to compose my thoughts and rein in my annoyance. We'd had less than five minutes of lighthearted conversation, and he was already trying my patience. What had I been thinking when I had accepted his invitation? *Be nice,* I cautioned myself. *But do set him straight.*

"Oh, but, Edward, Sarah was one of the dear advisors I consulted with before deciding to purchase a home in New Hampshire nearly sixteen years ago. I believe you were abroad when she and I traveled together to the Lakes Region of the Granite State. I had been previously in the spring, but this time was peak foliage season, and we felt strongly that it was a place we wanted to experience more of. We were both chuffed to bits," I said. I only embellished that last comment a bit, lapsing back into the parlance of my youth. Two could play at this game. Edward had the good sense to look sheepish.

"Well, yes, of course, it's lovely, I am certain. I've never been, however," he said with a shrug. Sarah's many visits over the years had frequently included their daughter, but Edward had never made the trip.

"Please plan to visit me in Jackson, won't you?" I said, leaning toward him with a smile. "You know you're always welcome."

Edward let out a low chuckle. "If you had asked me, I would have gladly considered driving north with you tomorrow," he said. "Perhaps next time you can give me a bit more advance notice." At this, I had to stifle a laugh, thinking back to the little white lie I had told Ariana that morning, as well as the fact that I could foresee no "next time." In my mind, this trip was it, both my maiden voyage and my swan song.

CHAPTER 4

I pretended to consider Edward's offhanded offer before shaking my head. "Oh no, my dear friend," I protested. "You are far too busy of a man to dillydally on a meandering route like I have ahead of me. Tomorrow night I'll be in Boston at the home of Priscilla Winters. Surely, you remember her? I've decided to stay a second night with her in order to attend a party hosted by my cousin Lucretia. Do you recall meeting her? Lucretia Preble, my first cousin on my mother's side? She married a solicitor from Gloucester. He works in her family's business. A pleasant chap called Curtis Vanderbilt—no relation, I'm afraid. Anywho, they are celebrating their fiftieth wedding anniversary. Can you imagine? At first, I sent my regrets, but then the more I thought of it, it seemed like something I could easily do. It will be held at the Parker House Hotel. And then I'll be . . . I'm sorry, I hope you don't think of me as rude, but may I make a quick call to my sister? You remember Ariana, I'm sure. She and Daniel are staying with their son Osborne and his family in New York. It's a lovely home on the Hudson River. I believe the town is called Rhinebeck. I promised to let her know the minute I arrived here in Taunton, and she'll be worried sick."

Edward nodded agreeably and rang a little bell on the side table. When the housekeeper appeared, he directed her to bring a phone to me. "Miss Wormeley has an important call to make," he informed her. Seconds later, an upright candlestick-style phone was placed on the marble side table next to me, and the woman scurried away quickly.

"I'll leave you to it," Edward said, liberally topping off his glass. "When you are done, please join me in the dining room. We'll dine precisely at six. So American of us, *n'est-ce pas?*" With a flourish, he left the room, and I picked up the mouthpiece and asked the operator to dial the number at the home of Ariana's son in New York. My sister answered on the first ring.

"Tell me you're okay," she said, sounding out of breath. "Are you at the Talbots'? In one piece?" The young girls we once were reappeared suddenly, and for a moment I considering having a go with her. How easy it would be to respond with, "No, I am quite lost, and the dark streets are so unfamiliar. Please help me, won't you?" The teasing of my oh so gullible younger sister was a skill that I had been quite brilliant at in my earlier years, but I thought the better of it. Poking the bear was likely not a smart move, given the approaching dinner hour and my current level of exhaustion. Still . . .

"Of course, silly. Edward and I are enjoying a pre-dinner glass of sherry in front of the fire. The drive was completely uneventful," I told her. "I told you I would be fine, and I am." Before she could respond, I covered the mouthpiece with one hand and called out, "Oh, is it time for dinner? I'm so sorry, Edward, I didn't hear the bell." Returning attention to my sister, I feigned an apologetic tone. "A? So sorry, but we've been summoned into the dining room. I hate to cut this short, but I must be off. I'll phone you tomorrow night from Priscilla's. No, my planned itinerary has not changed. Yes, the one I sent to you is still in effect. Good night, my dear." I ended the call and leaned back against the high-backed chair, enveloped by its elegant curves and plump cushioning. I recalled helping Sarah pick out the muted floral brocade fabric and insisting that she only use genuine horsehair in the upholstery, none of the dreadful steel springs and lashing wire found in mass-produced furniture. I closed my eyes ever so briefly, picturing my mercurial friend, spry as a fairy, as we examined the dozens of bolts of fabric in the upholsterer's showroom. I could hear her high-pitched voice as clear as day. "Are you sure, Katie? This one for certain? Do you think Edward will like it?" *Oh, my dear girl. I miss you so.*

Just then, I heard the unmistakable tinkle of the crystal dinner bell that I knew to be monogrammed with an etched *T* in an elegant cursive font. It was time to sit at Sarah's table and dine off Sarah's china and converse with Sarah's husband. I shook my head and moved toward the sound of the bell, feeling confident I could handle a couple of hours with my well-meaning host. I had survived the Peninsula Campaign, after all. Surely, the ghost of my best friend could see me through a couple of hours of desultory conversation before retiring to bed. It was not the fault of my host that my first day of travel had left me feeling quite worn out.

Mustering up what remained of my enthusiasm, I entered the dining room, walking briskly. "Is that roast lamb I smell? I'm positively faint with hunger."

Dinner, featuring a leg of lamb served alongside a colorful platter of roasted root vegetables, followed by a frothy meringue concoction and a respectable glass of port, was all quite pleasant. We discussed my trip, chatted about friends we shared, and I was brought up-to-date on the comings and goings of my goddaughter, Pamela Talbot Hastings. I had seen her fairly recently when she and her husband, Alexander, a Wall Street banker, had visited me in Newport. I already knew pretty much everything that Edward told me about his daughter, but I nodded and smiled throughout regardless. Yes, Alexander was doing well for himself in his career. And wasn't it lovely that they were planning a trip to Paris the following spring?

And certainly, while it was disappointing that the couple had never been blessed with children, one could not argue that the two led an enviable and charmed existence in their Park Avenue brownstone overlooking Central Park. Ah yes, Central Park!

"He was a friend of yours. Am I right, Katie? That Olmsted fellow?" I nodded, and he continued on. "Quite a legacy he left behind." Again, I simply gave a quick nod, having less than no desire to discuss Fred with Edward this evening—or any other, for that matter. Ours had been a complicated relationship, and if am being honest, I still haven't sorted it all out, what it all had meant and what we had meant to each other. While it was true that I had cared deeply for him, Fred was a married man and far too respectable to act upon anything inappropriate, save for a minor flirtation or two. The profound effect of war on personal relationships was certainly something to be considered in our case. It is quite possible that I had imagined the intensity of our attraction back then, caught up as I was in the drama and turmoil of serving on a hospital ship during wartime. And less than a year later, what had I done but fall in love with yet another unobtainable man? Not married, but completely unavailable nonetheless. It is certainly no mystery how I have managed to remain single all these years.

I changed the topic of conversation to the recent spell of delightful weather we had been enjoying in southern New England. It had been unseasonably warm, both calm and mild: a true Indian summer. My trip had been carefully scheduled around the hopes of mild weather this week, and it appeared I would be rewarded for my efforts.

"Well, it may be pleasant down here, but what about when you arrive in the frozen North?" Edward asked. "Have you really pictured yourself shivering and frostbitten?" he persisted. *Oh my.* Between Edward and my sister, the unsuitability of my living in New Hampshire was getting to be quite a boring topic of conversation. I informed him that my house had been winterized properly and that there were modern fireplaces in nearly every room. I bit my tongue and held back the one comment I wanted to make concerning the drafty barn of a home where we now sat. How often had Sarah complained to me about how much she dreaded the approach of winter here in Taunton? *Restraint,* I cautioned myself.

There was no reason to be rude. I changed the subject as quickly as I could.

"When we spoke last, you mentioned that you were starting to read one of the books I translated. It was written by Honore de Balzac, I believe. Tell me, did you enjoy it?"

Edward sniffed as if he had smelled something quite foul and shook his head at me as he responded. "No, my dear, I'm afraid that it was not to my taste. Not at all. The French, you know . . . so shallow, trite even." I managed to maintain a neutral visage, or at least I tried very hard to. Balzac was thought to be the founder of realism in European fiction and was much acclaimed for his complex characters. Trite? In a pig's eye! Apparently, I was not as successful as I'd thought at hiding my thoughts because Edward looked concerned. "Oh, my dear, that is not a reflection on your skills. After all, you can only work with the words that have already been written. Why, it's not like you actually create something on your own." I groaned inwardly, managing a tight smile. Years ago, when I had been offered the opportunity to translate into English, the novels of Balzac, the esteemed French novelist, I'd thought that receiving compensation for doing what I loved seemed silly, but I had decided to give it a try. It turned out I had a flair for translation and have since completed dozens of volumes for the late writer, as well as the celebrated playwright Moliere, Paul Bourget, Alexandre Dumas, and many more. I believe that it is my understanding of French life and the rich culture that make my translations successful.

"But it provides you a bit of pin money, I would imagine, and that's just ducky." Edward was still trying to correct his faux pas and failing miserably. The income I receive from this "little hobby" of mine has found its way into the coffers of several of the charities I work with. From birth, the belief that the ability to help those who were less fortunate was a privilege, as well as a responsibility, was deeply ingrained in me by our parents, and it has guided me in every phase of my life. I truly cannot imagine a better life than one spent in service for the betterment of our civilization. My, that sounds high and mighty, but it's true.

"How about a game of cards?" I asked my host. "I seem to recall you are quite the expert at whist. What do you say?" I could feel myself fading fast, but maybe after a quick game or two, I could slip off to bed. Edward had always been extremely competitive at everything he did, and I figured that, at the very least, keeping him focused on the game would prevent him from further critiquing my journey as well as my destination.

Edward agreed happily and minutes later began dealing from a deck of cards. "Thirteen cards each and nary a one from the bottom of the deck," he said with a mischievous glint in his eyes.

After two games, both of which he won handily, I could no longer keep my eyes open. I apologized profusely and bade Edward a good night. He seemed almost hesitant to let me escape to my room, reminding me to ring for Charlotte if I needed an extra blanket, more logs on the fire, or a glass of water for my bedside. I assured him I would be fine, just fine.

"We'll talk in the morning, then. Over breakfast," Edward called out, and I waved my hand in response. As I *was* his overnight guest, I certainly expected we would converse over breakfast. What an odd thing to say. I climbed the stairs to my room and, after staring at the ceiling while working out what I planned to say to S in a few days, slept reasonably well on sandalwood-scented Egyptian cotton sheets, the finest quality feather pillows, and a fluffy down comforter. If I dreamt, I did not recall any snippets when I awoke.

CHAPTER 5

Taunton, Massachusetts
Thursday, October 3, 1907

The next morning, I gathered up my belongings and headed down the stairs. Edward greeted me, protesting that he "had people to do that," referring to the transport of my luggage to the car. It was easier not to argue with him, so I left my bag by the door and followed him to a well-appointed breakfast room with a beautifully laid table and two chairs. He motioned for me to sit, and as I did, a young woman in uniform appeared with a carafe of coffee.

"Yes, please," I said to her with a smile, breathing in the aroma of freshly ground beans from somewhere exotic. Brazil, perhaps? Or possibly Costa Rica? A freshly brewed cup of coffee is one of the great pleasures of my life. Given a choice between it and an expensive French wine, I would choose a steaming cup of joe every time. I am also not in the least bit opposed to a square or two of chocolate. Dark and rich, I had always preferred Swiss confections, but I would gladly accept one of the newfangled Hershey bars now being made somewhere in Pennsylvania. At only a nickel, they were delicious and inexpensive and readily available to boot. I took an appreciative sip of my coffee and then another before returning my cup to its fine-boned saucer. I sat back, savoring the taste as Edward cleared his throat. I looked up expectantly. He appeared flustered as he again cleared his throat and fussed with the white linen napkin he had placed on his lap. Something was definitely amiss. "Edward, was there something you wished to discuss with me?" I asked. He nodded slowly.

"As a matter of fact, Katharine, there is." I frowned slightly. Last night I was Katie, the nickname most of my friends and all of my family used, and today I was Katharine. Still, it was a step up from "old girl." *Hmmm* . . . The swinging door from the kitchen opened and a young woman appeared, bearing a tray laden with an assortment of steaming hot dishes. She set the tray down on the sideboard and unloaded it, carrying over plates of eggs, grilled tomatoes, baked beans, back bacon, and fried bread to us. An authentic "full English" breakfast. Luckily, I did not see any of the dreaded black pudding, the scourge of my homeland. Who had ever imagined that blood sausage and oats concocted into rock-hard little discs would be appealing? Certainly not I!

"Will there be anything more, sir? Would you like—"

Edward's tone was sharp in his response. "That will be all, Daisy," he said. "Some privacy, if you please." The young woman flushed and scurried out of the room. I had never heard Edward speak so harshly to anyone, especially not a young woman who was simply performing her duties. I debated mentioning my concern, but Edward was once again clearing his throat and stammering. *What on earth?*

"Katie, before we have any more interruptions . . . I wanted to advise you, well, that is to make you aware of my, well, intentions." A deep red flush appeared out of nowhere and stained his pale cheeks. He paused, studying his own cup of coffee, seemingly unable to make eye contact with me, and I assumed it was now my turn to jump into our conversation.

"Intentions?" I asked. "Please don't keep me in suspense, old friend. Exactly what sort of intentions . . ." But before I could finish, the realization hit me. Of course, his intentions were . . .

"To marry you," he blurted out. "After a brief and socially acceptable courtship, that is. I mean, why delay the inevitable?" I stared at him, my mouth agape. What was inevitable about the two of us getting married? He continued on, seeming nervous at my look of surprise. "We shan't wait too long. I mean, honestly, you're certainly no spring chicken, my dear." I tuned him out, dazed at the reality of what he was asking me. *Marriage? To Edward Talbot?* I didn't know what to say, and even if I did, I was certain I would not be able to get the words out, my throat feeling thick and too full to allow anything to escape. I finally drew in a deep breath and let it out slowly.

"Marriage? Edward, honestly, what are you thinking?" I managed to utter. He looked crestfallen, then somewhat perplexed.

"Katie, it makes perfect sense. Don't you recognize that? Why, it's the logical next step for people like us."

"People like us?" I asked. Now he was looking impatient, as if he was growing tired of explaining something quite simple to someone quite dull. With steepled hands and a steely gaze, he shared his thoughts.

"Don't you see? We are perfectly matched; we are both cultured, well-educated, worldly adults with no financial burdens. We travel in the same social circles, have known each other for fifty years. You were Sarah's best friend, for goodness' sake. We own three homes between us, although I would strongly encourage you to give up your little cabin up north, sooner rather than later. I can't imagine we would ever want to spend any of our time up there. Not to mention my daughter adores you and I . . . well, am very fond of you as well."

"But how does all of that lead to marriage as a logical next step?" I asked. If it wasn't love or romance, shouldn't a proposal like this at least be based on a deep and abiding affection for the other person in question? My fondness for Edward was based on our memories and mutual experiences, which strengthened the bond we shared with dear Sarah. But as far as the future went, no matter how much longer I remained on earth, I did not imagine that this man would play any significant role whatsoever. And certainly not that of a husband. Edward was once again flushed and looking more and more peeved. Had he assumed I would fall into his arms and declare my undying love for him? That I would be flattered and simper like a blushing coquette? I could see he was more than a bit put-out, and his clipped tone reflected the very same.

"You're all alone, my pet, and so am I. Why else would you be traveling up to the hinterlands all by yourself, and why am I rattling around day after blasted day in this shrine to my dead wife?" I froze at the mention of my dear friend. I forced myself to stay calm and not let him ruffle my feathers. For all I knew, this might be the last time we spoke, at least face-to-face. This was no time for an argument or bruised feelings. I chose my words carefully.

"I know how much you miss Sarah," I said gently. "I miss her too. But shared grief is just that; it's not the basis for a happy marriage. I can't replace her, Edward. No one can. I understand how you might think . . ." He began to pace nervously.

"I'm not looking to replace my wife. I can't imagine that it could ever happen. But, if you were in favor, ours could be a marriage in name only. There would be no need for us to, well, share a bedroom." He was blushing furiously at this point. "I'm lonely, Katie, and I know you are too. I want someone to eat dinner with, someone to ask me about my day and accompany me to dinner parties. Someone to play cards with or read aloud to. Don't you want that as well?" Before I could respond, he held up a hand to stop me. "All I'm asking is that you think about it, yes? I'm sure it's a big decision, and, of course, you would need to sell your home in New Hampshire yet again. I didn't broach the subject last night as I knew you were tired, and, frankly, I didn't want to make things difficult between us. But you're leaving shortly, and you can consider what I have said and contact me upon your arrival in, what, five or six days?"

I nodded mutely. There was nothing else I could think of to say at the moment. Despite a few idiosyncrasies, he was a decent and honorable man and had been a good husband for many years to my best friend. I felt a touch of sadness at what I perceived to be his disappointment, but I had no desire to marry him—or anyone else, for that matter. I would let him down gently, but first, we had a meal to get through.

"My, this looks good." I served myself a fried egg, a single tomato half, and a couple of strips of crisp bacon. Breakfast was my favorite meal of the day, but I did not want to drag out this awkward silence any longer than necessary, and besides, our discussion had unsettled me and robbed me of my appetite. I picked at my food before giving up and pouring myself a fresh cup of coffee from the silver carafe Daisy had left. Edward's appetite did not appear to have suffered the same fate as mine. He spread a thick layer of butter on his bread, topping both slices with a liberal dollop of what appeared to be homemade blackberry preserves. He dug into his food as if famished, and perhaps, having gotten the discussion of our marriage off of his mind and onto the table, he was feeling both relief and hunger as well. I wondered how long he had been contemplating his proposal. Although I couldn't picture who exactly, the thought that I had not been his first choice for a second marriage came to me suddenly. Regardless, it was a moot point. Marriage to Edward Talbot was completely out of the question.

We finished our breakfast in silence, and I prepared to depart. He helped me on with my coat and gave my shoulders a friendly squeeze.

"You barely touched your food. Here's a little something to snack on." I accepted the hastily wrapped slice of fried bread he proffered and thanked him. At times like these, he could be so sweet. I turned to face him.

"Edward," I said. "I can't thank you enough for your kind hospitality. It was splendid to see you again. It's been lovely, just lovely to catch up." He leaned in, and for a second I thought he was going to kiss me on the lips, but at the last second I turned my face ever so slightly to the right. His kiss landed on my left cheek. I pulled back and forced a smile. He grinned broadly, looking quite pleased with himself. I stared at the breadcrumbs embedded in his mustache as he spoke.

"My dear Katie, I look forward to hearing from you when you get to where you are going. I hope you'll come to see what a suitable arrangement this will be for the both of us." A suitable arrangement? What a charmer! He took my arm and propelled me through the doorway, down the stairs, and over to where my car was parked.

He helped me up onto the running board and into the driver's seat before stepping back and studying the car closely. "It's quite a beauty, old girl. When you come home, perhaps we can take it out for a spin, pack a picnic lunch, and bring some champagne to celebrate our betrothal." I feigned a sudden interest in the fuel gauge to avoid having to respond.

"Almost half a tank left," I announced brightly. "They say these four-cylinder models are gas guzzlers, but in my experience that is just not the case." I turned on the magneto switch and set the choke, and Edward cranked the engine to get the car started. Even on a chilly morning, it only took a few tries.

"Thank you again, Edward," I said as I backed out of the narrow driveway. I waved, and he did as well.

"Farewell my dear. Safe travels," he called out. I turned onto the street, still dumbstruck over his out-of-the-blue offer of marriage. The first time I had received a proposal, I'd mulled it over for a couple of days before finally declining. This time? There had not been a split second of indecision. I hated the idea of spoiling our visit by turning him down on the spot, and I hoped that in a week's time he would have put the baffling notion completely out of his mind.

Following the signs along the well-marked route, I left Taunton behind me and made my way toward the next overnight stop on my itinerary: the city of Boston. No more surprises, I hoped. A marriage proposal was more than enough drama for one day.

CHAPTER 6

About an hour into my drive, I pulled off the road just briefly in order to adjust my driving goggles and tie my scarf more tightly around my head. I was certain that I looked a fright, with much of my shoulder-length gray hair having already escaped from the tight bun I had struggled with just a couple of hours earlier. Although never vain, I had always taken great pride in my appearance, but I had noticed that my standards were slipping a bit of late. Well, more than a bit, if I'm being honest. These days I knowingly wore stockings with small tears and often put on a dress I had taken off the night before, and what was the harm in that? All that time I had spent on primping over the years and where had it gotten me? Along with advancing years and more time spent in solitary pursuits, I felt more or less invisible a good deal of the time, and I had grown quite accustomed to that. There was no good reason to spend a single moment worrying about the way I looked. No, it was much more important that I focus on my work and my charitable endeavors.

I reminded myself that it was highly unlikely I would run into anyone, let alone anyone I knew, along this stretch of road. There was only one person on this trip whom I planned to get dolled up for, and that was several days from now. If windblown hair and a disheveled appearance was the price I had to pay to enjoy the fresh air and warm rays of the sun afforded by my open-top vehicle, so be it.

I took another look at my road map before attempting to fold it properly and return it to the glove box. This was not my first trip along this route, but it was the first time I had navigated it alone. I wanted to make certain that I was going to be arriving in Brockton soon, as I had determined that was where I would purchase gasoline. I could hear my mechanic's voice in my head. "Whatever you do, Miss Kate, don't let her drop below a half tank!" Not to mention that the prices would be higher the closer I got to Boston, I surmised. Possibly more than twenty cents a gallon. *Outrageous!*

A short while later, I took the turnoff into the bustling city of Brockton, known widely as the "Shoe City," with over a hundred separate shoe manufacturers located within the town's borders. I immediately began the search for a filling station, which I located after driving several blocks along the main street. I was delighted to note there was no line of motorists in front of me as I pulled up to the pump. I turned off the car and watched as the attendant shuffled my way. He was an older gentleman, probably in his mid-sixties, but still at least ten years my junior. His gray hair was badly in need of a cut, and his rumpled clothing suggested that he had recently chosen to sleep in his work overalls.

"Help you?" he asked. "Fill 'er up?"

"Good morning," I called out. "Yes, please."

His lined face scrunched up. "Not from heah?"

"No, I'm from Rhode Island, but I'm moving to New Hampshire. For good." It was the first time I had stated aloud my intention to leave Rhode Island permanently, and I felt a moment's thrill. I was actually doing this.

He shook his head at me. "No, ma'am," he stated flatly. "That's not it."

Now it was my turn to look confused. "Excuse me, but which part? I'm *not* from Rhode Island, or I'm *not* on my way to New Hampshire?"

He gave a low chuckle, and the years vanished from his weathered face. "I am fairly certain that both may indeed be true, but you sound like you're maybe Irish or English," he explained.

"You have a good ear, sir," I told him. "Yes, I was born in England, but I have lived here for close to sixty years."

He smiled broadly this time and extended his hand, still pumping gas with his other hand.

"That almost makes you a native New Englander. Billy," he said. "Billy Sullivan, at your service, Mrs. . . . ."

"Wormeley," I said. "Miss Katharine Wormeley, but please call me Kate."

Billy frowned as he replaced the hose and tightened the gas cap. "I'm sorry to be the one to inform you, Miss Kate, but you appear to have picked up a nail on your way here today," he said, shaking his head. I turned in my seat to see what he was pointing to. The back tire on the driver's side of the vehicle was floppy, and even from where I sat, I could see the head of a large, rusty-looking nail sticking out. *Oh dear.*

"Can you repair it?" I asked, certain that he would be able to come to my aid. A quick patch up and I would be back on the road.

"How far are you going?" he asked, and I told him I planned to get to Boston tonight.

"In time for dinner," I added, and once again he shook his head.

"If you were going to, say Foxboro, I might put a patch on it and get you on your way. But Boston? No, ma'am, no way. I would not be doing you any favors by sticking on something meant to be temporary. You hit one bump in the road, and bam, just like that you'd be sitting on the side of the road watching the rest of the world go driving by." *Drat!* I had known that I would likely need to replace a tire along the way, but did it have to be today?

"Then can you replace it with the spare I have in the back?" He brightened briefly and nodded.

"Now that I can do. But you have to promise me you'll buy yourself a new spare right away. Everyone always thinks they will, but too many forget and learn the hard way." He shook his head at the thought of such reckless irresponsibility. I promised him I would remember and eased myself out of the car slowly. I stretched, grateful to be free of the confines of my vehicle. The seats were the highest quality leather and very comfortable, but my legs were cramped after less than two hours of driving.

I was about to ask where there might be a restroom I could use when Billy turned to me and snapped his fingers.

"Say, I was just about to take my lunch break when you drove in. I've got more than enough. Would you join me for a bite? You have to eat at some point." He smiled shyly. "And then I promise I'll get you fixed up and on your way toot sweet." The invitation seemed to mean a great deal to him. Perhaps I reminded him of his mother or an ancient aunt.

"That is most kind of you. I really should get going," I said, "but as you said, I have to eat . . ."

"It's settled," he said. "You probably want to get freshened up first. There's a privy right over there," he said, pointing to a shed about fifty yards away. "It's not much to look at, but it's clean and will get the job done, if you know what I mean."

Indeed. I nodded gratefully. "Thank you, Billy."

As I started to walk away, he called out to me. "Don't forget about lunch."

I turned and waved before hightailing it to the privy.

CHAPTER 7

Minutes later, I sat across from Billy at a battered table partially shaded by a canvas tarp. He was busy taking food from a large metal bucket, and I stared at him, incredulous.

"You have enough food to properly feed an army," I said, and he laughed out loud.

"Well, it used to be my job to actually feed an army," he told me, a note of pride creeping into his voice. "So if anyone should know how to feed one, it would be me. Please help yourself."

I bit into the sandwich he had unwrapped, and a soft moan escaped my lips. It was divine. He was smiling at me as I chewed slowly and thoroughly. When I patted my lips with a roughly woven napkin, he asked, "Do you like it?"

I nodded vigorously. "Yes, it's delicious." I surveyed the half sandwich I was still holding carefully. "I know it's turkey, but what is that—" He cut me off, seemingly quite happy to share his culinary secrets.

"It's horseradish," he announced proudly. "I grow it at the house and blend it into my sandwich toppings."

"Genius," I told him. "So is that where you learned to cook? In the army?" He nodded and told me how at sixteen, he had lied about his age and enlisted, along with most of his pals from their Brooklyn neighborhood.

"It was right when all hell—I'm sorry, Miss Kate—when all heck was breaking loose after the attack on Fort Sumter and I got shipped out to Manassas, Virginia, right before the Battle of Bull Run. I just knew I had to join up and see what I could do to help the cause."

I nodded sadly, recalling all too well how chaotic it had been back then and how quickly lives had changed for the enlisted men and their families, as well as for volunteers like myself. But I had a question. "I hope you don't mind me asking, but if you were on the front lines, how did you end up working in a kitchen?" Billy hung his head, seemingly ashamed at what he was about to share. I smiled at him and nodded almost imperceptibly to encourage him to continue. I doubted there was anything this man could tell me that I hadn't already seen or experienced myself. War will do that to a person. My dear father used to say that it made a man old before his time. I had seen more evidence to prove that fact than I cared to recall.

"I got wounded. My, um, rifle went off when I was cleaning it, and it took off my left big toe." He sat back in his chair, crossing his arms, ready for my response, expecting surprise or even disapproval? I nodded sympathetically, having seen cases like his so many times.

"That's a shame. So I can assume they cleaned it with bromine to prevent gangrene, removed the bullet and any bone fragments, dressed it, and wrapped it up with strips of cloth bandages, tying it tight to your other toes?" He nodded thoughtfully. "And then, because they couldn't clear you for duty, I imagine they found work for you in the mess hall."

"Yes, that's it exactly. How did you know?" I explained that I too, had served in the army, as a nurse on a hospital ship. His eyes lit up.

"I know all about them. Were you one of those rich society ladies? The volunteers?" I nodded, but I wanted to clarify my position.

"I was a volunteer, but I certainly was no posh debutante. My friends and I were—"

"Was one of your friends, um, Georgy?" I was dumbfounded. That dear girl's name coming from the mouth of a stranger was the last thing I had expected to hear as I ate my turkey sandwich that day.

"Georgy, yes, of course." Georgeanna Woolsey had been my dear pal. She and her sister Eliza had roomed with me on board the ship, and the three of us had been inseparable. "But how did you know her?" I asked.

"Everyone knew Georgy," he replied. "We lived a couple blocks from her family in Brooklyn. When she announced she had joined the cause as a nurse, there was a big rift in her family. Her folks were outraged that she had signed up. They felt she was putting herself in danger." He shook his head. "But she was unstoppable, you know? We were real proud of that girl." I had been nodding mutely this whole time. My brave friend. The brightest and the best of us all. I missed her terribly at that moment.

"Yes indeed. I remember her telling us how disappointed her family was when she became a volunteer nurse. But they all had to be proud of her, yes? Why, after the war, she went on to become one of the founders of the Connecticut Training School for Nurses at New Haven Hospital."

Billy nodded in agreement. "Yeah, that's Georgy for you. She is really something. So what was it like on the ship?" he asked. Warmed now to the topic, I shared with him some of our experiences on the *Daniel Webster*, as well as the smaller transport and hospital ships down in Virginia. It is much more common today, but back then, we were among the first women ever to serve as nurses on transport vessels in an American war. I wouldn't go so far as to say that our efforts paved the way for future generations of women in the field of medicine, but I have heard others make that very same claim.

"It was a most exciting time," I told him. Exciting, dirty, loud, and frightening, if I am being honest. Never in my life have I recalled feeling so vital, so present among my surroundings. It was the human factor that made the horrors of war the slightest bit more manageable. The touch of a hand, a warm smile of gratitude, the sight of an injured soldier's health returning. I had tried to focus on those sorts of things during the Peninsular Campaign whenever I could. The gallons upon gallons of beef tea and milk punch that we served up in our efforts to soothe the men and help them regain their strength. The daily mail delivery, which was most always met with equal measures of excitement and trepidation. We nurses would rush to the mailbag, pleased as punch when we found an envelope addressed to us and down in the dumps the days that we came up empty. I received letters regularly from Mother and Ariana, less so from Eliza, and I answered each one I received the very same day. Some nights I could barely see the scribbles of my poor stubby pencil, and I always hoped it would be understood that it was exhaustion, pure and simple, combined with a lack of a proper writing surface that made my letters barely legible. Once, I tried to describe a meal that I'd just had to A, but the fact that our dining table was also the top of the stove and that our plates were actually pieces of stale bread got jumbled somehow. In response, she asked me exactly when I had learned to bake bread. "You were never suited for those sorts of household chores," she had chided me.

Years later, I had decided it was high time to share an account of my time with the United States Sanitary Commission. My family had saved the letters I had written them during that time, and after talking with a friend who worked for a publishing house, in 1888 I published *The Other Side of War:1862*. It was well-received, if I do say so myself. As it turned out, thousands of readers wanted to know more about the efforts we made to assist in the war effort by treating thousands of soldiers injured on southern battlefields. I have reason to believe that coming from the perspective of a civilian woman, it was a welcome recollection of the human side of the war equation.

I was well pleased with the favorable feedback I received, and the royalties helped to bolster the coffers of several charitable initiatives of mine. Very few good things come out of a time of war, but I liked to believe that my little book was one of them. I realized with a touch of panic that the opportunities to share my stories of that time were rapidly shrinking, but I did have a rather captivated audience of one here with me now. I sat forward, now in full storytelling mode.

"On my very first day on board, I was responsible for 250 men, their first day as well, most of them suffering from typhoid. The men with high fevers were the most difficult to help, moaning and incoherent. I gave them brandy and water and, if they could eat, bread and butter with tea. We took care of their diets, dressed their wounds, and comforted them. Mornings were a special challenge, as they all needed to be washed and given breakfast before the doctors made their rounds. Oh, and when they did . . . they would open up the wounds, apply ointments and liniments, and then replace the bandages. I have to admit that for the first few days, I sat with my fingers in my ears, trying to block out the sounds." If I allowed myself to be drawn back to those days, I could clearly recall the cries of pain, loneliness, and despair from the wounded and dying men. I had eventually grown accustomed to the noise and chaos, but I had never become numb to it either. Mrs. Griffin, the senior woman on the ship, had given me this advice, and I never forgot it. "You must work past the horror of all that we see and hear day after day, but you must never become immune to it either. It is what will inspire you to give your very best to these brave men every day of your service."

"That must have been awful," said Billy, and I nodded in agreement. "Awful" didn't even begin to describe the horrors we had witnessed.

"But it wasn't all bad," I told him. "When things settled down a bit, we nurses were able to chat with the soldiers or read to them. We even wrote letters to their loved ones for them." I smiled brightly. "That was my favorite activity, the writing of letters. Just to know that they could tell their families back home how they were faring . . . well, it was quite the rewarding experience I can tell you that." I felt tears well up in my eyes, and I quickly wiped them away. Many of those letters would have arrived at their intended destination long after the soldier who had dictated it had died from his injuries. I hoped that the last words they received had provided some solace to the grieving families. It had been an honor and a privilege to be involved in their lives in that way. I remembered trying and failing to imagine what it would have been like to receive a letter like that, dictated by a loved one, transcribed by a well-meaning stranger.

"It seems I was one of the lucky ones, I reckon," said Billy. "I served my time unscathed, except, of course, for losing my toe, and I got sent home when it was all over."

"You did your duty and served your country admirably," I assured him. "And developed a new skill with your cooking," I added.

He shook his head as if surprised by his relatively good fortune. "So what did you do after the war, Miss Kate?" he asked. "Go home, marry your sweetheart, and have a bunch of babies?"

I chuckled at that. "No, nothing at all like that, I'm afraid. I went home to Rhode Island, yes, made sure my mother was situated nicely, got unpacked, and had a week or two to rest up. Then I took a job at Lovell General Hospital in Portsmouth Grove, Rhode Island. As a matter of fact, Georgy became my assistant while I was there."

"Your assistant?" Billy asked.

"Yes, my title was superintendent," I confirmed. Billy looked suitably impressed. "We had 1700 beds, and believe me when I tell you they were always full. When I first arrived, I was appalled at the lack of organization and scarcity of supplies. Why, it was like being aboard the *Daniel Webster* all over again. But Georgy and I, we got right to work soliciting funds and donations of food and medicine from the surrounding towns." I was about to lament on the one battle I had lost back then; try as I might, I had not been able to secure funding for tar paper to cover the multitude of holes in the hospital walls. I realized I had barely stopped talking this whole time and had been completely monopolizing the entire conversation. "But that was so long ago now. How about you Mr. Sul—er, Billy? Where did your path take you after the war?" I took a large bite of my sandwich and chewed slowly, waiting for his response.

Billy shrugged before he began to speak. "I was kind of restless, I guess you might say. I went home for a while, but Brooklyn didn't really feel like home no more. Then everything changed." His whole face brightened, and I waited for him to explain.

"I met my Maureen," he said. "Maureen Kennedy was the most beautiful girl I had ever seen. She was visiting a friend in Park Slope, and I saw her cross the street. She was mailing a postcard to her mother. I followed her and asked her out, and she said yes. Then we got hitched, and two months later I moved here with her. We were happy, me and her. She couldn't have children, so it was just the two of us. This garage was her father's. When he died, I took it over, and well, here I am." He looked around at his workplace, its edges worn and tired, but nothing that a lot of elbow grease and a coat or two of paint wouldn't fix. I studied him more closely, imagining that his beloved wife must have died and recently, based upon his melancholy expression and shaggy appearance. Sadly, I was correct.

"Mo died this past spring. Only sixty-one. One minute she was just fine and then gone, just like that. It was an em, uh, embo . . ."

"Embolism?" I asked, and he nodded. "If it's any consolation, she didn't suffer," I reminded him gently. "She went quickly. I'm sure you must miss her terribly." He wiped at his eyes before getting up abruptly. He did not meet my gaze as he prepared to head back toward the garage.

"Lunch break is over for me. That tire of yours is not going to replace itself," he announced brusquely and, grabbing his tools, shuffled over to my car. I busied myself tidying up the remains of our lunch, packing most of the food back in the large bucket. I swallowed the remains from my cup of overly sweet lemonade and brought everything into the little office. While I waited, I washed the plates and cups we'd used in the tiny sink and set them to dry. Unsure of what to do next, I considered trying to locate a pay telephone in order to contact my hostess for the evening, but just a moment later Billy walked toward me, signs of his sadness gone. Except for his eyes. His blue eyes were tinged with red, causing his painted-on grin to look false. He was still very much in mourning, the poor soul.

"All set," he told me. "But don't forget what you promised me." I was confused momentarily before I recalled our earlier conversation.

"I will purchase a new spare tire. I promise," I said, and since he was apparently waiting for more, I added, "tomorrow in Boston." He nodded, satisfied that his work here was done, at least as far as I was concerned. I settled the bill, slipping a few extra dollars into his hand, unbeknownst to him. For lunch, I thought, and the opportunity to talk about Georgy with someone who had known her back in the day. That in itself was priceless.

"Say hello to Georgy for me," he called out as I started up the car. "Next time you see her, tell her little Billy Sullivan from the old neighborhood in Flatbush was asking after her." Too stunned to reply, I nodded noncommittally and turned onto the well-traveled road, heading north. "Don't forget about the tire," I heard him remind me.

I would have given anything in the world to pass Billy's greetings on to my dear friend. But sadly, she had passed away at her home in New Haven just last year at age seventy-three. "Rest in eternal peace, my darling girl," I whispered, grateful for the pair of oversized goggles for stopping the tears in my eyes from running down my windburned cheeks. Despite my fervent wish for new beginnings and a fresh start, it was quite obvious that I was still struggling with pain from the losses I'd experienced as well as more than a few regrets. Choices that at the time had seemed to be the most reasonable courses of action that I now questioned. This was truly my last opportunity to deal with all of it, to put my issues to bed once and for all.

Perhaps this was the real purpose of this trip of mine, I realized. I was running out of time, of that I was certain. If I could come to terms with my past and free myself to live out the rest of my days in peace, I would have succeeded mightily. Not to mention I could prove to myself and anyone who needed convincing that I was capable and self-sufficient enough to travel on my own. Doubters be damned!

CHAPTER 8

Arriving on the outskirts of Boston a couple of hours later, I realized I was more than an hour ahead of schedule. I had told Priscilla Winters that she could expect me in the late afternoon, but it was not quite 3:00 p.m. Despite my stop in Brockton and what had felt like a lengthy lunchtime discussion with Billy, I was still very early. No doubt my speedy departure from Edward's house this morning had contributed, leaving me with an hour to squander as I saw fit.

I counted Priscilla as a friend, but not necessarily one whose home I could invade this much earlier than expected. It was quite enough that I had extended my stay with her by an additional night and had even convinced her to attend tomorrow evening's soiree with me. With her husband away, she had seemed reticent at first to go out on the town unescorted, but I had convinced her it would be fine. Surely, if women would soon have the right to vote, we could appear out in public without the benefit of a male escort.

I decided to see if I could locate one of dear Fred's many parks in this city that he had called home for many years. From what I knew about his extensive work in Boston, I imagined it would not be a particularly difficult task. Along with most of the country, I had followed his career for years and was still in awe of his many accomplishments. His vision and determination had transformed

North America, and from what I heard, his stepson John and son Fred, Jr. were carrying on the family business, putting their own special touches on urban parks, public grounds, college landscapes, and private estates. It was a wonderful legacy we all could share in and appreciate. For the life of me, I could not picture a more enjoyable way to while away a free hour.

•   •   •

I had first met Frederick Law Olmsted when I volunteered as a nurse during the war. He had nearly completed his iconic park in the center of Manhattan and wanted to assist in the effort to bring unity to the country. Despite being newly married and a father to his wife's three children, he had accepted a position as the director of the United States Sanitary Commission, the civilian relief agency that my old chum Clara Barton later transformed into the American Red Cross. I was appointed to the *Daniel Webster*, the very first transport ship to be commissioned by the USSC. Little did I know the significant impact my time on board would have on my life.

One night early on in my assignment, Georgy and I were sitting in the mess hall, enjoying a cup of lukewarm ersatz coffee after a dinner of stew made with mutton and parsnips. We no longer complained about the food, as we were the ones most often responsible for its preparation. "That's our new boss," she said in a stage whisper. "Mr. Frederick Law Olmsted from New York City. He's the one who built that vast park in Manhattan from hundreds of acres of swampland, slaughterhouses, and pigpens. He is a genius, I'm telling you. Have you been? It's fabulous, just fabulous."

I had heard of the park and was curious to meet the visionary behind it, who also happened to be my new boss. I looked in the direction that Georgy had pointed to see a slightly built gentleman with graying hair and a pronounced limp entering the hall. As I watched, he glanced in our direction, and I got my first look at a pair of bright blue eyes. I stared at him, transfixed, drawn by his face, which was somehow both rugged and delicately beautiful at the same time. I blushed and looked away quickly. Not quickly enough, however, as my very astute friend had clearly not missed the effect that Mr. Olmsted had on me.

Georgy nudged me good-naturedly. "Don't get your hopes up," she said. "I hear he's married to his late brother's widow and has a whole passel of children." I bristled slightly at the notion that I had designs on any man, and certainly not on our newly appointed supervisor.

"Don't be silly," I told her. "I'm here to serve our men in uniform, not fall in love with a married man—or an unmarried one either, for that matter." But even as I said the words aloud, I felt a trickle of . . . sadness? Regret? Was it true that all the "good ones" were already married? *Don't be a ninny,* I told myself. *Men are dying, and you've developed a schoolgirl crush.* What was wrong with me? A short while later, Georgy and I were heading back to our room for our wraps before heading back up to the main deck. On nights while we were at sea, a group of us would meet to chat and enjoy the breeze and the gentle rocking of the boat. The men, doctors or hospital administrators, would smoke their pipes or cigars, and usually a flask or two would be passed around. I enjoyed the camaraderie and the gaiety, and a couple of swallows of brandy always helped me to fall asleep on a thin mattress on the top bunk in a dormitory room shared by a dozen nurses. I had never lived with anyone in the same room except for one or another of my sisters. Once I got over my initial shyness and familiarized myself with the layout of the ship, I let myself get swept up in the adventure of this brand-new chapter of my life.

As we traversed the deck leading to our quarters, we crossed paths with our director, a Mr. Knapp, who was accompanied by our new leader. Knapp, a good-looking fellow who we all liked and respected, stopped us. "Katie, Georgy, I want to introduce you to our new superintendent, Mr. Olmsted. These are two of our finest volunteer nurses, Miss Woolsey and Miss Wormeley." Mr. Olmsted smiled at us both, his blue eyes twinkling with mischief.

"Woolsey and Wormeley, you say? How on earth will I be able to tell you two lovely ladies apart?" Georgy stuck out her hand, shaking the newcomer's vigorously.

"I'm Georgeanna Woolsey," she said, emphasizing her last name. "But everyone calls me Georgy. And this here is Katharine Wormeley."

I extended my hand as well. "Please call me Kate, Mr. Olmsted," I said shyly. He was not a tall man, but there was something larger than life about him. His craggy face broke into a smile that softened his features.

"I will surely remember Miss Woolsey with the iron grip, and I shall remember Miss Wormeley with the lovely British accent, I believe. Where do you hail from, Miss, er, Kate?"

"From Suffolk, sir. Actually, Ipswich. It's on the—"

"Oh, I'm quite familiar with much of England," he said. "Why, before I got to work on Central Park, my late brother John and I traveled to many of your lovely public parks. So inspiring."

"Oh my, I'm so sorry to hear that your brother died. So did mine. His name was James." I reddened at my improper familiarity and earned a pinch from Georgy. Mr. Olmsted nodded thoughtfully and peered closely at me, his bright eyes looking directly into my own.

"One day we will need to share stories about our dear, departed brothers. I believe that I would find it most therapeutic. But for now, we need to resume our rounds," he said, looking at Mr. Knapp, who appeared ready to continue introducing our new boss to everyone on board. "We'll be off, then," he added, doffing his hat and bowing ever so slightly. "It's been a pleasure." The two men made their leave, and as soon as they were out of earshot, Georgy turned to me in astonishment.

"My brother died! That's what you have to say to our new supervisor? I simply can't believe you, Kate. I mean, why not ask how he acquired his limp, for goodness' sake," Georgy sputtered. I shook my head, embarrassed at my social faux pas. I had been raised in a proper household with rules of etiquette firmly engrained in all of us. When had I transformed from a well-bred woman into such a bumbling ninny? Was it fatigue, or had the newly arrived Mr. Olmsted gotten me all flustered? According to family lore, upon meeting my mother at the home of mutual friends, my father had taken one look at her, "so beautifully fair with such lovely brown hair," and had been immediately smitten. They had become engaged only a short while later and had been married that fall. Was history repeating itself? Was love at first sight even possible? *But he's a married man,* I reminded myself. I needed to steer this conversation in a whole new direction, I decided.

"I'll do better next time, I promise, my friend. Right now, let's retrieve our shawls and head up to the main." We linked arms and headed for the stairway. *Next time?* I wondered. How soon would that be? I quickly realized that we would be working quite closely together seven days a week. It was likely that he would be nearly impossible to avoid. I was right.

Working for Mr. Olmsted, as I continued to call him for a time before he finally insisted that I call him Fred, was never dull—an understatement if ever I'd made one. He was mostly affable and pleasant to deal with, but his rule was absolute, and no one dared to question any of his decisions. Some of the staff appeared to walk on eggshells when he was around, but not me. Of course, I was always respectful and exceedingly polite, but I'd never had an issue with seeking clarification of one of his direct orders, requesting minor changes to policies and procedures, and asking, as needed, for forgiveness instead of permission. He was, to my mind, always fair and courteous. I could easily forgive his occasional lapse into a thorough dressing down of the random worker or two when their behavior had negatively affected the care of one of our patients. I would have liked to give the offender a thorough tongue-lashing of my own, but I knew my role on board, and it was not that of an enforcer of the rules, nor was I allowed to mete out any punishment.

I was there solely for the purpose of assisting the doctors in our efforts to improve the health and lives of the wounded men. And that was fine with me.

·   ·   ·

The honking of an approaching car snapped me out of my reverie. I saw that I had drifted over a bit and twisted my steering wheel to get back to my side of the road. I was blushing, I realized, and my cheeks felt hot, but I was uncertain whether it was the result of being called out on my careless driving or the memory of meeting Fred for the first time, nearly fifty years earlier. *Concentrate on safe driving,* I warned myself.

A couple of minutes later, I saw a sign for Franklin Park and recognized it as one of Fred's. If memory served, the large public park was at one end of the long string of parks gracing Boston known as the Emerald Necklace. It got its colorful name for the manner in which the chain of parks hung from the "neck" of the Boston Peninsula. I had once imagined strolling along the entire seven miles of interconnected parks with Fred as my official tour guide. I smiled ruefully at the very thought. Why, with Fred's limp, which had resulted from being thrown from a horse-drawn carriage not long before I had met him, I could not imagine us getting all that far. Daydreams that preposterous were a silly waste of my time, even back then. I needed to get my head out of the clouds and focus on what was in front of my very nose.

I drove into the well-marked entrance off of Blue Hills Avenue, found a place to park, and got out of my car. I stretched and walked in circles for a minute to get my old legs working again. The afternoon sun had dipped lower in the sky, and the air felt chilly. I wrapped my coat around me and set off down a well-worn dirt path. Elm trees provided shade that I didn't need at the moment, and I moved along quickly. Seeing a break in the trees up ahead, I moved toward it, tilting my face up to the last remains of the sun. It felt glorious. I spent a few minutes strolling about the grounds, thoroughly enjoying the meandering paths and the large thickets of trees that graced the park. Hand-carved benches had been placed randomly about, and I spied one on an angle directly facing a lovely body of water. As I approached, I saw a wooden sign engraved with the name Scarboro Pond. A perfect spot to rest my tired feet and watch the Canada geese and mallard ducks and maybe even catch sight of a cormorant or a blue heron. So peaceful, just as my friend would have envisioned. I recalled hearing of the brouhaha that had ensued after Fred had been hired to begin working on the project. The money that Benjamin Franklin had earmarked for the park to be built in his name decades earlier had been frittered away on something else entirely. There had been a public outcry over municipal use of private funds, a real tempest in a teapot that Fred himself had managed to stir up. His efforts had been successful, the money had been miraculously "found" almost overnight, and the rest, as they say, is history. *Who says you can't fight City Hall?* I thought with a smile.

As soon as I sat down, a flock of pigeons and a couple of squirrels gathered as if waiting for me to offer them breadcrumbs or some other tasty morsels. I decided against offering them the lone slice of fried bread I had shoved in my bag this morning. It never hurt to have an extra snack on hand in case of an emergency. I had learned that the hard way years earlier.

"I'm sorry," I called to them. "I haven't got anything for you today." I sat there, and we watched each other for a time, a sort of *détente* hanging between us, an uneasy truce. I thought of the bucket of food Billy had offered up just a few hours ago. I hoped he had someone else to share it with, a neighbor or a friend. Good food is meant to be enjoyed with others. Solitary meals are strictly for the birds.

CHAPTER 9

A short while later, I was about to depart from my bench, both the ground and the water before me now deserted, when a young woman pushing a perambulator approached.

"Is anyone sitting here?" she asked, indicating the space beside me.

I looked around, trying to mask my surprise. There were at least a dozen perfectly empty benches within view. "No dear," I replied. "I am quite alone."

She smiled and slumped down on the bench, letting out a sigh of relief. "Thank you, ma'am. That's most kind of you."

I smiled back, a comfortable silence between us. She spoke up first.

"This is such a beautiful park. I just love it here," she said shyly. I nodded in agreement.

"The man who designed and built this magnificent park was Frederick Law Olmsted, a dear friend of mine," I told her.

"Oh, how marvelous." She was silent for a moment before blurting out, "Where are my manners? My name is Hannah. Hannah Doyle. And this fine little fellow is my son, Jonathan."

I smiled back at this young woman who had invaded my peaceful solitude, and I realized I was suddenly quite glad for her company. "My name is Katharine Wormeley, but my friends call me Kate."

Hannah stuck out her hand. "It's a pleasure to meet you, Kate. Do you live here in Boston?" I shook my head and explained briefly that I was traveling between my homes in Rhode Island and New Hampshire. She regarded me in total amazement.

"My goodness. I've never been out of Boston—unless you consider Somerville, that is. That's where we live," she added somewhat apologetically. "Charlie, that's my husband, thinks I'm crazy to waste the fare for a streetcar to come all the way out here. 'Why do you have to go to the city? There's plenty of parks here in Somerville,'" she said in a gruff tone that must have been reminiscent of her husband's. "But really," she said, gesturing to the gorgeous setting, "there is nothing like this in Somerville or anywhere else, for that matter, thanks to your friend. Charlie's just . . ." She let out a sigh of resignation and shook her head sadly. "I don't know what's wrong with him lately, to tell you the truth. He's changed so much since Jonathan was born. Always harping on me about money and staying closer to home. It's like he doesn't trust his own wife to take proper care of our baby."

"Isn't it just as likely that he cares about you and wants you both to be safe?" I ventured.

"Then why can't he just tell me that?" Hannah asked. I shook my head slowly.

"I don't know, my dear. The only thing that is clear is that the two of you need to talk more." She nodded and looked down at her baby. I thought it prudent to change the subject. "Tell me about Jonathan, if you would. How old is he?"

Her brown eyes lit up at the sound of her son's name. "He is eight months old, and he's already standing up and trying to walk. Isn't that amazing?"

I tried in vain to recall when my niece and four nephews had reached that milestone but came up blank. I would have to take his mother's word for it. "Indeed," I said. I turned to look at him. "You are quite an impressive young man." My voice sounded odd, even to my own ears. Forced and wooden. Despite time with my sisters' offspring, I had never mastered the art of talking with children. As a nurse and hospital administrator, my patients had all been grown men, and when I founded the Newport Industrial School for Girls, my youngest student had been fourteen. I turned to Hannah, who was watching me closely.

"I'm sure your son will continue to delight and amaze you," I said. "But you'll have to forgive me. I've never had children of my own."

Hannah's eyes grew wide, and she put a hand to her mouth. "Oh, I'm so sorry to hear that. You and your husband couldn't . . ."

"I'm afraid I've never had a husband either," I admitted. Hannah immediately started to apologize again, but I stopped her. "It's all right, really. Marriage and a family were never in the cards for me. But I've had a long and mostly happy life. I've traveled, spent wonderful time with my family and friends, and at the end of the day I believe I'll leave this world just a bit improved over when I arrived." I could see the question forming in her head and decided to answer it before she put it into words. "I'm seventy-seven, dear." Her eyes shone with something, admiration, perhaps?

"You don't look it," she said. "I mean, you don't seem a day over . . ."

I chuckled. "Seventy-six?" I asked with raised eyebrows and a smile. "And how old . . . ?"

"I'm twenty," Hannah told me. "I'll be twenty-one next month."

So young. Her whole life was ahead of her. I was about to ask about her plans for the future, her dreams and goals, when I realized that perhaps she already had what she wanted. My path had been very different, but as long as she was happy with her choices, hers was just fine.

"We women today, we have options. Why, my sister Eliza raised three children and still managed to work as a translator and an author. A very successful one too, I might add," I said with pride. "Your precious one won't always be so little, you know."

Hannah looked pensive but shook her head.

"You mean I could get a job?" she asked skeptically. "Charlie would never allow me to do that," she added. "No wife of mine . . ." she mumbled, not bothering to finish her thought. *Oh dear.* I knew I needed to tread carefully, lest I add the fuel of discontent to the flames that were clearly already licking at their marriage.

"Well, no, it doesn't need to be a job *per se*, but possibly a hobby or an interest of yours that you could take up when Jonathan is in school." Hannah wrinkled her pert nose in thought.

"Hmmm, you mean like needlework?"

"Why not, if you enjoy it? Or how about playing the piano or painting watercolors?" I suggested. "What is it you liked to do as a girl? A younger girl growing up?" I clarified.

Hannah smiled shyly, her whole face lighting up. "I like to garden," she declared. "Back home, we used to grow all kinds of flowers. Papa always said I had a knack for it."

"That's marvelous, my dear. Just think of the lovely floral arrangements you can place all around your home." As soon as my words were spoken, I realized the possible inappropriateness of them. It was quite conceivable that the Doyles were living in a tiny walk-up, with no space for a garden or room for lavish displays of flowers. But Hannah had thoughts of her own to share and seemed to have taken no offense at my words.

"Maybe your friend the park designer would hire me to work for him," she said, a wistful look on her face. "Why, working for him would be the very best job in the world. Even Charlie couldn't object to me taking a job like that! Do you think—"

I interrupted her before she could finish. "I am afraid that my friend died four years ago," I told her with a catch in my voice.

"I'm so sorry," she said. "It was a silly idea anyway. I probably should have stayed in school. I got good grades. I always wanted to go to college. To study, I don't know, maybe history or astronomy." She shook her head; her dreamy expression had vanished.

"What kept you from it?" I asked, certain that it was family finances, the frequent culprit when it came to young women and their goals of pursuing an education. She seemed like a bright and articulate young woman, but many like her had left school early to go to work in order to support their family.

She waved her hands in response. "Well, I guess you could say that Charlie happened. I met him through mutual friends one night. He was handsome and seemed, um, sophisticated. He was so lively and full of fun. He swept me off of my feet, and then I found out I was expecting a visit from the stork, so we got married, and seven months later Jonathan was born." A look of concern clouded her delicate features. "Oh, please don't get me wrong. This little boy is the best thing that ever happened to me. And Charlie too, of course," she added somewhat defensively. "But sometimes I get to wishing that, you know, I had waited. Had more time on my own to learn what I was capable of before becoming a wife and a mother."

I patted her hand sympathetically. "We all do that from time to time," I assured her. "Even if we are quite satisfied with the choices we have made, we can't help but wonder sometimes about the path not taken. It's human nature." Hannah looked mostly convinced, but she still had questions.

"What do you wish you had done differently?" she asked. "Any paths not taken for you?"

Well, certainly. Perhaps marriage and raising children would have been good choices for me, after all. Or I could have stayed on for much longer running the hospital and arranged for care for my dear ailing mother. Or traveled more frequently back to France when issues arose with translating all of those novels instead of relying on the slow and often erratic transatlantic postal service. I might have made the move to New Hampshire permanently several years earlier. I could have been a better sister and friend. Many paths not taken, but so many well-traveled ones too, for which I was truly grateful.

"Of course I have regrets, my dear. But with so little future left, I can't spend time mourning the past. You, on the other hand, have your whole life ahead of you. You have plenty of time to explore many paths." Hannah looked agreeable to that.

"You're right, Kate. Thank you. I just needed to hear that. Charlie . . ." She shrugged. "I don't know . . ."

Before she let herself become morose again, I deftly changed the subject from his shortcomings to his occupation. "What does your husband do for work?" I asked.

She wrinkled her freckled nose. "It's kind of hard to explain. He works in a big factory. He runs some kind of machines. Well, mostly he stands guard over them to make sure they are working properly. They make brass tubes, I think. And, er, copper too."

I nodded, trying to seem enthusiastic. "Oh my, yes, brass and copper tubes." I did not know what they would be used for, and apparently neither did Hannah. "It certainly sounds like your Charlie has a very important job."

Hannah shrugged at that. "I guess so. He comes home all tired and filthy. I try to tell him about little Jon, how he's standing and trying to walk and all. But he just waves me off, tells me he needs to get cleaned up. Then after he eats dinner, he wants to go lie down, like he's ready to go to sleep, though it's still light outside. And the next day? He does it all again. I don't understand him." She threw up her hands.

I nodded, sensing that she had more to say.

"What should I do, Kate? I don't want to go crawling home to my parents' house, but I'm sick of being ignored and criticized all the time. I'm at my wit's end." The poor girl looked positively miserable, much worse off than when she had sat down beside me a short while ago. Sometimes getting things off your chest resulted in them landing square on your shoulders. What could I possibly say to help her feel better? Certainly, I had to at least try. *Let's see . . .*

"I am probably the last person qualified to give relationship advice. But since you're asking me, I'll tell you what I think."

Hannah sat forward, listening expectantly. "Go home. Not to your parents', but to the home you share with Charlie. Talk to your husband, but wait until he's had a bath after work. And maybe serve him a special dinner too. It's much easier to talk to someone who's well-fed." Hannah's brows drew together, and twin red dots appeared on her pale cheeks. I held up my hand to stop her. "I know what you're thinking. You've got a little one to keep fed and clean, and now you've got Charlie too?" She nodded but let me continue. "Dear, I'm not saying you have to run his bath or cook a three-course meal every night, but you both have a job to do. Currently, his is to go to work every day in a factory that I can only imagine is loud and dirty, get his weekly pay, put food on the table, and keep a roof over your heads. Yours is equally important, but for the time being it lacks much in the way of tangible rewards. But it's vital work. Caring for your son, tending to your home, loving your husband: it's all very important." Hannah seemed unconvinced, so I tried a different, more direct approach.

"What I'm saying in a nutshell is, it's time to grow up. You chose to get married, and that comes with responsibilities. You're not playing house, my dear. Real life is hard, and now you've got a third person added to the equation. One that relies on you for absolutely everything. You are his entire world. You must tell Charlie what you need from him and, at the same time, assure him you're quite capable of running the house and caring for your son. Can you do that, Hannah?"

She nodded slowly. "I think so. And you're right. I chose this life; I realize that. I just didn't expect it would be so . . ." She trailed off, and I found myself guessing how she might have finished her thought. Messy? Boring? Relentless? I wanted to tell her that life was short and over all too quickly, that our time with loved ones was precious and that most of us would give anything to enjoy just one more day with that one special person. Certainly, Billy Sullivan felt that way about his beloved Maureen, and Edward, despite proposing to me, would clearly move mountains to see darling Sarah again.

And S? Surely, feelings of loss hounded him daily. As for me, I would soon have the chance to spend time with . . . The silence between us was suddenly interrupted by the distinct rumbling of Hannah's stomach. *Hungry,* I thought. *This poor girl is hungry.*

I dug around in my bag and unearthed the bread that Edward had pressed upon me, wrapped in a white napkin. I knew it would serve a better purpose than merely providing crumbs for the squirrels and pigeons. "Can you help me? This entire trip, I've gotten into a bad habit of forgetting to eat lunch. By dinnertime, I'm more than a bit peckish. Would you like to share this with me? It would be impolite of me to eat alone." Hannah glanced at Jonathan, who was sleeping soundly, his small chest rising slowly beneath a thin blanket.

"Well, if you insist," Hannah answered. She took the larger piece I held out to her and proceeded to devour it. As the turkey sandwich from earlier had left me feeling quite full, I nibbled on my portion, wondering if I should offer it to her as well. She didn't appear malnourished, so it was likely that she just had not packed anything when she left the house earlier in the day. During the war, I had witnessed abject hunger on the faces of the soldiers in my care. And now some many years later, I was projecting that same dreadful state on Hannah, though I saw no actual proof of it. *Stop being a nurse,* I told myself. *This young woman needs a friend right now.*

We sat and talked for a while longer, and whether it was the food or the fact that she had been listened to, Hannah seemed much more positive and energetic than she had earlier. She vowed to share her concerns with her husband and to be more open with him about expressing her needs.

"I want him to know that I am a wonderful mother and can handle things, but I need for him to believe it too. And also, I still need alone time with him." She blushed and added, "We both need it."

"Yes, dear. Of course you do." I patted her hand and stood to leave. The way the sun was positioned in the cloudless sky, I had to assume that it was past 4:00 p.m. A quick glance at my watch confirmed it.

Then Hannah surprised me by pulling me into an embrace. "Thank you for listening to me," she whispered in my ear. "For someone who was never married, you give great marriage advice."

"It has been a delight to make your acquaintance today, my dear. I hope that our conversation helped. You take care of yourself and get your little one home all safe and sound." Hannah said she would.

"Goodbye, Kate. Safe travels," she called out as she pushed the pram down the path.

"Goodbye, my dear," I said. *Count your blessings, ask for what you need, and have a happy life.*

CHAPTER 10

Twenty minutes later, I pulled into the driveway of the Winters' stately home. As newlyweds, Priscilla and her husband, Gerald, had planned to fill up the house with children—"a face in every window," Priscilla had written in a note to me—but fate apparently had other plans. The couple had never been blessed with children, and the home that had been built for large families and holiday gatherings had never reached its full potential. I had visited on a number of occasions over the years and always felt that it more resembled a mausoleum than a family residence. Still, it would be good to catch up with Priscilla and enjoy a nice dinner. She had always been a first-rate hostess, although I hoped she had not felt the need to plan a multi-course meal along with properly paired wines selected just for us. I would be quite content with a bowl of hot soup and maybe a glass of port, thank you very much.

I heard my name being called, and I looked up at the house. And there she was, looking elegant and so well put together, waving to me from the veranda that ran the entire width of the home. I exited my car and stretched before retrieving my overnight bag and heading toward her.

"Hello, Pris. I made it, and all in one piece," I said proudly, in a tone that brooked no argument. Priscilla had been a vocal member of the recently assembled Greek chorus, the one whose sole purpose had been to question my decision to make this trip on my own. I was hoping to hear nothing more on that particular topic this evening. It had been a long day, and I was of no mind to defend myself.

"Hello, my dear Kate. You look positively radiant. And none the worse for wear," she called out. I looked down at my mud-splattered tweed coat, dusty black boots, and dirty leather gloves. I didn't believe her, not for a minute, but had to admit it was nice to hear.

After I removed my coat and gloves, we hugged and I told her she looked quite marvelous, and she did. Priscilla Winters, née Worthington, had always possessed an ethereal beauty with her thick mane of flowing golden hair, pale blue eyes, and delicate frame. Our paths had first crossed when Mother and I began volunteering at the Ladies Union Aid Society in Newport before the war broke out. Priscilla and her mother had joined as well, and the four of us had become friends, often visiting each other's homes for dinner or a game of bridge.

I had been able to secure a government clothing contract, which provided paid employment for the wives and daughters of our enlisted men. I recall boasting that we could produce ten thousand flannel shirts but was chuffed to bits when we ended up with five times that amount. After the work had ended and we ceased production, Pris and I drifted apart, especially after I volunteered as a nurse stationed in Virginia and she started seeing a man ten years her junior. I had only met him a handful of times; he was quite dashing, but honestly? I found him to be shallow, certainly no match for her sharp wit and intellect. I had been unable to attend the ceremony when they tied the knot, and they'd moved to Boston shortly thereafter. I rarely heard from her over the years, but she had written to me soon after Mother died, and we had begun a regular correspondence which endured to this day. Whenever she traveled back to Newport, she stayed with me. Her husband did not join her on these jaunts, and I only saw him occasionally when I visited. He was frequently away on business. I imagined he had now retired, but I wasn't certain.

I offered to remove my boots once we stepped aside, but my concerns were waved away. Priscilla was chattering on and on as she led me through the house, pointing out the new wallpaper in the large, elegantly appointed foyer and a mahogany sideboard, recently inherited from Gerald's side of the family, in the formal dining room. I asked after her husband and was informed that he was in Albany, visiting his sister, who was recovering from a nasty bout of pneumonia.

"Gerald's visit is such a blessing to his poor sister. I miss him so," said Priscilla, sounding as if she didn't actually miss him one little bit. "But this will give us ladies time to visit." A uniformed maid appeared, and despite her diminutive size, she reached for my valise. Hoisting it over her shoulder, she headed for the stairs, and I followed behind.

"Charlotte will help you get settled, my dear. Then join me in the parlor for a cuppa," Priscilla called to me with what I assumed was her attempt at a British accent. Was it my imagination, or was everyone using colloquialisms from across the pond these days? *Please stop,* I begged silently.

I huffed and puffed a bit on the last few stairs. Surely, this was not one of the symptoms my doctor had warned me about. Being out of breath was no doubt due to my cutting back on my usual routine of twice daily walks on the beach. It had been an unseasonably hot summer, and more than ever the promise of crisp mountain air felt rejuvenating. I followed the maid into a lovely room complete with cabbage-rose wallpaper, thick Persian rugs, and a four-poster bed that required a portable set of wooden stairs to climb up to.

"Thank you," I told Charlotte as she started hanging clothes in the closet in the corner of the large room. She took special care with the sapphire-blue silk organza gown that I planned to wear tomorrow evening. It had served me well for a number of years, and if it was perhaps a wee bit dated, well, so be it. I had never been a slave to fashion, and as I was nearing eighty years of age, it was highly unlikely that I would start now.

"My pleasure, ma'am," she said with an accent I found oddly familiar.

"Call me Kate," I implored. "And tell me, if you would, where are you from?"

She appeared flustered as she gathered up my disreputable outerwear and boots to take back downstairs. I knew that everything would be returned to me first thing in the morning, all spic and span. "I live here," she finally said, reaching for my hat and scarf, adding them to the pile.

"Oh yes, but your people? I was born and raised in Suffolk, and your accent reminds me of home."

Charlotte's eyes grew bright, and she told me she had grown up in nearby Essex. "My whole family still lives there," she said, a note of wistfulness in her voice. "I plan to go back there someday, but for now . . ." She glanced around the room, shaking her head sadly.

"Well, at the very least you have a lovely home to live and work in," I said cheerfully. "I'm certain that Mrs. Winters appreciates your hard work." Charlotte seemed unconvinced, but the distinct ringing of the crystal bell from downstairs shook her from her reverie.

"It's been lovely to meet you. I should head back down," she said. And with that, she hurried out of the room and headed for the staircase. I certainly hoped that Priscilla appreciated her. Growing up with maids, cooks, nannies, and governesses, the four of us children had been raised with our parents' excellent example to be nothing short of kind and generous to our staff. Why, they had been a part of the family. I maintained that same practice today with the year-round, live-in help at both of my homes. I had shared with the three members of my Newport staff that they would receive generous severance pay from me and that I would do my best to see that they were hired by whomever purchased my home. They would be well taken care of, that was for certain. I changed into a pair of leather-soled pumps and smoothed my full-skirted traveling dress. There was no need to primp or change into evening attire for dinner.

I heard the bell again and assumed this time it signaled that my presence was expected downstairs for tea. I splashed cold water on my face and washed my hands, looking in vain at my windblown hair. At least it would be a quiet evening tonight. Just two old friends, chewing the proverbial fat.

CHAPTER 11

"I have a delightful surprise for you, Kate. Would you like to venture a guess?" Priscilla asked once we were settled in front of a blazing fire with cups of steaming hot tea. I leaned forward and placed my cup on the marble-topped table.

"Goodness me, Pris. At my age, I'm surprised that I recognize where I am when I awake in the morning. Or even that I do awaken." She pouted, and I remembered how strong her flare for the dramatic had always been, so I softened my tone. "I am sorry, dear. Tell me, please, won't you? A new dessert recipe, perhaps? Maybe some recently inherited china place settings?"

She smiled, appeased. "No, you silly girl. Something much better. We're expecting a special guest any minute now for dinner." When I failed to start guessing who it might be, she blurted out, "It's Mary. Mrs. Frederick Law Olmsted." *What on earth?* My look of surprise was hard to hide, and Priscilla immediately grew concerned.

"Kate, oh my goodness. Did I make a mistake in inviting Mrs. Olmsted? She's a lovely woman, lost her husband a few years ago, and she's on her way back up to Deer Isle, Maine. We ran into each other at a luncheon to discuss the new hospital they're building in the South End. We got to talking, and I mentioned how my good friend Kate Wormeley was going to be visiting and she said, 'Oh, I would love to see her while she is in town.' So I said . . . Kate, you've gone pale. I assumed you were old friends. Please, dear, say something, won't you?"

Surprised as I was, I still felt the need to reassure my hostess. "It's all right, Pris. Really, it will be fine, truly fine. It's just that I've never actually—" I was interrupted by the sound of the doorbell, and as I watched, Charlotte scurried toward the massive oak front door. Priscilla rose and, with an apologetic look, left the room to greet her guest.

"I'm sorry, Kate," she murmured as she passed me. Seconds later, I heard her welcoming Mrs. Mary Perkins Olmsted, widow of the illustrious landscape architect Frederick Law Olmsted. Since our time working together at the USSC, Fred and I had become friends and confidantes, although I had never met his wife or any of their children. For a second, I regretted not asking for a glass of sherry instead of tea. If there was ever a moment when my jangled nerves might benefit from a bracing sip of alcohol, this was most definitely it. I stood as the two women entered the drawing room, and I felt myself being silently appraised by Pris, worried that I might be upset, as well as by the newcomer, with much curiosity. I stood in place as they approached me. Although we were all roughly the same age, Mrs. Olmsted appeared much younger than Priscilla or myself. The few wrinkles she had did nothing to mar her porcelain complexion, and her bright blue eyes seemed to not miss a thing. She was a tiny woman, several inches shorter than me at five feet four inches. Delicate but with a core of steel, if everything I'd heard about her for nearly fifty years was accurate.

"Kate, it is my honor to introduce you to my friend Mrs. Frederick Law Olmsted. I had thought the two of you had been previously acquainted, but no matter. Mary, this is Miss Katharine Wormeley, a dear old friend who is passing through on her way to her second home, way up north in New Hampshire."

Mrs. Olmsted nodded in my direction. "Ah, one more thing that we have in common, my dear Miss Wormeley." She paused, and I found myself anxious to know what she meant. "I enjoy heading up north as well. Later this week, I'll be on my way to Maine, to the home I shared with my late husband Fred for a number of years." I couldn't tell if she had emphasized the possessive nature of the relationship, but I tried to focus on remaining calm, at least on the outside. I felt a wave of . . . was it guilt? There had always been something between her husband and me. Not romance certainly, but a connection of sorts. Over the years of our friendship, Fred had rarely spoken of his wife, at least not to me.

"I was so sorry to hear of Mr. Olmsted's passing. I do hope you received my note of condolence?" I asked. She appeared to ponder my question for just a moment before shaking her head.

"As I'm sure you can imagine, Fred's death ushered in a tidal wave of letters, cards, and floral arrangements. Why, the entire first floor of our home in Brookline still reeks of lilies," she said, her nose wrinkling in distaste. "And it's been four whole years," she added, almost as if speaking to herself.

"I'm not surprised by the outpouring of mourners that you describe. He was highly regarded by so many," I said. "And please, won't you call me Kate?" Her blue eyes were shrewd as she regarded me thoughtfully before nodding.

"And naturally, I'm Mary," she said matter-of-factly before turning her attention to our hostess. "I see there is a pot of tea at the ready, but I was hoping for a glass of sherry or perhaps some mulled wine, my dear Priscilla. I find tea keeps me up at night, while a nice glass of sherry on the other hand . . ."

"Oh, of course, where are my manners?" Priscilla rang a tiny silver bell and instructed Charlotte, who appeared almost instantaneously, to bring a decanter of sherry and three glasses. "You'll join us, Kate, of course," she declared, not waiting for an answer. Motioning for us to join her, she sat and faced the crackling fire in the hearth. "Is there anything lovelier than a late-day fire? This old house gets so drafty," she admitted. "But nothing like the Talbots' home in Taunton, am I right, Kate?" She turned back to Mary. "Our Kate just spent the night with Edward Talbot," she said before realizing how that might have sounded. She became quite flustered as she attempted to correct herself. "Oh, I mean, well, he was a host to her . . ."

Mary chuckled heartily. "For a moment, I thought we were in for some juicy gossip. A single woman overnight in a recent widower's home? My, that would get some old Brahmin tongues wagging."

I bristled at the implication of anything untoward occurring. Marriage proposal aside, Edward had been a perfect gentleman.

"Surely, my friends know me well enough to vouch for my behavior. Why, I've known Edward since before he married my oldest friend, Sarah Andrews. Nearly fifty years," I responded, trying to maintain a calm and tranquil demeanor.

"Thou dost protest too much, my dear Kate," Mary replied with a twinkle in her blue eyes. "But scandalous affairs aside, just how is Edward these days? I first met him and his wife when we moved here from Manhattan years ago. I was saddened to hear of dear Sarah's passing. I do hope he's coping reasonably well?"

"He is doing just fine," I said. "Hale and hearty as ever." *And itching to get married again,* I almost added.

Mary leaned forward and spoke in a conspiratorial tone. "And tell me, does he still interject those ridiculous British phrases into his speech?" I laughed aloud at that and found myself warming to this woman. She had a razor-sharp wit, and it was obvious that she didn't suffer fools lightly. She was quick and quite charming, and I imagined she would have been excellent company for Fred and independent enough to withstand his prolonged absences.

"Blimey, guv'nor," I said, breaking into a Cockney dialect. "Yeah, he's a right prat, a'right." Now it was Mary's turn to laugh, and I watched as she cast me an appraising look. *She likes me too,* I realized. *Or at least finds me likable.* I was enjoying getting to know her.

Priscilla looked back and forth between us, appearing a bit confused as to the lighthearted turn of the conversation between two relative strangers. "Excuse me, won't you, ladies? I need to go check on dinner," she announced as she stood and hurried out of the room. The resultant silence between Mary and me was not an uncomfortable one. Just as the quiet seemed to go on for a touch too long, Mary spoke up.

"Do tell me, won't you, how do you spend your time up north? I imagine you've made friends with some of the locals?"

"Oh yes," I said. "Jackson is a lovely small town, and I've met so many of my neighbors over the years. Some local folks, farmers and tradesmen, but a fair number of transplants like myself. Artists, writers, poets . . . all drawn to the natural beauty and fresh mountain air. It's quite exhilarating," I concluded.

"Then I'm certain you must fit in there quite nicely," Mary pronounced, and I nodded in agreement. Indeed, I felt that I did. I was so looking forward to reconnecting with my neighbors and friends in Jackson. It offered all of the charm and conviviality one could hope for and was surrounded by mountains and forests of trees. *Heavenly!*

Priscilla returned to let us know that dinner was being served. As we followed our hostess into the dining room, she turned to smile at us. "Look at the two of you," she said. "Barely just met and already thicker than thieves."

"Who knew we had so much in common?" I said, and Mary and I shared a laugh, joined after a brief pause by our mystified and somewhat relieved hostess. During dinner, a lovely leg of lamb, this one served with a tangy mint jelly, Priscilla shared with Mary that she would be attending the anniversary party of Curtis and Lucretia Vanderbilt the next evening as my guest.

"Can you imagine?" she crowed. "A proper married woman parading around at night without her husband?" Realizing her faux pas, she tried to remedy the awkward silence that had greeted her comment. "Oh my, I mean, Mary, I'm so sorry. Your husband has passed away and, Kate, my goodness, you've never had a husband, so it's not as if . . ." She trailed off miserably. "I apologize ladies. It's just highly unusual to see women alone at night."

Mary cut her off smoothly with a wave of her hand. "You should quit while you're ahead, dear Pris, and certainly before you put your foot squarely in your mouth for a second time." She winked at me, and we exchanged a glance of mutual support. "Tell me, Kate, how did you manage to wangle an invitation to one of the premier social events of the fall season?"

"Lucretia is my first cousin on my mother's side," I explained. "I imagine I'll be one of the few guests in attendance tomorrow evening who also attended their wedding ceremony fifty years earlier."

"I'm sure it will be just lovely, and the two of you the absolute belles of the ball," said Mary as she reached for her glass of sherry.

The conversation turned to events of the day before branching out to popular songs and books. As it turned out, Mary and I had similar tastes in both music and literature. She even shared that she had read and thoroughly enjoyed many of the novels I had translated. "You manage to imbue the culture and nuance of the French people in a manner that makes the reading most enjoyable," she told me. Her praise thrilled me to my very core, and I thanked her. *Ha, take that Edward Talbot,* I thought. I had imagined a quiet evening with Pris, but it had developed into something memorable and lively.

CHAPTER 12

After our dinner plates had been cleared, we returned to the library with its crackling fire, and Mary and I ended up sitting together on the velvet settee. Priscilla was flitting about, overseeing the stoking of the flames one minute and checking on dessert in the kitchen the next. I had stopped drinking after a half glass of sherry, knowing that imbibing any more was *verboten*, according to my doctor, and likely to have me dozing instead of enjoying this lovely evening. I wasn't consciously keeping track, but I was fairly certain that the diminutive Mary was currently enjoying her third glass. She leaned toward me, and in the firelight I could see her blue eyes were very bright and her cheeks were flushed. Possibly her fourth?

"I'm sure you know how much he admired you," she said in a tone that brooked no argument, despite a distinct slurring of her words. "I believe he may have even loved you in his way." Ah, so we were having this conversation this evening.

"I can assure you, Mary. Nothing ever—"

She silenced me with a wave of her tiny hand. "Of course it didn't. My husband was a decent and most honorable man. He would never have disrespected me in that way." I sat back, relieved I was not required to defend neither myself nor her late husband. "But, nonetheless, requited or not, I believe he loved you and that you loved him as well. There was correspondence between you, letters over the years. I never read the ones I found in his things after . . . However, based upon the sheer volume, I have to imagine there was . . . something. Am I correct in my assumptions?"

I let out a breath and chose my words carefully. "I respect you too much to tell you anything but the truth. Yes, it's true. I loved your husband." She was watching me with the oddest expression on her face. A combination of sadness and something else. Respect, maybe? "I'm sorry," I added. Not sorry to have loved him, I wanted to clarify. No, I was only sorry that I had to admit it to her all these years later. She nodded almost imperceptibly.

"I was not his first choice for a wife. Are you aware that he had been engaged previously?" It was my turn to nod. Fred had told me of his broken engagement to a Miss Emily Perkins, no relation of Mary's. "And that I had been married to his younger brother John? He died at only thirty-two years of age, can you imagine that?" Again, I nodded. Fred had done the honorable thing by marrying his brother's young widow and adopting her three children. They'd welcomed four more babies into the family, but only two had survived past infancy. While not a love match, at least initially, their marriage had been sound and healthy by all reports. In the years I had known Fred, through hundreds of conversations and many dozens of letters that had passed between us, I had never heard him utter or write a single cross word about his wife. I leaned in and smiled at her.

"He loved you very much," I told her, and after a moment she responded with a touch of annoyance.

"I am very much aware of that fact," she said crisply. "I don't need you to tell me that my husband of forty-four years loved me." Stung, I looked down at my lap, unsure of how to respond. I stayed silent long enough for Mary to get the last word in. "Apparently, he loved us both, in his way." She stood, brushing her hands down her full-skirted dress as she studied me closely. I stayed quiet, having no clue what was expected of me.

"That's another thing we have in common," she said. Confused, I stood as well. She motioned toward my own full dress. "Not giving a damn about the fashion trends of the day. No slim skirts for me. How does one enter or exit a motor vehicle, I ask you? Or board a sailing skiff or even ride a horse, for that matter?" I smiled at her. A genuine smile this time, relief flooding my veins and warming me to my core.

"Well, I may be dressed appropriately, but I believe that my sailing days are over and I have hung up my saddle for good as well. But you go right ahead," I added with a wink.

That got a laugh from Mary, and she wiped at her eyes with a lace handkerchief retrieved from her skirt pocket. "You know, don't you, that I may have misrepresented the nature of our relationship to our hostess just a smidge."

"Yes," I said. "Clearly, Pris had been led to believe that you and I were old chums."

"And now we are," said Mary with a smile.

"And now we are," I agreed. I doubted I would ever see Mary Olmsted again after this evening, but I was very glad to have spent time in her company. Fred's married state had negated any possibility that he and I could have had some sort of future together, and it made me glad that it had been to a strong woman, clearly worthy of his devotion. And if not for Mary, I never would have fallen in love for a second time just one year later.

It was an early night since Mary's son John arrived in the family carriage to fetch his mother shortly before 9:00 p.m. We embraced warmly and said our goodbyes. As I was falling asleep an hour later, I replayed snippets of our conversation and found myself smiling.

CHAPTER 13

Boston, Massachusetts
Friday, October 4, 1907

I slept well in the comfortable room I had been provided with, and in the morning, after washing up, I headed downstairs, where I joined Priscilla for breakfast. I was looking forward to coffee and— *hmmm, let's see*—a delightful warm scone served with fresh strawberries and clotted cream. *Heavenly.*

"Would you have preferred lemon curd?" Priscilla asked me. "It's fresh and, I'm told, very delicious," she added. I assured her I would sample it tomorrow morning, provided scones would be available once more. I noticed she'd made do with a cup of tea with lemon and a single slice of unbuttered toast.

"If I continue to dine like this, I'll need to expand my skirts even farther," I said with a grin.

"Why, you must weigh the same as you did all of those years ago when we first met."

It was close to being true, I conceded. I had been blessed with a very speedy metabolism, inherited from both of my parents, and had enjoyed, until quite recently, a very active lifestyle.

"Nevertheless, once I arrive home I'll need to increase my level of activity. I am certainly not getting any exercise by driving my car." That got an immediate response from Priscilla. She leaned forward expectantly, her pale eyes full of mischief.

"Did you see the look on Mary Olmsted's face when she discovered you were driving on your own?" she asked. "She was flabbergasted and more than a bit in awe of you."

I nodded and took a sip of my coffee. Yes, that had been quite satisfying. I turned my attention to the scone in front of me, breaking it into smaller pieces and slathering it with cream. "She was actually quite lovely."

"Yes, she's had such a hard life though, the poor dear. What with her husband traveling all over the country, I can't imagine that he was around all that much," she said with a disapproving sniff. I was about to jump in and defend him when she continued. "And those babies she lost, and her older daughter confined to an insane asylum and the one son dying out west after graduating from Yale . . . why, her whole life has been one tragedy after another." She shook her head in disbelief.

I couldn't imagine the pain of losing children at any age, and Mary Olmsted had certainly had more than her share of adversity. But she was fortunate in that Fred had been by her side through all of it, at least in spirit, and I hoped that his presence had eased even a modicum of her grief. I picked at the sliced strawberries, lost in thought. *To have and to hold, from this day forward.* Words from the popular wedding vows came to me unbidden. What had I missed out on, never being witness to those words being spoken about me?

"So how will we spend the day, then?" I asked brightly. We had talked about doing some shopping, followed by a late lunch. "Shopping at Filene's and lunch? Does that still sound good?"

"Yes, let's stick to the plan," she said gaily. "I'll have Douglas bring the carriage around in, say, half an hour. Will that give you enough time to get ready?" she asked, deftly appraising my appearance from head to toe. I looked down at the serviceable gray wool shirtwaist dress I had already worn a couple of times on this trip. As far as I was concerned, I was ready to go.

"That will be fine," I told her.

•   •   •

William Filene's Sons & Company was a large, modern, and stylish store offering the best and latest merchandise and exceptional customer service. It was, according to Pris, the *only* place to shop in Boston. I had noticed several other retailers dotting the neighborhood, including Jordan Marsh and Gilchrist's, but I decided I would trust her judgment and exquisite taste. The only item on my shopping list for today was a gift for the Vanderbilts. What on earth do you get the couple that has everything? With Pris's help, I selected a delicate pair of Lalique crystal swans. They were far too *chichi* for my personal tastes, but I recalled that my cousin Lu always favored anything that looked expensive, and to my relatively untrained eye, these swans appeared nearly as expensive as they actually were.

"They mate for life, you know," I told Pris, who looked puzzled.

"What's that now?" she asked, and I explained what little I knew about the mating life of swans.

"Well, isn't that just ducky?" she chuckled. "You learn something new every day."

I would have been more than content to go to lunch while waiting for my gift to be wrapped, but Pris had her heart set on a new pair of gloves for this evening. She had once confessed to feeling self-conscious about her liver-spotted hands that she believed aged her considerably, so we spent the better part of an hour while she steadfastly tried on pair after pair of evening gloves, or as she called them, opera gloves, before finally deciding on a silk-lined, cream-colored pair, the very first she had been shown. I considered purchasing a pair myself to replace the already worn pair of gauntlet gloves I had purchased specifically for this trip but decided that I truly didn't mind if my old-lady hands were on display this evening. After collecting my beautifully wrapped gift, we entered the restaurant. I had pictured a simple café with maybe a counter and some stools, but it was nothing but the best for our dear Pris.

Uniformed servers swarmed around the space, which was elegant and softly lit, designed specifically for the society ladies who lunched.

"Our special today is chicken *a la* king served on toast points," confided the young man assigned to our table in a most conspiratorial tone. Was the "special" truly so special that it was meant to be kept a secret? "I haven't sampled it myself, but I understand it is simply divine." Pris raised an eyebrow as if to elicit my interest, but I shook my head. I knew that separating out the requisite peas from the sauce would be time-consuming and would call attention to my dietary quirk. The roast chicken served with dumplings caught my eye, and after confirming the lack of any tiny green nuisances, I placed my order. Pris ordered the lobster cocktail with a side of celery and radishes, which I knew from experience she would push around her plate while chattering nonstop. "Please eat a sandwich," I frequently wanted to say to her, but that was the unspoken rule between us. Her restrictive diet was her business and hers alone. I knew full well that I could not address it even indirectly, despite my concerns.

While we sipped our water and waited for our lunch, we couldn't help but overhear the conversation between two women in the booth across from ours.

"Well, excuse me for saying, but if Edward Filene expects women to trudge down to the basement to pick at second-rate merchandise, he'll have a rude awakening," the older of the two women said.

"What on earth do you suppose he's thinking?" asked the other woman, shaking her head in amazement. Now I am not one to gossip, but I do pride myself on being knowledgeable about certain subjects. I decided I had to know more about this one.

"Excuse me, I couldn't help overhear. What is being planned for this store? Some sort of bargain basement?" I asked before Pris could stop me, her sense of proper behavior of a higher standard than mine. The two turned their attention to me, clearly interested in hearing more from this outspoken interloper.

The older women spoke up. "Apparently, next year they are going to open a bargain annex in the basement to sell off excess merchandise, things that wouldn't sell upstairs, at low prices. He's even developed some sort of automatic markdown schedule."

"So the longer an item goes unsold, the more it gets marked down. Can you even imagine?" the younger woman asked.

Pris shuddered visibly. "How crass. They'll be shutting their doors after a month," she predicted. The two women nodded in agreement, but I was intrigued by the idea. Not everyone could afford the full-price clothing and household goods that Filene's offered. Why, the price of the pair of gloves Pris had purchased would feed a family of four for a week or more. The swans? Probably six months. And then there were the frugal ones like me who liked nice things and appreciated quality but would prefer to see their funds go to help others, not simply to line the coffers of the Filene family. I might have to plan a trip back to Boston next year, after all.

Our meals arrived, and I tucked right in, watching as Pris nibbled at a quartered radish.

"This is delightful, Pris. Would you care for a bite?" I held up my fork as an open invitation, but she shook her head and patted her lips with her napkin.

"I'm saving room for what should be a lavish buffet at the Vanderbilts' this evening," she said with a wink. After pushing around a chunk of lobster, pink and glistening, with her fork, she gave up the pretense of eating altogether. "I don't know where you put it, Kate," she said. My mouth full of soft, pillowy dumplings, I shrugged my shoulders and chewed contentedly.

CHAPTER 14

We arrived back at the house in the middle of the afternoon to find Gerald Winters having what my dear mother would have referred to as throwing a wobbly. Working himself up to a full lather of annoyance, he paced back and forth in the foyer, glaring at the two of us and trying like heck to find out what we had purchased and where we had been. I wondered if either of us had produced a gift for him, if he would have calmed right down. But all we had to show for our time was an anniversary gift and a pair of leather gloves.

"I couldn't imagine where you had gotten off to," Gerald said, his voice stiff with barely hidden ititation, causing Pris to go into a long and drawn-out explanation of Filene's various departments, how I had purchased a gift and she'd bought gloves for this evening's celebration. She began to extoll the virtues of her lobster cocktail, which she had barely touched, when Gerald cut her off.

"What sort of party are you referring to? I recall nothing on my calendar for this evening," Gerald said with a note of finality in his tone. I decided to speak up on her behalf.

"Your wife has generously agreed to accompany me to an anniversary gala this evening," I told Gerald sweetly. "Have you ever met my cousin Lucretia Preble? She and Curtis Vanderbilt, no relation, are celebrating their fiftieth anniversary this evening."

"I'm sure I told you, darling. What with your poor sister's health on your mind, it must have slipped," Pris stammered, clearly made nervous by her husband's truculence.

"Far be it from me to recall all the comings and goings you rattle on about, Priscilla," said Gerald coldly. "But since I have been away for several days, I came home to see my wife. I did not know that you would be off gadding about, tonight of all nights."

"I can call over if you like," I said. "I'm certain that an extra guest would be most welcome."

Gerald looked as if he had tasted something quite rancid. He shook his head and answered me through pursed lips. "That will not be necessary, I can assure you, Katharine. Priscilla and I will stay in this evening. I have already alerted the staff."

Priscilla looked about to say something, but decided against it. Clearly, her husband's mind had been made up. I would be going solo this evening.

As soon as I could, I excused myself to get ready. While I drew a bath, I placed a call to the Parker House, inquiring if they had any available rooms for the evening. Based upon the current level of tension in the home, I thought it prudent to make myself scarce. But no, I was told, there were no rooms available as there was a huge social event planned for the evening and rooms had sold out quickly.

"It's the Vanderbilts," said the operator in a tone edged with awe. "It's a big swanky to-do for *the* Vanderbilts." I wanted to correct her assumption with a "no relation" response, but let her have her fantasies. Far be it from me to burst someone's bubble for no good reason.

I drew a steaming hot bath, aware that I could have asked for help from one of the staff. When the day comes that I am no longer capable of running a bath for myself, well, it would certainly be high time I start looking at pine boxes for my eternal slumber. After a good long soak *sans* assistance, I toweled off and began the process of pulling on the layers of underpinnings, topped off with a perky crinoline and my trusted gown of silk organza. The deep blue was flattering, I knew, as I had received dozens of compliments in the years that I had been wearing it. I was about to ring for Charlotte to assist me with the long row of back buttons when there came a light tap on the door, followed by, "Kate? It's Pris. May I come in?"

"Of course," I replied quickly, and the door opened. Pris's face, lined with concern, peered around the frame. She softened somewhat as she studied my evening frock.

"I've always liked you in that dress," she cooed, and I smiled at her.

"It's all right, you know," I said. At her look of confusion, I continued. "Not attending the party this evening, I mean. I understand, and it's fine."

Pris forced a smile. "I am so sorry, Kate. If I had known Gerald was coming back a day early, I never would have—"

I interrupted by turning my back to her. "Priscilla, you do not need to apologize, but I would appreciate your help with these dratted buttons, please."

She got right to work, and soon I was all buttoned up and ready for a night on the town. At least I thought I was, but Pris started making adjustments immediately, first to my dress with a couple of well-placed safety pins and then to my hair, undoing my serviceable bun and twisting it into some sort of chignon, and finally to my face, dotting my cheeks with a rouge and applying a dusting of lightly scented powder. I stood in front of the mirror, surveying her work, and had to admit that I looked better for her efforts.

"Would you like to borrow one of my furs?" she asked, and I shook my head after realizing I would need to check it into the cloakroom unless I wanted to carry it around all evening, and besides, it wasn't all that chilly. She looked disappointed, as if she so desperately wanted to do something nice for me to make up for leaving me unescorted. Poor Pris. She already had a spouse who wanted her to feel guilty. She didn't need me piling on more of the same.

"I have asked Douglas to drive you tonight. It's the least I can do. I can't imagine you'll want to have to deal with your car and trying to park it over on Beacon Hill; it's bound to be more of a challenge than you need," she insisted. I was about to turn down her offer, but I relented. I hadn't ever gotten used to driving at night, and my eyesight was not all that it had once been.

"That would be lovely," I assured her.

"He'll wait for you, if you like, or you can call here when you're ready to come home," she pressed, as anxious as a mother seeing off her socially awkward daughter. I assured her I would make arrangements with Douglas and that there was no need for her to worry about me.

She pressed on, undaunted, determined to assist me in any way she could. "I've asked Chartlotte to attend to you this evening when you return. To assist you with your boudoir." I was about to tell her I needed no assistance, but recalling the long row of buttons that would be standing between me and a good night's sleep later this evening, I agreed.

"Thank you, Pris. I shall try to not be out too late," I said with a smile.

"Gerald says to have a lovely evening and to give his best to the happy couple," Pris told me smoothly. I sincerely doubted that he had voiced either of those sentiments, but I nodded my thanks and prepared to depart. Douglas, looking every inch the nattily attired society chauffeur, was waiting for me at the bottom of the stairs and escorted me to my waiting carriage. I looked over at my car parked near the gazebo. Just for a moment, I could imagine myself hurrying over, getting in, and driving off into the night. Then I realized it was pitch-dark, and I didn't enjoy driving at night. *See you tomorrow*, I silently messaged the car. *We'll be back on the road first thing.*

"I feel a bit like Cinderella going to the ball," I told Douglas as I got settled.

"I'll be sure to get you home by midnight, then," he said with a smile. And off we went.

CHAPTER 15

We were still a block or two from the Parker House, the elegant hotel on the corner of School Street and Tremont in the city's heart, when traffic came to a complete halt. I looked around, amazed at what I was seeing. A heady landscape of color, from the brightly hued gowns of the well-dressed women to the outrageous floral displays lining the sidewalks, the streets were brightly lit and jammed with people. Mostly partygoers, if I had to guess, based on the top hats and tails worn by the dozens of men who walked, or at least tried to, arm in arm with the gowned and bejeweled women. My blue dress looked drab in comparison, not at all surprising due to the fact that it had been shoved in a back bedroom closet for years. How long had it been since I'd had the occasion to wear it—seven or eight, possibly ten years? Oh well, it was likely that no one would be looking at me this evening, that was for certain.

Douglas skillfully inched ahead, maneuvering around cars, horses, and carriages, his shoulders hunched forward, his gaze unflinching. I leaned toward him and tapped on the glass that separated us. He half turned to look back at me.

"Can I help you, Miss Wormeley?" he asked. "Is there anything you need?"

"Please call me Kate," I pressed. "I just wanted to tell you how much I appreciate your driving me. I had planned to take my car, but all this . . ." I shuddered. "I would be a wreck. You, on the other hand, look like you're enjoying the challenge." He chuckled at that.

"You're right. I am. We're less than a half block away from the entrance. What would you say if I were able to pull up just past that street sign ahead? I could walk you into your party and be back before any of the street patrol noticed me." I watched as a dozen uniformed guards and police officers strolled around, instructing the drivers of any stopped vehicles to get moving.

"It's your call, Douglas. I am capable of walking from here. Believe me, I'm much heartier than I might appear to be."

"I would never underestimate you, Miss Kate. You strike me as a woman who can accomplish anything you have a mind to," he said.

"Well, thank you. What a lovely thing to hear." And his timing couldn't have been any better, I thought. Arriving unescorted at a posh party, a ball, where I wouldn't know a single solitary soul save for the hosts: a cousin I hadn't seen in probably twenty years and her husband, whom I had met only a handful of times. My confidence waning, I wondered why I had said I would be in attendance this evening.

"Let's do this, Miss Kate," said Douglas, and I saw he had pulled off on the side of the road. Right in front of us was the Parker House Hotel. He tied up the horse while I gathered my evening clutch and the elegantly wrapped anniversary gift. Douglas helped me out of the carriage, and we were about to cross the busy street when a patrolman called out for us to stop.

"Where do you think you're going?" the beefy young man asked Douglas.

"Why, officer, I am merely helping this lovely lady into the party going on, and then I'll be right back to move my horse and carriage," replied Douglas smoothly, but the man in uniform clearly would not allow that to happen. He shook his head emphatically.

"Yeah, sorry, pal. I'm gonna have to ask you to move. I will be glad to help her across the street and up the stairs, but you and your horse and buggy are causing a traffic jam out here. Time to go, buddy." I panicked at the thought of being on my own, having hoped that I could arrive at the party on Douglas's strong and steady arm, but that hadn't worked out.

"Are you going to be all right?" Douglas asked, clearly upset by the turn of events.

"I'll be fine," I told him, mustering up all the confidence I could. "Can we meet back here in a couple of hours? I just want to make an appearance, offer my best wishes, and drop off my gift." Douglas looked at his watch.

"I'll be here at 10:00 p.m. on the dot, and don't worry, I'll wait for you in case you're busy dancing and having a gay old time." I scoffed at the image, but our friend the police officer was decidedly more vocal in his response.

"You'll not be waiting here for that long, buddy. Not on my watch, which actually ends at 9:00 p.m. Well, I guess you'll be someone else's problem by then. C'mon, then, mother. Tell your son good night and let's get you across the street and inside." I grinned, suddenly feeling lighthearted and a tad mischevious.

"Good night, dear sonny boy," I called out with a wave, which Douglas returned.

"Good night, Mother dearest," he replied with a wink before untying his horse and climbing back up onto the wide bench.

"C'mon, then, ma'am," my police escort pleaded. "Let's get this show on the road, yeah?" I took his arm, and we started across the street.

The hotel lobby was teeming with people: tuxedoed gentlemen bellying up to one of the three cocktail bars for glasses of wine or sifters of port or brandy, women whose long dresses and jewels glittered even more in the brightly lit space. I noticed all this while I stood on the wrong side of the entrance, unable to convince the smartly-dressed maitre d' that I was *not* a party crasher.

"Madam," he said smoothly but showing just a touch of annoyance with me, "I'm sorry, but you are not on the guest list, and you cannot produce an invitation. It was mailed to all guests several weeks ago. I'm afraid I have to insist that you please go back home."

"My name is Katharine Wormeley, my good man, and as I have already told you, I packed the invitation away shortly after it arrived. I sent my regrets, but then my plans changed and I sent word that I would attend after all with a guest." His bushy eyebrows raised suspiciously, he frowned at me.

"Then where is your guest, madam?"

"Her husband returned unexpectedly, and she couldn't join me this evening. But guest or no guest, Mrs. Vanderbilt is my first cousin, and I'm sure that she would—"

"The Vanderbilts are very important people, madam. Surely, they don't—"

"They're no relation," I interjected quickly, which earned me another frown.

"You just told me you were a cousin," he said, not even trying to hide his growing suspicion.

"I *am* a cousin. When I said 'no relation,' I meant that the hosts for this evening are not true Vanderbilts, is all. They are not the famous millionaire Vanderbilts. They are merely the regular ones. No relation." I saw by his look of disdain that I had run out of arguments.

"Be that as it may, tonight's hosts were adamant that no one be allowed to enter who was not on the list." I was about to turn away and go back outside when I heard a young male voice call out.

"Auntie. There you are. We have been so worried. What are you doing out here? Come in and join us. You must be exhausted, traveling all this way." The speaker was a tall, very good-looking man with fair hair and pink cheeks. I had never laid eyes on him in my life. I studied him closely, emboldened by his confidence and the devilish gleam in his blue eyes. I reasoned that if my chauffeur could pretend to be my son, surely this young stranger could play the part of my beloved nephew.

"Oh, my dear, it's so good to see you again. I seem to have forgotten my invitation, and this gentleman claims I'm not on his guest list," I said with a pout.

"Sir, I am Thaddeus Vanderbilt, and this is my dear aunt. I will vouch for her presence here his evening. She has traveled a respectful distance to be here celebrating with her family on this most joyous of evenings, and I am going to have to insist that you let her join us. Now," he added decisively, which caused the gentleman to flush with embarrassment.

"I'm so sorry for the confusion, Mr. Vanderbilt. I don't know how it happened, but if you say that this woman is welcome, then by all means." With a flick of his wrist, the red velvet rope that had kept me out fell to the ground.

"Come now Auntie," my "nephew" proclaimed and, taking my arm, led me through the lobby into the ballroom. As soon as we were safely inside, I turned to him.

"Thank you for coming to my rescue, young man. My name is Miss Katharine Wormeley, and I can assure you that I was indeed invited this evening. Now tell me, please. Your name is not familiar to me. Thaddeus, you said?"

He laughed aloud at this and leaned down to whisper in my ear. "Pleased to meet you, Miss Wormeley. I am James Collins, ma'am. I heard that tosser giving you a hard time, so I thought I would have a go with him. And now, as no good deed goes unpunished, I need to find my fiancée and a drink, not necessarily in that order. It is her father who is a business associate of Mr. Curtis Vanderbilt. You know," he added in a conspiratorial tone, "they say that despite his claims to the contrary, he is *not* one of *those* Vanderbilts, merely a run-of-the-mill, garden-variety Vanderbilt. But you didn't hear that from me," he added with a wink. "You have yourself a good evening. I hope you are able to locate your cousin." With a brisk salute, he turned on his heel and started to disappear into the crowd. I watched his retreating back, amazed at my good fortune. I had a sudden thought and called out to him.

"James. James Collins," I said, and he turned immediately. With a quizzical look on his face, he sauntered back to stand in front of me. I thrust the wrapped gift I had been carrying around with me into his hands.

"Let's call this a wedding present, shall we? Congratulations to you and your future bride." He studied me closely before shaking his head.

"Why would you give me what appears to be a very expensive gift?" he asked. "I'm a total stranger."

"The couple celebrating tonight has already had all the good fortune any of us could hope for," I said. "I would love to think the two of you will appreciate it more."

"Thank you, Miss Kate." He leaned down to plant a light kiss on my cheek. "Elizabeth will be thrilled."

I beamed up at him. "Best of luck to you both, James." With a wave, I turned and slowly began to weave my way through the crowd. As I approached a wall of glass windows, the number of partygoers seemed to diminish a bit. It appeared all the action was in the center of the room, where guests stood shoulder to shoulder. At large events, I had always preferred to be on the outskirts, right on the edge, where I could enjoy the music and the camaraderie and still hear myself think. I accepted a glass of champagne punch from an elegantly dressed server and drank it down far too quickly. It was icy cold, bubbly, and very refreshing. I stood there holding on to my nearly empty glass for just a minute or two when another server approached, whisking my glass away and handing me a new one, full to the brim. I took my time with this one, as the last thing I wanted was to congratulate my cousin Lu while tipsy. What on earth would she think of me, showing up after all these years in a state of drunkenness? I wandered around, sipping champagne and looking for the hosts of this fancy soiree. Twice, I thought I'd heard Lu's horsey-sounding laugh from within the clusters of women, but try as I might, I could not locate either of the Vanderbilts. According to the clock on the wall, it was just a few minutes past 9:00 p.m. Perhaps it was time to find something to nibble on and soak up some of the champagne I'd consumed as well.

I had promised myself that I would sample the Parker House's signature dessert, a cake-and-custard confection they had christened Boston cream pie, so I strolled along, looking with interest at the various food stations and at the trays being carried by countless numbers of servers. Finally, I found what I had been seeking, a three-tiered tray, each level loaded with thick pieces of cake. I drank the rest of my punch, and within seconds a server had taken it from me. With my small clutch in one hand, I approached the table. I took a fork and a gold cloth napkin and selected a piece of cake. I made my way to the small cluster of tables in the corner, sat down heavily, and sampled my dessert. It definitely lived up to its reputation, I decided as I ran my fork through the sinfully thick chocolate ganache, artfully glazing the moist cake and creamy custard. I savored every single bite. Before I realized it, I had downed half of the new glass of punch that had appeared on my table as if by magic.

There were several couples and small groups who apparently were waiting for a table, so I gladly abandoned mine. I took one more stroll around the ballroom floor in order to find and congratulate Lu and Curtis. But locating them was clearly not meant to be. I finally decided I'd had enough of the stuffy ballroom, so I made my way around the lobby and out through the intricately carved oak doors. The night air felt wonderful on my skin, and I breathed in the whole of it: car exhaust, horse manure, and salty sea, combined with a heavy overlay of fancy French perfumes and musky-scented men's aftershave. It was intoxicating and a welcome relief from the the overheated ballroom.

I glanced over in the general location where Douglas had promised to be waiting and saw him waving at me. He hurried over to meet me and, taking my arm, led me to the carriage.

"How was your cousin?" Douglas asked after helping me to get settled comfortably. "Was she happy to see you?"

"I would like to think that if she had seen me, she would have been happy," I assured him. At his look of surprise, I attempted to clarify. "It was mobbed, and I couldn't locate her or her husband. I'll send her a note when I get home," I assured him. If I really wanted to have a go, I could ask her if she liked the gift that I'd left for her. She would go batty trying to find it, but I knew I wouldn't do that. It gave me quite a chuckle, however. Even at my age, a practical joke was still a great deal of fun. I closed my eyes, lulled into total relaxation by the gentle swaying of the carriage and the steady clip-clop of the horse's hooves on the relatively empty streets.

I was asleep before we had even reached the first turn in the road, and the next thing I knew Douglas was gently rousting me awake in the Winters' driveway.

"We're home, Cinderella," he whispered and, taking my arm in his, led me into the house, where Charlotte was waiting to free me from the confines of my gown. A short while later, I was once again dozing, happily ensconced under an eiderdown comforter in my four-poster bed. *Delightful!*

CHAPTER 16

Saturday, October 5, 1907
Boston, Massachusetts

When I awoke the next morning, my head was fuzzy due to the effects of either too little sleep, too much champagne, or some combination thereof. I stumbled into the empty breakfast room in search of coffee, which I located on the sideboard. I poured myself a cup and breathed in the fragrant, slightly bitter scent. I turned as I heard movement in the doorway. It was Gerald, appearing well rested and relaxed in his dressing gown and slippers.

"I saved you some coffee," I said. "Can I pour you some?" Without waiting for his response, I brought the steaming carafe over to the table and filled the cup on his right. He nodded in my general direction, and I took it as tacit approval to seat myself across from him.

"This is nice," I said as I sipped my coffee. There was no response from my host.

One of the neatly uniformed maids arrived, carrying a tray containing our breakfast. She placed a folded newspaper to the left of Gerald's silverware and he waited as she unfolded it and left him to it. She then busied herself serving up healthy-sized portions. It all looked wonderful.

I thanked her as she placed a plate laden with poached eggs on those lovely English muffins everyone seemed to be buzzing about lately and a rasher of crisp bacon in front of me. We had always called them toasted crumpets, but either way, they were quite delicious. I love a substantial breakfast, so I dove in, savoring the lemony sauce drizzled over the eggs and the buttery muffin.

"Well now, isn't this most interesting?" Gerald remarked from behind his newspaper. I was uncertain if he was actually speaking to me or just thinking aloud, so I waited a moment before responding. Swallowing a bite of my eggs, I took a sip from my water glass before I spoke.

"What's that, Gerald?" I asked. He peeked out from his copy of the sports section of the *Boston Globe*, looking almost surprised to see me. Had he been talking to himself? Did he imagine that I'd simply disappeared? Before coffee? *Not bloody likely.*

"The Boston Red Sox. What do you think of that?" *What?* He looked at me as if my blank stare and lack of a response was enough to brand me as the village idiot. "The baseball team? America's favorite pastime?"

I wiped my lips with my napkin, trying to hide my annoyance. "I may be British, but I know what baseball is, Gerald. And I'm aware that Boston has a team of young men who play it. The Americans, yes? But what did you call them? Red socks?"

Somewhat mollified, Gerald put down his paper and told me that the Boston Americans had played their last game of the 1907 season last night against the New York Highlanders.

I was perplexed. "But what of the red stockings?" I asked. Gerald appeared to be amazed that I could possibly be that dense.

"That was the last game they ever played as the Boston Americans. Their new name is the Boston Red Sox."

Well, that explained that, I thought."So I would imagine their sporting costumes will include red stockings, then?" I asked.

"Yes, Kate, their uniforms will include a pair of red stockings," Gerald said agreeably.

"And what of the New York Highlanders?" I asked. "Will their name be changed as well?"

"Who cares about the Highlanders?" Gerald asked derisively. "They're just a bunch of damn Yankees."

"Who are damn Yankees?" Priscilla asked, breezing into the room in a silk dressing gown and a pair of what appeared to be ostrich-feathered mules. She bent and kissed her husband on the top of his head, winking at me as she did so. "I hope you didn't wait for me," she said, clearly seeing that we had not. I mopped up the last of the sauce with a final square of delectable muffin and popped it into my mouth.

"We were talking about baseball," I told her. She looked puzzled before smiling sweetly.

"Well, I'm glad to know the two of you found some common ground this morning," she said. I nodded, and Gerald's harrumph from behind his paper sounded agreeable as well. For Gerald, that is.

We finished our breakfast, punctuated by idle chitchat and more coffee. After turning down Pris's halfhearted invitation to stay the weekend, I returned to my room and prepared to leave. I changed into my driving ensemble: a spotlessly clean tweed duster, shiny black boots, gloves, hat, and scarf. It was all beginning to feel very familiar. When I returned to the front hallway, I found Pris waiting. I hugged my old friend close to me.

"Thank you, Priscilla," I said. "It has been a pleasure, and I'm sorry if I caused Gerald any agitation." She insisted he was tied up at the moment but had asked her to offer me his heartfelt thanks for being such a good sport last evening. Of course, he had said no such thing, but I smiled politely in response.

"You'll just have to come back and soon. Perhaps in the springtime," she said. "On your way home to Newport."

I pretended to give her suggestion some serious thought but chose not to disclose that I had already decided to make New Hampshire my permanent residence from now on and, except for a visit or two to Rhode Island, planned to stay there full time. Traveling between the two residences was something I had done for years. At seventy-seven, I had to admit that it was, at times, simply exhausting, and if my doctor was correct, it would soon become increasingly so. I had no intentions of sharing my recent diagnosis with anyone, at least not at this time, except for Ariana, Hilma, and of course S, but I could always blame the rising costs of maintaining two households for my decision to sell Red Beech Cottage.

Having inherited money from both of my parents' estates and generally preferring to live frugally, I had spent most of my adult life figuring out the best ways to give money away. I had donated my salary as a hospital administrator as well as proceeds from my books and translations to a number of causes over the years. And now I would have the proceeds from the upcoming sale on my Newport home. I had spoken with my solicitor last week and had asked him to suss out a potential buyer for the Rhode Island property. With the utmost of discretion, I had insisted. He had promised to have an offer for me by the time I arrived in Jackson.

"A lot can happen between now and then," I said and kissed her on both cheeks.

She hugged me to her one last time and whispered, "Please take care. I worry about you out there on the open road all by yourself. It's simply terrifying." She shuddered for extra emphasis. So dramatic was our Pris.

I pulled back and pasted a smile on my face. I knew that she genuinely cared for my welfare, but the constant disapproval from my family and friends was wearing on me. "I'll be fine, Pris. Thank you again."

I walked out to my car, and after settling myself in the driver's seat, I pulled on my goggles and pushed the lever into gear. And I was off! Within minutes, I had maneuvered around the congested city center and was soon out on the open road, as Priscilla had predicted. Not in the least bit terrifying, I noted. It would be a relatively long day, but I felt confident that I would be fine with today's drive. I had reserved a single room with a private bath in Haverhill, a good-sized town close to the New Hampshire border. I was happy to once again be alone, as I had so much to reflect on. It had been a most interesting trip so far. A wedding proposal from an unexpected source and an entire evening spent with the woman who had held the heart of a man I had once loved. I had met a grief-stricken Billy Sullivan and had given marriage advice to a troubled young bride named Hannah. Enjoyed a night out among Boston's version of "the Four Hundred," shopped at Filene's, and held a conversation about baseball with Gerald Winters. What a hoot!

Today's drive would serve as an excellent opportunity to mull over the events of the past few days. I had hoped to find an escape or two from the tedium of a week of driving, but all that occurred so far had exceeded even my wildest imaginings. Surely, nothing could top all of this.

CHAPTER 17

I am not a superstitious woman by nature, but upon careful reflection, I realized I had been perhaps a tad too flippant when vocalizing my thoughts on how well my car had been performing. When I was but an hour into my drive, I heard the telltale sound of steam releasing, and as I watched, a cloud of it escaped from underneath the hood of my car. I pulled over almost immediately onto a fairly wide shoulder of road and turned off the magneto switch after putting it in neutral and engaging the parking brake. Yes indeed, my car was most definitely overheating. It would appear that I had been deficient in checking the fluid levels, despite Jasper's frequent reminders to do so.

I leaned against the driver's side door, looking in both directions. The last sign I'd seen had indicated I was near the town of Wilmington Junction. It was midmorning on a weekday, and traffic had been light. This was as good a place as any to be detained. Jasper had told me that if the car were to overheat (but that, of course, it would not, as I would be most vigilant and prevent that from happening, I had assured him more than once) I needed to let it cool down before adding water. I had a jug of water in the back for that very happenstance. I would have to wait a while, judging by the steam that continued to pour from my hood. Sighing, I unearthed my Dewar's flask from behind the seat and poured myself a sip of cold water. It quenched my parched throat, but lest I overindulge, I screwed the top back on and returned it to its place. I had vowed to carefully monitor my fluid consumption while driving. It was often many miles between proper rest areas, and I was far too old and civilized to squat behind a tree. I shook my head, groaning at the unsightly image that briefly crossed my mind.

I leaned back, lifted my face to the sun, closed my eyes, and thought about S. We would share a laugh about my carelessness, of that I was certain. He would tease me and have me laughing in no time. And how about Fred? What would he have said about my current predicament? Never the most practical of men, he had been ruled by both his imagination and bottomless wells of inspiration, *not* everyday practicalities. I could clearly picture something like this happening to him. It was still difficult to imagine that he had been gone for four whole years.

Opening my eyes, I saw a red-haired girl of about eight or nine approaching me, running and stumbling over the uneven dirt path. It looked as if she was coming from one of the nearby farms. Her freckled face was flushed, and she seemed agitated.

"Hello there," I called out. "I'm afraid I'm stuck. Maybe this is your land? I hope it's all right that I'm parked here for a bit, just until my car cools down."

"Yes, ma'am," she mumbled as she stopped short a few feet from where I stood. "But can you help me? I mean, help my pa?"

I studied her face carefully. "Child, where is your father? What sort of help does he need?" She shrugged and looked down at her feet, which were bare and coated with several layers of dirt. Unless I was terribly mistaken, she had missed more than a few baths of late. "What is your name?" I asked gently.

"It's Addie," she said. "Addie Kelliher. But it's my pa that needs help. He's cut hisself. Can you help him?" She looked at me pleading, her clear green eyes huge in her narrow face. *Oh my.*

"I can certainly try," I said. "Where is he?" She motioned for me to follow her and took off running up the dirt path that I presumed led back to her house. I took a last look at my car, knowing it was not drivable at this point and therefore was unlikely to be stolen out from under me. I pulled my floral carpetbag out from the back seat and slung it over my shoulder. "I'm right behind you, Addie," I called to her and followed as best I could, knowing that my thin leather boots, while still somewhat stylish, were not constructed for the rocky terrain before me. After several minutes of climbing, I saw the outline of a cabin that I judged to be about a hundred yards ahead. A wisp of smoke was visible from the chimney, and I spotted an enormous pile of freshly split logs meant to feed that fire. On the ground only a few feet away was a man. As I got closer, I could hear him moaning and saw an axe lying at his side, its blade covered in blood.

"Addie, what is your father's name?" I asked, drawing ragged breaths from the climb.

Her face scrunched in confusion, she whispered, "It's Pa."

"Yes, but what do others call him, dear?"

"Er, Kelly, I reckon."

I knelt next to the man and saw that he was conscious, but just barely. Based on the amount of blood pooling around his injured foot, I surmised that the accident had occurred less than an hour earlier and that he was going into shock. At least the warmer weather would prevent the effects of hypothermia. I spoke softly but firmly. "Mr. Kelliher, er, Kelly, my name is Miss Katharine Wormeley. Your daughter asked me to help you. It's been years, decades actually, but I am a nurse, and I would like to inspect your foot. Is that all right with you?" I watched, and he nodded faintly. I realized he was quite young, possibly still in his twenties. "Let's see what I can do to make you more comfortable," I said as cheerfully as I could.

Turning back to the girl, who looked slightly less terrified than she had just a few minutes earlier, I spoke briskly. "I need your help, Addie. Would you be my assistant today?" She nodded gamely as I continued. "Can you heat a large bucket of clean water and bring me as many rags as you can find? Towels too and a bedsheet, if you please." She nodded again but appeared stuck in place. "All right, then. Hurry now, won't you? Be quick."

She took off at a run, and her father forced out a low chuckle.

"That little gal? She's like a jackrabbit," he whispered through clenched teeth. "The wife and I used to say that she was born to run, never could sit still." *Just like me.* I squeezed his hand in a manner so reminiscent of my bedside behavior with countless numbers of our dear wounded soldiers. Whenever time permitted, I would sit close by, holding their hands, sometimes chattering away about this or that and other times sitting silently or praying with them. Today would require prayer and lots of it, I predicted. I wondered where Mrs. Kelliher was.

As we waited for the bucket of water, I removed his worn leather boot and sweat-stained sock in order to study his right foot closely. The axe had sliced through several layers of skin and tendons, but his boot had protected him from losing all of his toes. As I worked, I told him about my time as a nurse during the war. How we'd had to become adept at pilfering in order to keep a stock on hand of everything we needed to do our jobs, all of it in short supply. "Beef stock, brandy, tea, linens, ointment, liniment, clothing, corkscrews . . . why, nothing was safe among the bunch of us kleptomaniacs." I was yammering on, but I knew I needed to keep my patient both conscious and distracted. Kelly was growing even more pale, and it sounded like his breathing had become increasingly labored just in the time since I had arrived. He was continuing to lose blood at an alarming rate. I would need to turn things around and quickly if this young man was going to survive.

Unwilling to leave him to go check on the water, I reached under my skirts and located the thin fabric of my petticoat. There was no time for modesty, and honestly, my time on a medical ship that served as a floating hospital had robbed me of any last vestiges of propriety. Using both hands, I pulled with all of my might and ripped off a strip that was about four inches wide by two feet long. His eyes were fluttering, and I was afraid he might lose consciousness, so I kept chattering away. I told him how shortly after I had joined the crew on board, Georgy and I had bonded over the most mundane of topics—the job requirements for the volunteer nursing positions we both occupied. I had made an offhand comment, questioning who in their right mind had decided that we were well suited for this work. "It's part nursemaid, part scullery maid, part social worker," I had said, counting off our slate of duties on my fingers, which had been raw and red from all the cleaning supplies and ointments we'd used.

Georgy had laughed. "Well, if it's our job description you're questioning, that is the creation of none other than Dr. Elizabeth Blackwell." I had been so surprised I had fired back at her.

"Georgeanna Woolsey, are you telling me we actually have an official job description written by the best-known female doctor in the United States?"

Georgy had scoffed at my reaction. "What do you think? That we're just flying by the seat of our pants down here?" That is exactly what I had thought. I smiled at the memory, suddenly so vivid in my head, but sobered quickly as I watched my patient grimace with pain. I wiped his forehead, now covered with sweat, despite the chilly morning air up on the hilltop.

"Kelly," I began in my most conversational tone. "Did I tell you about the time when— well, of course I haven't as we have only just met. Anyhow, it was when Georgy and I resigned ourselves that no matter how diligent we were, no matter how conscientiously we experimented and tinkered with the recipe, the turnip soup we ladled out to our patients would never win a blue ribbon at a county fair." As I talked, I positioned the cloth directly above the gash right below his toes. "And do you know what she said to me?" I pulled the cloth tighter and fashioned it into a knot. "Hells bells, Kate, can't Uncle Sam spare a joint of beef once in a blue moon?" When I gave one last tug, his eyes opened wide and he let out a sharp cry of pain. His daughter was close by, struggling to hold on to a bucket of steaming water with both hands and balancing a stack of towels and rags on her head. She ran toward us, somehow managing to spill not a drop from the bucket.

"Aren't you the clever one?" I complimented her as she hurried to get closer to her father. She threw herself at him and buried her head in his shoulder. He tried to pat her back but gave up after a couple of tries, his face drawn with pain.

"Is he gonna be all right?" she asked, her bright eyes wide in her pale face. What could I say to this poor child?

I busied myself dipping one of the cloths in the water and, with practiced skill, ripped his canvas pants to gain better access to his injured foot. I dabbed at the wound, trying to clean the twigs and sawdust off as best I could. I found a faded but clean bedsheet at the bottom of the pile of linens. "I need you to rip this sheet," I told Addie. "About this wide," I motioned with my thumb and my index finger, "and this long," I added, spreading my hands out as far as I could. "I'll need as many as you can manage—and quickly too."

She got right to work, and we soon had a half-dozen tourniquets at the ready. I removed the original one that was now soaked through with blood and repeated the process, causing my patient to gasp once more. Addie's stoic expression appeared frozen on her face as she concentrated on ripping the bedsheet into strips.

"You're very brave," I told her, and she nodded. I imagined that this was not the first time she had been required to act as an adult in her isolated home on this hill. "I want to make your father more comfortable," I assured her. "During my days as a nurse, I bandaged up countless young men who were much worse off than him." While I worked, I saw her watching me closely, so I shifted my body so that she could observe what I was doing. It was clear she was very protective of her father, and it was likely she would have to serve as primary caregiver for him, assuming he would survive this. She would need to learn how to take care of him on her own, unless . . .

"Is it just the two of you, then?" I asked gently. There was no response, and I was about to repeat my question when she cleared her throat and spoke up.

"Ma passed last year. Went up to heaven to see my little brother," Addie said, shaking her head as if still not believing it. I wanted to keep her talking as it was a distinct possibility that her soft words would serve as a comfort to her father, who had passed out minutes earlier. I had always been a believer that the voices of loved ones could make their way through to a patient, conscious or not. It certainly couldn't hurt.

"Oh, my poor child. I am so very sorry for your loss." She looked up at me, confusion marring her features.

"It weren't your fault," she protested before studying me closely. "Ma'am, is my pa gonna be all right?" I looked at the man's foot and saw that the bleeding had stopped. The fresh cloths remained dry and clean. But the likelihood of infection was still high, and I felt I owed it to her to be truthful.

"I believe he will recover, but he's not out of the woods yet." Again, a look of total confusion. "What I mean to say is we will need to address a few things first. Your father requires medical attention as soon as is humanly possible. Are there any neighbors nearby who can help us or at least summon a local doctor?"

Addie shook her head. "Nah, Pa says they're all just a bunch of busybodies. No one comes around all that much anymore since Ma left us for her heavenly reward. But I can take care of him. You can tell me what to do, can't ya?" There was no mistaking the pleading tone in her voice. Unfortunately, aside from trying to make him comfortable and keeping his leg stable, there was little else that could be done up here on the hill. I was about to gently tell her that, try as she might, all the best intentions in the world would not aid us in getting her father moved down the hill, into my car, and to a hospital.

"Well, dear," I began but was interrupted by the unmistakable sound of approaching footsteps. Was it too much to hope that help had arrived?

CHAPTER 18

We turned to watch two men walking toward us at a leisurely pace. The tall one called out as they rounded the bend in the path. "Excuse me, ma'am. Is that your vehicle down on the road?"

"Yes, it is," I assured him.

"What happened to your driver? Is he indisposed?" His friend chuckled at that, but I answered quickly.

"I am the driver and sole occupant of the vehicle. Is there something wrong?" The men exchanged glances, and the shorter one shrugged as his friend responded.

"Oh no—well, yes, I mean, your car was overheating, so I found the jug of water you had and I took care of it. Didn't no one tell you to check the fluids?" I let out a sigh. *Patience*, I cautioned myself. *This is someone who is trying to help, and heaven knows we need all of the help we can get.*

"Yes, I had been warned, but I've had a lot on my mind, I imagine. Thank you so much. I appreciate your concern, but I'm afraid that I need further help from you both." I gestured to the unconscious man sprawled on the ground at my feet and now only partially hidden from their view. "Mr. Kelliher here is injured. Severely injured. Would you be able to assist me in loading him into my vehicle? He needs immediate medical attention."

The men looked at their neighbor with a mixture of concern and indifference. The shorter man scoffed. "Mr. Kelliher don't need no one's help, ma'am." The other man nodded his agreement as Addie approached them, tears leaving clean white streaks down her face.

"My pa is too proud fer his own good," she managed. "That's what my ma always used to say. But he's hurt. Hurt bad. Please, can you help this nice old lady and get him to a doctor? Please," she added, her hands clutched in what looked like a prayerful pose. I watched the men closely for signs of agreement, my "nice old lady" face hopeful, pleading.

The tall man turned to his friend. "We gotta to help him, Bud. C'mon. We'll grab him by the arms and get him down the hill." The two men began dragging a barely conscious Kelly when Bud had a thought.

"Are we gonna let him bleed all over this nice lady's car?" he said in a tone that was more of a statement than a question. "I'll go get the wagon and we can load him in. I'll hook up old Duke and we can have him to the doc's in no time flat. Don't worry none, li'l gal. Your pappy is going to be just fine." They made quick work of navigating the path leading down the hill, with little Addie and me trailing close behind. At the bottom, they laid their neighbor down gently on a grassy area in the shade. Bud took off at a run across the road, heading toward a large red barn.

"I'll be back in no time flat," he called out.

"Well, that was quite a change of heart," I said, wiping my brow with a handkerchief from my pocket and trying to catch my breath. "I'm sure Mr. Kelliher will appreciate your help, Mr. . . ." The tall man turned his attention back to me.

"I'm Nate Tetrow, ma'am. Pleased to make your acquaintance," he said, extending his hand to me. I took his calloused and oil-stained hand in mine and shook it gently.

"Thank you, Mr. Tetrow. You are a true gentleman." He reddened at the compliment but held my gaze.

"That's what neighbors are for, I guess," he said with what I had already come to recognize as his customary shrug.

"Don't sell yourself short, sir. You are going above and beyond today. You helped me with my car without my even asking, and now . . . well, if I had to guess, you'll be the ones responsible for saving this man's life," I told him.

"It seems like the least we can do. Poor fella. Never all that friendly. Keeps to hisself even more after the missus died from the typhoid. We tried to help at first. My wife sent over pots of soup and some pickings from our garden, but we never got so much as a simple thank-you. I finally told her not to bother anymore." Addie stepped forward, tugging on his sleeve to get his attention.

"I liked the stew you sent over that time. So did Pa. Said it was better than any he'd had ever before."

Tetrow flushed, looking pleased. "Well, that's something, then. I will tell the wife you said so," he promised, giving Addie a smile. "And next time she makes up a batch, you and your pa can come over and join us. How's that sound?" Addie nodded enthusiastically.

We watched in silence as Bud expertly rode his horse, now tethered to a wagon, toward us. As soon as he was close enough, he hopped down and asked me to mind the horse while he helped get Kelliher on the open bed of the wagon. "Of course," I told him. "I've been around horses growing up where I did in England." I grabbed the reins, and the enormous beast stopped in his tracks. He was a good-looking animal, a Belgian, if I had to guess, and probably sixteen hands tall. I stroked his mane, and he whinnied softly, swishing his massive tail.

"He likes you," said Addie, and I smiled back at her. We watched as the two men lifted Kelly onto the wagon.

"Shall I follow you in my car, then?" I asked. I wondered if I should have the child with me. "How far away is the doctor's office?" The two men exchanged glances before responding.

"Doc don't 'xactly got an office. He works from home. From his barn," Nate said sheepishly. *His barn?*

"What kind of doctor is he, exactly?"

"He's what you would call a vet, I guess. He mostly works on animals, like cows and horses." Oh my, a veterinarian was going to stitch up poor Mr. Kelliher.

"Well, if you think he's up to the job . . ." There was little more I could say. The two men nodded knowingly.

"Oh yeah," said Bud. "Why, the one time my wife was in labor and there was more'n two feet of snow on the path, Doc came charging in and he had that baby out in no time flat. And when Nate here's young'un swallowed that—"

I cut him off after glancing at our patient. I did not want to appear rude, but time was of the utmost importance. The tourniquet was once again soaked through with fresh blood, and our patient was semiconscious and writhing in pain.

"You should get him to the doctor," I suggested with what I hoped was the right amount of urgency. "Quickly."

Addie settled the question in my mind when she hopped up on the bed of the wagon next to her father.

"I wanna stay with him," she said, and that was that. Bud took the reins, and Nate climbed up next to the Kellihers.

"Be safe," I called out as the horse trotted down the road.

Addie turned and waved to me. "Thank you, Miss Kate."

I waved back and, having already decided I would follow them to the vet's, got in my car, which, thanks to the helpful neighbors was once again able to be driven. I followed behind them as they turned off onto a dirt road about a half mile from where we had started. I felt hopeful that the young man would recover fully. I had seen worse injuries in my day, and if this veterinarian was worth his salt, I predicted that Kelly would be up and walking, as Bud would say, in no time flat. Perhaps along with his physical healing, he could learn to open up to his neighbors more and allow Addie the comfort of friends. That little girl would need as much companionship as she could get if she were to thrive up here on this secluded hill.

CHAPTER 19

I pulled up alongside the wagon and emerged from my car in time to see Kelly being carried into the barn by the two men as well as a tall, distinguished fellow who I imagined was the veterinarian. I looked down to see dear Addie squeezing my hand and watching me closely.

"Do ya think he'll be okay?" she asked me with a catch in her words, and I saw that she was valiantly holding back her tears. I turned and pulled her close to me, patting her head gently as she sobbed into my full skirt.

"I think it's time we say a prayer of thanks that your father is receiving excellent medical care and perhaps another prayer that he'll be good as new long before the first snowfall. Do you agree?" Addie nodded, and we spoke our prayers aloud and thanked God for looking out for the two Kellihers. Satisfied we had done what we could, I perched on a large bale of hay and pulled Addie up to join me. Exhausted, she sprawled against me, her red hair spilling over my lap and her long legs curled up like a kitten's.

"My ma used to tell me something happy when I was feelin' sad," she whispered and I nodded knowingly.

"So did mine," I told her. I thought for a minute. What would be a happy story for a young girl her age? I brightened as an idea came to me. "I'm going to my home in New Hampshire, and do you know what will be waiting for me?" Addie appeared deep in thought before responding.

"Your ma?" she asked in a hopeful tone. I chuckled at that.

"No, my dear. But there will be a new litter of kittens. My housekeeper told me that our barn cat, Miss Lucy, was going to be a mother and very soon. What do you think of that?" Addie grinned at me.

"You're lucky. We got a cat, but his name is Tom, and Ma said he can't have no kittens cuz he's a boy." I squeezed her hand and smiled back at her, certain that old Tom had fathered his own share of local kittens. We sat quietly for a few minutes before the doctor emerged from the barn, looking quite somber. He nodded at me but spoke directly to Addie.

"Your pa is doing just fine, little lady. He said to tell you not to worry about nothin'. He'll be able to get around just fine before you know it." Addie jumped off the hay bale, just as excited as you please. I let out a sigh of relief at his words of encouragement.

"Can I go see him?" she asked and, at the doctor's nod, raced off to the barn. He turned to me, a quizzical look on his lined face.

"Samuel Thompson," he said, extendeding a gnarled hand to me. I shook it and introduced myself. "So if you don't mind my asking, Miss Kate, where did you get your medical training?" he asked. "You saved that man's life, sure as I'm sitting here." I told him about my days as an army nurse, and he nodded sagely. "I guessed it was something like that."

"So he'll be all right, then? Mr. Kelliher? Do you think he'll be able to take care of his little one?"

The doctor shook his head slowly. "For the time being, she'll be the one looking after him, I'm afraid. I got him all stitched up and there's no sign of infection yet, but he could have easily lost that foot. We'll have to get him fixed up with crutches, and it's probably best that someone looks in on them a couple times a day, at least for the first month or so. Now Bud there, he's got a wife who's sharp as a tack. I could show her how to change bandages and keep the wound clean, and maybe she could bring a meal over now and again. But . . ." He frowned as he reflected on what to say next. But I already knew.

"What if I were to pay for his care? And help out with some of their household expenses? We could keep it between us. We could compensate Bud's wife for looking out for them, keep them fed and all. Maybe you could make a house call or two? What do you think?"

Doctor Thompson looked more than a little surprised at my offer. "Why would you do that, Miss Kate? You barely know these people."

I shrugged, channeling my new friend Mr. Tetrow. "I've been blessed with more than I could ever need, Doctor. These are good people, and I'm able to offer them assistance until he's back on his feet. Why wouldn't I help them?"

The doctor shook his head, smiling for the first time. "Thank you," he said simply. "I'll make certain that he gets the best care we can provide."

"And if the occasional all-day sucker or Hershey's chocolate bar just happened to make its way to Miss Addie, well, that would be lovely too, don't you agree?" The doctor's smile grew even wider as he nodded his agreement. I thanked him and handed him a small wad of cash from my purse. "I'll send this same amount to you each month, and you can decide how it should best be spent. How does that sound?" He agreed, and after writing his address on a card, we went into the barn so I could say goodbye to the Kellihers and their neighbors. Addie smiled up at me from where she sat keeping vigil next to her father. He was sleeping peacefully, his breathing slow and even. Addie put a finger to her lips and hopped up, beckoning me to follow her outside. Bud and Nate joined us and, after a quick talk with the doctor, made their leave. Addie and I waved to them before the little girl turned and hugged me.

"Thank you, Miss Kate," she said, her voice clear and bright. "Pa and I really 'preciate everything you did for us."

I assured her that it was my pleasure. "I'm very pleased to have made your acquaintance, Addie," I told her, giving her thin shoulders a final squeeze. I hoped that Bud's wife's cooking would put a little meat on those bones. As she turned to run back into the barn, she called out to me.

"Have fun with your kittens, Miss Kate." Indeed, I would. I said a final goodbye to the doctor and returned to my car. I checked everything before cranking the engine and taking off. *No more surprises,* I told myself. I vowed to be more vigilant to the needs of my car. But honestly, if I hadn't been so negligent, I would never have been able to help the Kellihers. I would need to remember to tell this story to Jasper as the silver lining to my folly . . . if I chose to tell him at all.

CHAPTER 20

By the time I was back on the road, it was already close to noon. As I had promised myself I would, I stopped at a corner drugstore in the center of Lawrence, Massachusetts, in order to fill up my now empty jug with water. I availed myself of the facilities, and while washing up, I noted that the white cuffs of my gray shirtwaist dress were spotted with blood. Hilma would surely have a devil of a time trying to bleach out those stains. And I knew I would hear all about it. I considered pulling my dusty coat back on to hide the bloodstains, then laughed at my questionable logic. Which was more socially acceptable—bloody cuffs or a dusty duster? Back on the street, I stowed all of my outerwear inside the car and took a closer look at my surroundings. I felt restless and was itching to take a quick stroll around.

Despite the relatively poor progress I had made on my planned itinerary so far that day, I could rationalize that I had the best possible reason for the delay. I decided to treat myself when I spied a small tea shop just two doors down from the drugstore. I was hungry and reasoned that a light meal would provide me with just the boost I needed to drive through the afternoon in order to arrive in Haverhill before dark. As I opened the door and crossed the vestibule, a tiny bell tinkled overhead. I realized the café was bigger than I had originally thought, and the thirty or so seats were mostly occupied. It was a bustling lunchtime crowd, all women, well-dressed ones, stopping for a break between shopping and errands, judging by the many bags and parcels surrounding them. A few looked up at me, the obvious stranger in the room, but resumed their chatter almost immediately. A harried-looking woman in a pink uniform with a starched white apron approached me.

"You can sit wherever you can find a seat," she said briskly. "The menu is on the wall. I'll be over to take your order as soon as I can." She scurried away, and I returned to scoping out a chair at an unoccupied table. There was none. I was just about resigned to heading back out to my car when a trio of young women at a table by the window waved me over to them.

"We've got an extra seat, and you're welcome to join us," the brunette with the sleek bob assured me. "C'mon, it's okay, we won't bite." I chuckled and lowered myself into the chair she had gestured to.

"Well, thank you kindly. I thought I might have to resort to visiting a local tavern for a stick of beef jerky or one of those dreadful hard-boiled eggs from a glass jar," I said with a smile. I noted all three of them were staring at me. The brunette spoke first.

"Where are you from? Not from around here, that's for sure." The other two women nodded in agreement. The petite one with blond hair worn in a stylish chignon took the lead.

"We are not meaning to be rude, ma'am. But you sound like our boss's wife. Mrs. Sinclair. She's from England."

"As am I," I said with a smile. "I'm Miss Katharine Wormeley, most recently of Newport, Rhode Island, and soon to be Jackson, New Hampshire. But yes, I was born in England. A town called Ipswich. It's one of the oldest in the country. And please call me Kate."

"I'm Babs—well, Barbara," said the blond, extending her hand, "and this is Elizabeth, but never call her Betty." She gestured to the brunette, who nodded emphatically.

"And I'm Penelope, but you can call me Penny," the young woman with the reddish-brown curls cut in. "Have you ever met the queen?" she asked.

Elizabeth cut her eyes at her friend. "Dumb-dumb, that's like asking me if I have lunched with the governor of Massachusetts," she said with a tone of exasperation. "Just because I live here doesn't mean—"

"You don't even know the governor's name," Babs scoffed, and when all three of them laughed, I joined in.

"Well, actually I have met the queen, the former queen that is," I admitted and chatter at our table and the surrounding ones came to an abrupt stop. I felt all eyes upon me as I continued. "I met the late Queen Victoria when I was a young girl. We were in London to attend the funeral of King William IV, and we watched as Victoria entered Westminster Abbey for her coronation." The three young women gaped open-mouthed at my story. "My father, you see, was a rear admiral in the British Navy," I added. Nearby patrons had been hanging on my every word, and several watched me closely as I unfolded the white linen napkin and placed it in my lap. I studied the half-empty plates of my luncheon companions with interest.

Chicken pot pie, meatloaf, and a ham sandwich, unless I was mistaken. "What do you recommend?" I asked as I glanced up at the handwritten menu on the blackboard. It looked as if the pot pie had been partially erased, but that was fine, as I was unlikely to order it. It would no doubt be full of peas. Not for me, unless they were garden fresh and still in the pod.

"Oh, Miss Katharine," Babs implored. "You should order the meatloaf. It's so good. And it comes with soup too. Would you like to try mine?" She pushed her plate toward me. The meatloaf did look good, and it came with a side of mashed potatoes, according to the menu and confirmed by the remnants on Babs's plate.

"I'll take your word for it," I assured Babs, and seconds later I placed my order for the very same with the harried waitress. I sat back and smiled at the three lovely faces of my luncheon companions. Babs wore a bit too much face paint in my humble opinion, but the other two were clean-scrubbed and as wholesome as the day was long. Such bright, inquisitive faces. I couldn't help compare them to myself and the two Woolsey sisters so long ago. "What do you girls do?" I asked with interest.

As I sipped my water, they regaled me with the stories of their lives. My tenuous connection with British royalty long forgotten, I quickly learned that a leisurely lunch like the one they were having today was a rare occasion, and that on workdays they were lucky to gobble down half of a sandwich during their all too brief lunch breaks. They worked at the Liberty Insurance company, its corporate headquarters right here in the city of Lawrence. Elizabeth was a secretary to the vice-president, while Babs and Penny were telephone operators. They had all three grown up together and had attended the same public schools. Elizabeth was a newlywed, Babs had a steady beau that she was likely to marry—"If he's lucky," she drawled—and Penny lived with her widowed father and a younger brother.

Penny, the most outspoken of the three, asked if I thought the women's suffrage movement was making any actual progress of late. It was quickly clear that she did not. "Women should have every right, the same as men," she declared, causing several women from nearby tables to look up from their meals in surprise. "Why is this whole thing taking so darn long anyway?" *Oh my.* I chose my words carefully. Suffrage was quite the divisive topic for polite, public conversation, today and every day for as long as I could recall.

"I agree with you, of course, Penny. This battle has been fought for far too long. And the loss of Elizabeth Stanton and just last year Susan Anthony, well, that has set things back considerably, I believe." All three young women looked glum as I continued. "But it's not all bad news. Perhaps you have all heard that Mrs. Stanton's daughter Harriet has been very active of late. She recently founded the Equality League of Self-Supporting Women, and I believe you'll see some actual progress from her and her members soon." I certainly hoped so. I had all but given up the idea of voting in my lifetime, but looking at these bright, young faces, I hoped with all of my heart that the day was quickly approaching when they would have the same rights as their husbands and brothers.

"But in the meantime, what can *we* do, Miss Katharine?" Penny asked, and once again I was careful in my response. There were no easy answers to solve this ongoing struggle.

"Women across America are writing letters to their elected officials and organizing marches and lectures. But I would caution you that you would need to do careful research, get all your facts squared away, and read everything you can on the history before you begin any kind of public outreach." Penny nodded, a gleam in her brown eyes. *That one is a doer,* I thought. If push came to shove, Penny was someone who could get things done.

"How about a hunger strike?" Babs asked as she continued to pick at her mashed potatoes. "That would get their attention for sure."

Elizabeth mocked her suggestion. "A hunger strike? Who are you kidding, Babs? When exactly is the last time that you went for more than a few hours without some sort of sweet or snack?" she asked.

Babs blushed, and I changed the subject. Our little caucus had gained a good deal of attention from the other patrons. I had seen crowds turn ugly with significantly less provocation.

"Tell me more about yourselves," I said, just as the waitress approached.

"Well, Babs is the pretty one, of course, and Elizabeth is the smart one," said Penny in the most matter-of-fact of tone. I looked up from the steaming cup of chicken noodle soup that had been placed in front of me.

"Which one are you?" I asked, and Penny frowned, speechless for the first time since I had met her. "We're all more than one thing, you know," I added. Penny looked at each of her friends and shrugged. "For example," I continued. "Elizabeth is clearly very attractive." The girl's cheeks colored at the sound of her name. "And from what I have witnessed, Babs appears to be very intelligent and well-spoken. So that makes the two of you both pretty as well as smart." All three were nodding now, as if the thought had never occurred to them. "I grew up with both an older sister and a younger one. My older sister, Eliza, was thought to be the intelligent one. She got the best grades, the awards at year's end, all that and more. She became a noted writer, an author of history. She also grew into her looks and was quite a handsome woman. Eliza was happily married, and she and her husband raised three children. Their daughter is a doctor," I added with pride, and all three girls looked impressed.

"My younger sister, Ariana, well, she was considered the true beauty of the family, took after our dear mother. She had men falling at her feet while she was still a girl in school. But I came to realize fairly early on that she was as clever as they come. Smart as a whip and a noted playwright to boot. She met and married a wonderful man named Daniel Curtis, and they are very happy together to this day. They have two grown sons and spend most of their time at their villa in Venice. So you see, no one of us is just the one thing."

"What are you, then?" asked Penny, who had been munching away at the soda crackers that had accompanied my soup, the remains of her ham sandwich forgotten. "Which one are you?" Her plain face was glowing with interest, and her brown eyes sparkled. I could tell she would grow into her looks, as had my sister.

"I'm sure when you look at me, you see a stoop-shouldered, gray-haired old woman, and you would be right." I held up my hand to stop their feeble protests. "But at one time, I was considered pretty and intelligent as well. I turned a few heads in my day. My friend Fred referred to me as lively and quite fetching, and I've had my own level of success as a nurse and a hospital administrator and a translator of French novels. In fact—"

"But then why are you a Miss, not a Mrs.?" asked Penny. "You don't have a wedding band, and you introduced yourself as Miss—" Both Babs and Elizabeth tried to shush their friend, but I smiled.

"It's all right. It's a perfectly reasonable question, girls. Just because I never married doesn't mean I never had a great love or two," I assured them with a wink. An enormous platter of meatloaf, mashed potatoes, green beans, and a dinner roll was placed in front of me. I tucked into my meal, allowing the weight of my words to settle. Perhaps I had given these pretty young things something to think about.

"It's past one, girls," Elizabeth shrieked, catching sight of the clock on the wall. They had plans to visit a co-worker who had just had a baby, and they needed to arrive before the new mother and her son went down for their 2:00 p.m. naps. They each started digging about for coins to pay for their lunch, but I insisted it was my treat.

"Please put your money away. You have made what I had imagined would be a quiet and most solitary meal into a lively and most memorable one. It is my pleasure."

"Thank you, thank you, Miss Katharine. Have a safe trip to New Hampshire," they called out as they gathered their wraps to depart. As the other girls waved and rushed out the door, Penny hurried back to me.

"You asked me which one I was," she reminded me, nearly breathless. "I think that I'm the lively one. Just like you." She gave my hand a quick pat and dashed after her friends.

Lively? Yes, you are indeed, I thought as I cut into my meatloaf with renewed gusto. *Don't get bogged down by the minutiae, my dear girl. And while you're at it, reach for the stars.*

CHAPTER 21

By late afternoon, I arrived at the Riverside Inn in Haverhill, Massachusetts, as I had planned. I was provided with a small room on the second floor, and I quickly set about unpacking only what I felt I would need for the evening. Riverside indeed. Alas, there was not so much as a stream onsite, let alone a river, at least from what I could see from my tiny single window that faced the street. Well, I hadn't planned to do more than sleep in this room anyway, so it didn't matter all that much. I had high hopes for the evening ahead. I washed my hands and then headed back to the lobby and approached the receptionist, who looked up as I drew near.

"Excuse me, Miss, but would you be so kind as to direct me towards the Orpheum Theater?" The stoop-shouldered young woman looked confused by my question.

"I think you have the wrong town, ma'am. The only theater we've got is the Gem, and it's closed for renovations," she said, her accented words sounding both clipped and flat at the same time.

"Yes, the Gem. That's it," I said. "I read that a young man by the name of Louis Mayer had purchased it and was going to reopen it as a movie theater. His first of many, I believe."

The young women looked doubtful. "I still don't know if we're talking about the same place. It's a rundown pile of rubble right now. I sure hope you weren't planning on seeing a picture show tonight." My spirits sagged, as that was precisely what I had hoped to do.

"It would seem that what I read about a grand opening was incorrect. Well, be that as it may, I would like to use your telephone, please. I need to make a call to my sister." I was led to a small table and chair in the corner of the lobby. She pointed to the phone on the wall.

"I'll have to get the charges when you're done and add it to your bill," she warned me.

"Of course, dear. And thank you," I replied. After I recited the phone number to the operator, Ariana answered on the second ring, and I asked jokingly if she had been waiting by the phone.

"Well, of course I was," she responded. "Where are you?" I described the day's journey for her, wisely leaving out any mention of my meeting with the Kellihers and my car problems. I would certainly do my level best to avoid adding more fuel to spark her already vivid imagination of the horrors and dangers she had predicted I would encounter on my trip.

I had just finished describing my lovely luncheon companions when she asked, "And how did Edward feel about your insinuating yourselves into a table of young career girls?" I gulped nervously. Damn, it appeared I would have to backtrack a bit.

"Oh, A, I thought I told you that Edward isn't, um, with me at the moment." Silence on her end, then:

"I don't understand. Did he have to return home this morning? It barely made sense for him to make the trip for just . . ." Another awkward silence. "Are you telling me, Katharine, that Edward did not accompany you? That you left his home alone two whole days ago, and this is the first I'm hearing of it?" For the second time in only a few days, I stared at the telephone receiver I was holding, wondering when my sister had become so tightly wound.

"I never said that he would definitely join me, merely that it was a possibility," I argued, knowing that there was probably nothing I could say to silence her. Except . . . "And besides, he proposed marriage to me, and I told him I needed some time alone to think about it." It must have worked, as the only sound I could hear was my sister's labored breathing. "A, are you all right?"

I heard a burst of laughter and then listened as she announced to her husband, "Edward asked for Katie's hand. Can you believe it? Yes, her hand in marriage!" This was followed by a masculine snort of laughter and more laughs from Ariana.

"Oh my, Katie. What on earth possessed him to . . ." Apparently, finishing her question was too much to hope for, as my sister was now suffused with uncontrollable gaiety. Now I was offended. It was one thing for me to be shocked by an out-of-the-blue proposal, but an entirely different matter when my happily married sister and her husband made a mockery of it. The audacity!

"Is it really so shocking to think that someone would want to marry me?" I asked, mustering up as much indignation as I believed the situation deserved. *And it's not the first proposal I've received,* I barely stopped myself from adding.

"Oh, Katie, no. I'm so sorry. I didn't mean to imply . . . It's just so ludicrous that . . ." As she dissolved once more into peals of laughter, I decided I had heard enough.

"There is someone waiting to make an important call. Good night for now," I said and hung up. I turned to the receptionist, who had to have heard both sides of the conversation. She shrugged in a "What can you do?" sort of gesture and asked if I wished to be seated for dinner. I wasn't particularly hungry after my generously portioned lunch, as well as my disturbing talk with A, so I turned down her suggestion. "Can you point me toward the Orpheum, er, the Gem Theater please?" She looked at me as if I had asked her for directions to the moon but told me to take a right upon exiting the hotel and it would be two blocks down on the left-hand side of the street.

"It's not open for business yet," she reminded me as I nodded my thanks and pushed my way through the large double doors to the street. I strolled along slowly, looking at the various storefronts and shops that dotted the street. A few folks nodded at me and smiled, and I returned the gesture happily. I took my time, taking in the sights as I walked. There was nothing conventional about the architectural style of the structures that lined the street. I appreciated the unique characteristics and finishings that the various design styles embraced. Perhaps in another life, I would have been an architect. Despite the challenges, the dust and debris and the back-breaking work that went hand in hand with home renovation, seeing the finished product and knowing what you had contributed to it would be most rewarding.

Shortly after fixing up the farmhouse, my first purchase in Jackson, with the help of half a dozen local handymen, I realized it was not at all suited to my needs, so I sold it and continued my search. As I truly wanted something new, I reached out to my friends at the preeminent architectural firm McKim, Mead, and White in New York City. Mr. Charles McKim had designed my beloved home in Newport and now sounded enthusiastic about the opportunity I presented. We named the project "Satyr," which translated to "upland meadow" in Norwegian, for reasons that if I knew back then, I have long forgotten, on a plot of land on Thorn Hill Road. His design, which I found quite pleasing, contained several signature features, including a low gambrel roof and exterior shingles that were all the rage at the time. The interior was going to be spectacular, a conflagration of color, texture, and space. Anyone who lived there or visited would be well pleased. Unfortunately, despite the lovely views provided by the home, the winds that virtually buffeted the house had me a nervous wreck. I felt as if I might blow away, new house and all. So, reluctantly, I sold the home and once again looked for something more suitable. I came across a sheltered lot farther down the road and immediately purchased the property. The lot was tucked away and would not expose the home to the winds that had queered my interest in my last home. Once again, I needed an architect.

Mr. McKim claimed to be too busy to work with me, although I was certain that he was more than a bit miffed at how quickly I had sold his beloved "Satyr," not to mention that it probably had reached his ears that I'd made a tidy profit on the transaction as well. A young and up-and-coming partner of his, a Mr. Stanford White, expressed an interest in my latest project, so I hired him to develop plans for what I hoped would be my last home in Jackson. I named it Brookmead because I just liked the way it sounded. During the winter of 1894, we got to be quite friendly, Stanford and I, and I felt a sense of enthusiasm and passion for both the building and the man with a level of intensity I had not experienced in some time. He was separated from his wife, Bessie, at the time, and it was commonly known that they were considering divorce. Before you judge me for having designs on yet another married man, let me assure you that ours was just a mild case of flirtation, nothing more. Why, at more than twenty years his senior, I was old enough to be his mother. But his attentions were quite flattering and I enjoyed our time together, spent going over the designs for my new home.

Stan favored bulkier buildings than I was accustomed to, so despite my better judgment, I let him have his way. Whether I was swayed by the fact that he had designed mansions on Fifth Avenue in Manhattan for the likes of the Astors and the Vanderbilts or that he was a charming companion, I can't honestly say. Regardless, I was glad that I had trusted his instincts and was thrilled with the end results when Brookmead was completed in 1895. Our friendship stuttered a bit, as he was once again living back in New York, before it quickly ran out of steam. I saw him out socially a few times over the years, but we rarely spoke more than a few words in passing.

I was shocked to hear the news last summer that Stan had been carrying on an affair with a sixteen-year-old chorus girl named Evelyn. While it was true that I had been a mere eighteen when I embarked on a short-lived affair with a much older William Thackeray, I would like to clarify that I had been of legal age and he had not been a married man. It had all been quite proper, that is if sleeping with a man twice my age could be characterized as proper.

Naturally, Stan's affair had ended in tragedy. Another of the girl's suitors had accosted Stan while he was dining on the rooftop of the Madison Square Garden in New York City, his most celebrated design. The jilted lover produced a gun and shot Stan three times in the face, killing him on the spot. What a horrific end to the life of such a talented, albeit deeply flawed, man. A child of only sixteen indeed. Why, you think you know a person. What in heaven's name had he been thinking? *Outrageous!*

CHAPTER 22

Wrapped up in my thoughts of my forever home and my musings on a former friend, I stopped walking, realizing that the theater was directly across the street from where I was standing. A hastily written post on a wooded plaque proclaimed that this was "the future site of the soon to be famous Orpheum Theater." Still not looking forward to the solitude of my room at the hotel, I waited for a couple of cars to pass and made my way across the street. I walked down to the end of the block, all the while agreeing with the desk clerk. This building was definitely *not* open for business. The foundation looked intact, and the skeleton framework hinted at what would be a large entertainment space. I turned and almost ran into a young man who had suddenly materialized, seemingly out of thin air. He, too, was inspecting the structure with a critical eye.

"Good evening, ma'am," he said. "And how are you doing on this most lovely of evenings?"

I had been the recipient of many nods and smiles since arriving in town a couple of hours earlier but had not yet been greeted so enthusiastically as this. I took a quick measure of the man, barely taller than myself, slight with dark hair and dark eyes. I calculated him to be in his mid-twenties. His face was very familiar to me.

"And a very good evening to you, sir. I am well. Thank you for asking," I responded with a smile.

"So what do you think?" he asked, gesturing to the shell of a building taking up an entire city block. "I hear they're building a brand-new theater in this very spot." His brown eyes twinkled merrily. "Can you believe that?"

"Yes, that is what they are saying," I said with a decisive nod.

"And who, pray tell, is saying that?" he asked inquisitively. "What have you heard?"

"Well, in addition to the sign directly behind you, the 'they' I'm referring to is anyone who has read a newspaper in the past month or two. Mr. Mayer," I added slyly. Many of the articles that had run had included his photograph, and unless this man was Mayer's doppelganger, I was conversing with the man himself. He reddened and thrust out his hand.

"And here I thought my true identity would be kept secret for a while longer," he said. "I am Louis Mayer, formerly of New York City, and I am very pleased to make your acquaintance, Mrs. . . . ?"

I shook his hand and introduced myself. "Miss Katharine Wormeley, formerly of Newport, Rhode Island, and soon of Jackson, New Hampshire, Mr. Mayer."

"And what brings you to town, Miss Wormeley? Might I be so bold as to hope it was visiting the site of my future theater?" he asked with a wide grin that turned to a look of total surprise when I nodded. I explained I had planned the stop in Haverhill to hopefully coincide with a show at the newly renovated venue.

His concern was genuine as he explained that budgetary issues and delays in securing building materials and the permits had pushed back the planned opening until next spring. He shrugged his shoulders with a "What can you do?" look. "Please come back next year," he pleaded. "As my guest, of course."

I explained I was traveling north and it was unlikely I would be back in town anytime soon. Or ever, I realized.

"That is a damn shame, Miss Wormeley," he said with genuine disappointment. "This will be the first of many theaters I plan to open across the country. Not bad for a boy from the ghetto," he added with a smirk. "Can I describe for you what the Orpheum will be like when we do finally open? I would love to get your thoughts on my plans."

Always a fan of building design and blueprints, I nodded enthusiastically and followed him over to a nearby bench. He pulled out a large rolled-up document from his battered leather valise, and as we sat in the growing darkness, he pointed out where the stage would be as well as the mezzanine, the balcony, including the very prestigious royal boxes, the concession stand, and even the dressing rooms. It was obvious that he was extremely proud of his very ambitious project.

"I plan to offer the finest chocolates available along with an assortment of salted mixed nuts, ice-cold bottles of Coca-Cola, and I even ordered a steam-powered machine to pop corn. Made fresh daily and just five cents a bag," he added with a wide grin.

"That sounds very exciting, Mr. Mayer. You appear to have impeccable taste."

"I grew up poor, and my father was, well, I guess you could say less than equipped to support his family. So I quit school at the age of twelve and joined the family business." At my raised eyebrows, he clarified. "We were junk dealers, you see. New Brunswick's best," he added without an ounce of irony.

"You're from Canada, then?" I asked.

"No, actually, I was born in Minsk in Eastern Poland," said Mayer. "My given name was Lazar Meir."

"That all sounds lovely, Mr. Mayer. I hope that all of your exciting plans come to fruition and I can say I knew you when," I said. "And now I should probably take my leave and return to my hotel. It's getting dark, and I'm not familiar with the neighborhood. I very much enjoyed our conversation. It has been a pleasure," I added as I stood.

"Please, Miss Wormeley. I am nothing if not a gentleman. Won't you permit me to escort you?" he asked politely, and I allowed him to take my arm, grateful for his steady presence as we made our way down the darkened street. While we walked, he told me that he wanted to make movies someday, good wholesome entertainment for all ages. "Why, if I can build up a roster of theaters and produce the movies that will air in them, I'll be the head of an entire entertainment empire!" he said, and although I'm not one to make snap judgments or trust someone solely on first impressions, I truly believed at that moment that he would live to see his dreams come true. Enthusiasm for the grueling task ahead positively oozed from his pores. And I could well imagine that he would need every bit.

We said good night at the entrance to my hotel, and he repeated his offer for me to be his guest in the new year. I wished him luck and thanked him for his chivalry, entering the lobby and feeling a rush of warm air. It was only then I realized how chilled I had gotten during my walk. I approached the desk, where the same harried clerk was on duty. As I approached, she looked up warily.

"How was it?" she asked with just a touch of cheek, no doubt expecting me to confirm that, despite all of my high hopes, it was indeed a sad pile of rubble. Just as she had predicted.

"It was lovely, just lovely. The concession stand promises to satisfy even the most finicky of epicureans, and Mr. Mayer was nothing short of delightful as well. Meeting him was a happy surprise. Now I find my appetite has perked up considerably. May I be seated, please?" She nodded, mystified at my account of the last hour, and I followed her into the dining room.

"Table for one," she called to the passing server, causing the three couples in the room to look up in interest. I have traveled a great deal in my life and have had the occasion to eat many a meal with only myself for company. It rarely bothered me, as I usually had a book with me, and besides, I loved to watch the other diners as well. But tonight, as I sat facing away from my fellow patrons and picking at my meal of Dover sole and creamed potatoes with an unrequested side dish of dreadful peas, I felt totally and utterly alone. Unmoored, adrift. I felt strangely unsettled by my chance meeting with the young Polish man with the larger-than-life dreams. My own accomplishments seemed paltry in comparison, considering I had been born with all the privileges of both money and a loving family, while he'd had none of that. I'm sure the fish was delicious, but I could barely taste, let alone swallow my food. When had living on my own suddenly turned lonely? Why was my receiving a marriage proposal a cause for hilarity? Why was I in the middle of a ridiculous road trip that no one, not even me at the moment, felt was a good idea?

I left money for my mostly uneaten meal and a generous gratuity and left the dining room. No one was at the desk when I passed, for which I was grateful, and I slowly climbed the stairs to my room. Once inside, I dispensed with my usual washing, brushing, and cleansing routine. I took off my dress and crinoline and slipped into bed in my chemise. After I turned down the oil lamp on the bedside table, I said a prayer for Hannah to find happiness as a wife and mother, another for Penny to follow her passion wherever it led her, and one for Addie and her father for a speedy recovery. I said a last prayer for young Mr. Mayer, wishing him much success as a movie mogul or entertainment emperor or whatever he deemed an appropriate title. And then I slept. Or at least I attempted to.

After a half hour of literal tossing and turning, I decided to give my brain a little exercise in the hopes it would help me fall asleep. I have never been a believer of the "counting sheep" practice of falling asleep. It has always seemed like an absolute exercise in futility to me. All the damn sheep look exactly alike, and in my mind they rarely stood still long enough to be properly counted anyway. As an alternative method, I prefer to pick a topic and think of everything I know about it. Of course, some are more successful than others. Trying to name all forty-five of the state capitals had given me a raging headache. I could never remember that Pierre was the capital of South Dakota and Frankfort was Kentucky's.

I got better results with other subjects, such as the names of the various trees that are commonly found in New Hampshire. Let's see, there's arborvitae, balsam fir, eastern hemlock, eastern white pine, red pine, pitch pine, Douglas fir, sugar maple, blue spruce . . .

CHAPTER 23

Haverhill, Massachusetts
Sunday, October 6, 1907
The next morning, after a positively dreadful breakfast of horribly weak coffee and a plate of runny eggs, I drove away from the Riverside Inn heading north, determined to make haste and arrive in Dover, New Hampshire, in time for an early check-in at the inn where I had reserved a cottage. Based upon my current level of exhaustion, I wanted to arrive as early as possible and try to get in a nap before dinner. I had slept poorly, despite a comfortable feather bed and a light-as-air down comforter.

As I drove closer to the border of the Granite State, I saw that the effects of autumn were greater here, more magnified. The colors on the trees were vibrant and, to my casual eye, near peak. But despite the beauty of the day, I felt anxious, my spirits still deflated and my good mood long vanished. I could not shut off my brain, playing and replaying the conversation with my sister. I have never been a particularly sensitive person and have generally lived my life not giving a whit about the impressions I made on most people. I have tried to be honest, and being single by choice was just part of who I was. I was blessed with—or cursed with, depending on the individual making the judgment—a stubborn streak of independence. The very idea that I would need to consult another person when it came to where to live and, more importantly, *how* to live was preposterous. What to eat and when? To travel abroad or not? To purchase a brand-new featherbed or simply replace the feathers in the existing one? No, thank you very much. I preferred the ability to make those types of decisions all on my own. If I made the right choice, I alone would reap the benefits. If I made the wrong decision, it would be my responsibility to shoulder the blame and live with the consequences. And perhaps I had seen the future, or, more likely, I had shaped my future based on the dozens of decisions I made over the years. Most of the men I knew during that time were less than ideal candidates for marriage, and to be honest, that was a big part of their appeal. The two men I had actually fallen in love with were both wholly unavailable, albeit for completely different reasons.

To my dear mother's disappointment, I became what polite society would label an "old maid." By the ripe old age of twenty-five, my single state was virtually set in stone and had become a moot topic for discussion. There was no longer any sort of expectation concerning my future, and it actually came as a sort of relief to me. I was quite happy with my life, thank you very much, but in my mother's opinion, my sisters had fared substantially better than "poor Katie." So why had A's laughter about Edward's proposal stung so much? Surely, I had much bigger fish to fry, what with my recent decision to move permanently to New Hampshire and sell my beloved home in Newport. I had a checklist a mile long of calls to make and details to work out in order to make it happen. This kind of negative thinking would get me nowhere, I decided. What had Mark Twain, one of my favorite writers, once said about worry? I racked my brain until it finally came to me. Oh yes. "Worrying is like paying a debt you don't owe." Such a wise man, that Samuel Clemens. I had met him once long before he became such a household name after introducing readers around the world to the small-town charms of Tom Sawyer and Huckleberry Finn. We had dined together at the home of mutual friends, and I'd found him to be witty and full of fun.

As I navigated my way through the town center in Merrimack in the early morning fog, I noted that my gas tank was dangerously close to being empty. I tried to recall if I might have passed a filling station already this morning, just as I saw a small line of cars in front of a filling station. Perfect. I knew some places also offered coffee and pastries to their customers, and I hoped that this was one of those. I needed additional sustenance that my dreary hotel breakfast had not provided. I pulled off the road and took my place at the end of a line of three cars.

It was a beautiful day, and I enjoyed the opportunity to study my fellow travelers as I waited for my turn. The car directly in front of me was occupied by a couple with two small children. Their license plate had been issued in North Carolina, which meant they had been on the road for a couple of weeks at least. I wondered where they were heading. Lost in thought, I started when a young man with pink cheeks and curly brown hair tapped on my windshield. "Hello, ma'am. What can I do for you today?" he asked.

"Oh yes, of course. Can you please fill my tank with gasoline?" I asked, and he nodded curtly. After he turned and began lugging the hose toward the rear end of my car, I called out, "And by the way, do you offer coffee to your customers?"

He shrugged, then nodded halfheartedly. "I guess so. My sister is in the office," he said, gesturing toward a small building roughly an additional fifty feet back from the road. "She'll get you taken care of. If you want to head over, I can fill your car up and then park it over there." He was pointing to a small paved area to the right of the office.

"Thank you. That sounds perfect." I gathered up my bag and smiled as the young man held my arm as I stepped off the running board. Someone was raised with very good manners, I thought.

I walked over to the office, limping slightly. Hours of driving and lack of proper exercise were definitely taking their toll on me. I would be so happy to get home and resume my normal routines. I tapped lightly on the door and, hearing a muffled "come in," pulled open the door and hobbled into an overly bright room of maybe a hundred square feet. A large desk dominated the space, and sitting behind it, I saw a young woman with the same pink cheeks and curly brown hair as her brother. From her vantage point, she would have seen me clearly as I hobbled over to her door.

"Good morning. Your brother said you might scare up a cup of coffee for me," I began. "I am sorry to bother you, but I thought—"

She stood and hurried over to me, a look of concern marring her attractive features.

"Oh, please sit, ma'am," she begged loudly and pulled her chair around the desk. "Please." She gestured at the chair. I was about to demur, feeling like some physical activity might help me to work out the kinks. But she seemed insistent, so I sat. "Are you all right?" she asked, her voice sounding a few decibels louder than necessary, especially given the small room and the fact that we were separated by only a few feet.

"Why, yes," I assured her. "I'm perfectly fine, just a bit of a charley horse, you know?" At her look of confusion, I hurried on. "I'm just not used to sitting for so long, and I'm feeling unsteady on my feet. Would you have any coffee that you can spare? I stayed at the Riverside Inn last night, and I'm sorry to report that their coffee was as weak as dishwater. I was hoping—"

She hopped up and disappeared behind a door I had not noticed. I heard water running.

"Of course," she called out. "I'll put on a pot right now." A moment later, she emerged and approached me once more. "It will just be a few minutes, ma'am," she said in the same louder than necessary voice, clearly enunciating each syllable. I presumed she viewed me as even older than I was, no doubt because of the temporary limp I had exhibited when I had entered a few minutes earlier. I supposed I could allow this charade to continue for a bit longer, provided that I earned a bracing cup of coffee for my efforts. But then, what of my earlier claim to living an authentic life? I stood and walked *sans* limp over to where the young woman was placing cups and saucers on a tray, along with a half-dozen shortbread cookies.

"You have no idea, my dear, just how much I appreciate your efforts. I am Miss Katharine Wormeley," I began. "Perhaps you would call me Kate."

She turned quickly, a look of surprise on her pretty face.

"I'm Kate as well," she announced. "Don't you hate it when they call you Katie?" I personally had no problem with the nickname myself, but I nodded noncommittally. The entry door opened just then, and Kate's brother stuck his head in.

"Katie, did you set this lady up with coffee?" he asked, and she rolled her eyes and nodded.

"Yes, Mikey, I am brewing it now," she said crisply and headed to the back to retrieve the promised pot.

"I told you not to call me Mikey at work," he said peevishly. "I'm your boss and—"

"Well, Michael, I asked you not to call me Katie, at home or at work, and yet here we are. Kate," she said sweetly, "please join me for some refreshments outside on the patio, won't you?" She swept grandly past her brother, and I followed her back outside. We set up our midmorning snack at a rusted metal table in the middle of a crumbling concrete square next to the office. I pulled out her chair with a flourish and she sat down, pretending to fan herself.

"Isn't this lovely to enjoy a spot of tea on this lovely day?" she asked, attempting a posh accent. I returned it in spades, playing along with this delightful young woman.

"Oh yes, my dear. Why it's been donkey's years since we've had a proper chin-wag," I trilled. When I realized I had carried things a bit too far based on her look of confusion, I explained quickly that all I had meant to say was that I was looking forward to our time together this morning.

Michael had been watching our play-acting with a look of total disbelief. He shrugged as he headed back to the gas pump, where more customers were now lined up. "It's coffee, not tea," he mumbled loud enough for us both to hear. "Oh, and ma'am? I filled your tank, and I topped off your fluids too. You should be all set to go. It comes to ninety-five cents. You can pay my sister, if you would. Have a good day now."

As we watched him go, we dissolved into giggles. Kate scoffed. "Big brothers are the worst," she mock-complained, and I thought naturally of my late brother, James, gone these many years.

"Oh, they're not so bad," I said and took a long sip of steaming hot coffee. *Heavenly!*

CHAPTER 24

Kate pushed the plate of shortbread toward me, and I took one gratefully. It was lovely to be enjoying a tasty repast with this clever young woman. I sighed, allowing myself to relax against the confines of the battered metal chair.

"Where are you heading to?" Kate asked, and I told her about my plans to move permanently to the White Mountains of New Hampshire. "That sounds wonderful," she said dreamily. "If it were me, I would love to burrow in all winter with an enormous stack of books and mugs of hot tea and just shut everyone out."

Well, well. "I plan to do just that," I told her. "But with coffee, not tea, and I won't shut everyone out, at least not entirely. But back to books. Which authors do you enjoy?"

Kate grew even more animated as she listed her favorites. Several were mine as well, including Jane Austen, the Bronte sisters, and my chum Lou Alcott.

"Louisa was a friend of mine," I told Kate, who almost spit out a mouthful of coffee.

"Louisa May Alcott was your friend?" she all but shouted. I smiled and nodded.

"She was a war nurse like me before she became such a well-known author."

Kate shook her head, eye eyes wide with wonder and her small mouth turned in a smile. "What was she like?" she asked. "Was she a storyteller even back then?"

I thought about the slim, dark-haired woman I had known and nodded. "I would say that she always had a flair, yes, certainly. When any of us had a spare moment, we wrote letters to our loved ones back home, but not Lou. No sir, she was always writing in that journal of hers. I asked her one time what she was writing, and she said it was a disjointed mishmash of thoughts, rambles, impressions, and the like. 'In case I decide to write a book someday,' she had added with a wink."

Kate leaned closer to me, her drink and cookies forgotten. "Tell me more about what it was like. Please."

I relented quickly, never wanting to miss an opportunity to talk about the adventures I'd had and the friends I had met along the way. I thought for a moment before I continued.

"Certainly nothing in my upbringing had prepared me for the time I spent on board. Growing up, ours was a civilized household where private matters occurred behind closed doors and were rarely discussed. You can only imagine the shock I experienced when I came face-to-face with hundreds of half-dressed men, all needing personal care, medical treatment, and sponge baths. It was quite the eye-opening experience to not only perform the duties required of nurses, but to share accounts of what I had done with my colleagues and to keep accurate medical records as well. The first time I treated a wounded soldier for ulcerated bedsores on his bottom, I'd followed the established protocol without issue. It was only when I had to tell the on-call doctor the results of the examination that I'd been overcome with embarrassment and found myself unable to describe exactly what I had seen and precisely where I had seen it. Thank goodness modesty could be unlearned quickly. Out of sheer necessity, I learned how to rattle off symptoms, describe bodily functions and secretions, and examine even the most private of bodily orifices."

"Oh my, that all sounds dreadful, but so exciting as well," Kate said with a shy giggle.

"Oh yes, it was indeed. But despite the fact that we were overworked volunteers with insufficient supplies and woefully inadequate medical facilities, we nurses did have a good deal of fun," I said. "Perhaps it was to minimize the pain and suffering all around us, but we were constantly joking with each other, playing little tricks. We were civilians, you see. We were part of the USSC, and as such we were not subjected to some of the stricter requirements of the military. I'm sorry, I should explain that the USSC—"

"The United States Sanitary Commission," Kate recited from memory. "The civilian-run nursing organization that was formed in 1861 to improve the health and living conditions of the Union soldiers," she added.

"Most impressive," I told her.

She blushed and shook her head. "I know all sorts of things," she said with an air of diffidence. "I read a lot."

"Indeed," I said with a smile. "Just be certain to get plenty of fresh air and exercise to balance out all that reading." My parents had always made certain of that, and I had nearly always been happy to comply.

"Oh, I do," Kate assured me. "I'm healthy as a horse."

"Louisa was never a particularly robust woman," I mused, half to myself. I recalled frequent instances of exhaustion, headaches, and digestive pain, the latter causing the poor dear to miss many a meal and suffer in silence through countless more.

"Miss Alcott died the year I was born," Kate said with a note of sadness.

Yes, of a stroke, I recalled.

"That would make you . . ." I thought back quickly, "nineteen," I announced, and Kate nodded.

"On my next birthday, yes," she said.

We smiled at each other, and I held up my coffee cup in a toast. "To our good health," I said, and we clinked cups.

"Do you know any other famous writers?" asked Kate, and I smiled. Where to begin? Well, at the beginning, naturally.

"Are you familiar with Mr. William Makepeace Thackeray?" I asked, and Kate shook her head. "No? So you have not read *Vanity Fair*?" Again, Kate shook her head. "Oh, my dear, but you must. Why, *Vanity Fair* is the penultimate portrait of British society. It's satirical and a brilliant, albeit cautionary tale of egotism and the desire for constant admiration and praise."

"That sounds wonderful. And you knew him?" I blushed in response. Yes, I had known him well.

"We were, er, friends in Paris. A circle of friends, if you will." And at eighteen, this older and wildly sophisticated man had captivated me senseless. I must have fancied myself in love with him at the time, or I would never have allowed myself to be seduced. Oh, what a silly child I had been back then, roughly the same age as my new friend Kate. My parents may have only suspected, but I believe it was my infatuation with William that caused their decision to speed up plans to move us to the States following my father's sudden decision to retire. Our family never spoke of such things, as calling attention to potentially scandalous behavior would just make it that much more scandalous. No, we Wormeleys believed in covering things up and paying no attention to elephants that may have been residing in the room with us. Stiff upper lip and all that. All I knew for sure was that the original plan was to spend one last winter in Paris, and suddenly there we were, celebrating Thanksgiving, of all things, in our new home in Rhode Island. I had always wondered about the sudden change. I barely had the chance to say goodbye to William. Letters that I mailed to him had been returned to me unopened. Clearly he had moved on, and so I did as well.

I busied myself with the dregs of my cold coffee, as I was certain I was still red in the face. Vivid memories, like they had happened yesterday.

"You've had such an exciting life," Kate said. "I'm just dying to leave here and travel, you know?"

"Where would you go first?" I asked, and her face lit up. Suddenly, she couldn't get her words out quickly enough.

"Oh my, well, the Great Pyramids, of course. And the Colosseum in Rome . . . and Stonehenge, the Grand Canyon, the Statue of Liberty . . . but the very first place?"

"Yes. The spot at the very top of your list," I said.

Her face turned dreamy. "France, especially Paris. It's so romantic, and it's where all my favorite authors are from." I was momentarily confused as the authors we had been discussing were either Americans or Brits.

My very perceptive young friend explained her last comment before I had the chance to question her. "There's another type of books that I truly enjoy, but they are difficult to come by," she said somewhat shyly.

"Do tell," I urged her, and she grinned.

"Everyone thinks I'm an odd duck anyway," she said, clearly not caring. "Maybe I'm crazy, but I love the French writers. And no," she added quickly, misinterpreting my look of surprise, "I don't read them in French. I can pick out certain words and phrases, but that is about it. The ones I have read and those I have heard about have been beautifully translated into English. But they still feel French to me. Do you know what I mean?" she asked, watching for my reaction.

Did I ever!

"What are some writers you favor?" I asked, attempting a casual tone.

"Where do I begin?" Kate asked. "Balzac, of course. He is my favorite. And Moliere, Daudet, Dumas . . . I love them all. They . . . speak to me," she said slowly before shaking her head. "I feel so foolish. I've never said those words out loud before. And honestly, who would I tell? All I hear is 'Katie, you'll ruin your eyes with all that reading. Katie, stop lallygagging around and put down that book. The table needs set. The clothes need washed.'" She looked up suddenly and saw me watching her closely and hanging on her every word. "I'm sorry," she said, clearly embarrassed. "I don't mean to complain, but I just . . ."

I put my hand over hers. "I understand completely. I heard those same words growing up." Granted, my parents had been most gentle in their reproach, being voracious readers themselves. But I did understand. Kate smiled, still shy, and reached for another cookie. I finished my cup of coffee and patted my lips with the napkin I had been given. "Time to settle up," I said briskly. I extracted my billfold and pulled out a crisp five-dollar bill. "This should cover it nicely." I held up my hand to stop Kate as she began to protest that it was far too much. "It is my sincere pleasure," I told her. "And now, if you'll excuse me, I need to fetch something from my car." I stood slowly and waved off her offer of support. I limped over to my car and, digging around in the back seat, found what I was looking for. I opened it and jotted a few words inside. I pocketed the item and went back into the tiny office.

"While I use your restroom one last time, perhaps you'll write your full name and address down on a piece of paper. Can you do that for me, please?"

"Of course," she agreed, a tad confused, and when I emerged a few minutes later, she handed me a small square of paper. I nodded and thanked her for her hospitality. I looked outside, where Michael was once again knee-deep in customers. "Thank your brother for me as well. And trust me, my dear. Sometime soon, you'll find that your brother can be your greatest ally." I extended my hand to her, and she surprised me by pulling me into a quick embrace.

"I enjoyed talking with you, Kate," she said. "I feel you understand me somehow." I nodded, gave her hand a last squeeze, and walked to my car. Without meaning to, my departure resulted in a large cloud of dust, but when I turned briefly, I could just barely make out the figure of a young woman waving to me. A reader, a dreamer, an odd duck. Just like me.

I smiled as I turned back onto the main road heading north. Right about now, Kate would be checking the restroom to see if it needed servicing before the next customer. She would find a copy of *Catherine de Medici* written by Honoré de Balzac and Katharine Prescott Wormeley, with my hastily scribbled note on the inside cover.

Don't stop reading and dreaming, dear Kate. And trust me, you're never alone.

Your friend, Kate

As soon as I made it home to Jackson, I would write to my publisher and ask him to send signed copies of my translated novels, more than forty in all, to my new friend Kate Findley.

I knew that she would be thrilled. We *were* kindred spirits, after all.

CHAPTER 25

I realized I was humming as I drove along, tunelessly, I'm certain. I am a perfect example of someone who can't carry a tune in a bucket. But there was no one to hear me, so I sang the words aloud. "Give my regards to Broadway, remember me to . . ." Wait, to whom had the composer wished to be remembered? I racked my brain, but I honestly could not recall the lyrics. These bouts of forgetfulness were happening with an alarming frequency, I am sorry to say. Well, never mind. It would come to me when I least expected it. I knew that the song was featured in the play *Little Johnny Jones*. I had seen it at a community theater in Providence, Rhode Island, and had thoroughly enjoyed it. I had yet to see a show on Broadway, and at my advanced age, there was literally no time to waste. Perhaps in the spring, I could wrangle my goddaughter Pamela into escorting me around her city. It had been years since I'd visited her. Certainly, it would be something to look forward to after the cold winter months, which I planned to spend inside, save for my twice daily constitutionals. If she were amenable, I would stay with her and her husband in their large and airy brownstone, or perhaps I would take a suite at the Plaza Hotel. We could enjoy high tea before the show and a late supper *après*. How much fun would that be? I had not stayed up that late in ages, but for an evening like the one I envisioned, I would gladly make an exception.

It suddenly came to me. Herald Square! Yes, that was it. *Remember me to Herald Square.* It must be a park of sorts. I would add it to my itinerary, along with Fred's *pièce de résistance*, Central Park. I'd heard stories and seen paintings and photographs, but I had yet to visit the large urban public space that drew millions of visitors from all over the world each year. This spring for certain, I vowed.

I glanced around, suddenly aware of the clouds that had to have been forming for more than an hour. The sky was a dark gray, and the wind started to pick up. About an hour outside of the town of Dover, New Hampshire, I felt the first drops of rain start to fall. Being a practical woman, I had naturally purchased the canvas top that had been offered when I bought my car last month. But had I asked Jasper how to set it up or held on to any directions that might have been provided? No, sir, I had not. It would appear that I was going to learn, and hopefully very quickly, how to put the top on my automobile. A baptism by fire, I decided as I pulled off the road onto a wide-open shoulder.

As I sat there like a ninny, considering what to do first, the skies literally opened up. Between the heavy rain and the strong wind, I was soaked to the skin in less than a minute. Reasoning I could not possibly get any more drenched than I already was, I climbed slowly out of the car and stretched to get my sea legs. I saw the cover where it had been hiding in plain sight since day one, folded back and resting on the top of the back seat. Honestly, how hard could it be?

Fifteen minutes later, I had my answer. It had been very hard indeed. I am not a tall woman, and I had been cursed with arms that were quite short. Although they had never proven to be much of a challenge in my life until this point, today, of all days, my stunted limbs prevented me from getting a good grip on the cover and pulling it over the car. If I stood behind the car, I couldn't reach it and the same if I approached from either side. I tried to hop in order to examine the top more closely and succeeded in thoroughly soaking my boots, my stockings, and the hem of my duster when I landed in a muddy puddle. Finally, with less grace than a newborn colt, I scrambled into the back seat, where I stood and pulled up with all of my might. Finally, the top unfolded and I could fasten it to the windshield in a manner that seemed correct. Flushed and shivering, I cranked the engine and climbed back into the driver's seat. Seconds later, I was driving north.

Once the rain stopped, the midafternoon sun broke through the clouds and I craved the warmth from the fading rays, but of course the blasted car cover prevented that. And then I saw it, clear as day through my rain-splattered windshield: a spectacular rainbow in all of its glory. A magnificent circular arc of vibrant hues, all of the colors in the spectrum. It was nearly as beautiful as the one I had seen in Virginia during the war. Memories of that afternoon in 1862 came flooding back.

I had accompanied Fred to pick up supplies after a heavy rain. A horse and carriage had been arranged after Fred (I had stopped calling him Mr. Olmsted unless I was referring to him in general conversation) had said he wanted to go into town. He asked a few of us if anyone had a hankering to walk around on dry land for a bit. I must have shown more enthusiasm for the task than Georgy or Mrs. Griffin, so he and I arranged to meet at the end of the pier in a half hour's time. I hurried back to the room I shared with the other nurses to grab a shawl but also to freshen up a bit. I pulled a comb through my tangled brown hair and twisted it back into the low bun I generally wore. I studied my reflection in the cracked mirror that stood over the washbasin. I had not been feeling like my usual energetic self lately and was looking forward to a quick nap in my bunk, but in spite of myself, I felt flushed, excited. *Don't be a ninny,* I told my blurry reflection. *You're simply an extra pair of hands to carry bags of cornmeal or a bushel of onions.* My head knew this all too well, but then why was my heart beating so darn fast?

I earned a wink from Georgy and a cautionary "don't do anything I wouldn't do" warning as I hurried down the gangplank, passing her along the way. Fred was talking with an older gentleman, the two of them standing next to an old gray mare, so I hurried over. I was greeted warmly by my boss.

"Ah, you made it, then. Kate, I would like to introduce you to Thomas Cronin. He's a New Yorker with a horse farm here in Virginia and has graciously offered to transport us into town. You know better than anyone how low we are on flour, tea, and, well, I have a list here somewhere. Tom, meet Kate Wormeley, one of our very best nurses, who has graciously given up a well-deserved break in order to help with the provisions. Shall we be off, then?"

I clambered up on the running board and slid over on the large bench seat, ending up being crushed between Mr. Cronin's bulk and Fred. The two of them talked over me for most of the ride, only about fifteen minutes, about farming, this year's tobacco crop, and the weather. It was quite pleasant, and the fresh air felt good on my face. I was feeling relaxed, not my usual whirling-dervish self, and shortly before we reached the town center, I felt myself drifting off and my head fell to the right and landed on Fred's shoulder. Startled awake, I jerked upright in time to see him cast me an appraising look before he stepped down out of the buggy. He held my arm as I disembarked, and I couldn't meet his eyes at first.

"I'm so sorry," I stammered. "It was inappropriate of me to—"

Fred cut me off with a wave of his hand. "I should be the one apologizing to you, Kate. With the hellacious hours that you keep on duty, it was inappropriate of me to wrangle you into doing this errand with me."

"Oh no, sir," I assured him. "There is nowhere else I would rather be right now than here, um, with you . . ." I trailed off as I watched him look around at the dusty lot where we stood and the town center, which boasted a general store and a café, aptly titled "EATS." He gave me the oddest look and seemed about to say something in response when Mr. Cronin came bustling over.

"I'm sorry to interrupt, but we should move things along, I'm afraid. Looks like we've got some bad weather moving in, and with this heat that usually means a thunderstorm. I don't want to spook old Patches here, so . . ."

"Say no more, my friend. Let's be quick, Kate, and see how many of the items on the list we can find." Taking my arm, Fred propelled me across the lot toward the store. His limp was much more pronounced than on the ship, and when I asked him, he said it was probably the bad weather heading our way. "This leg is shorter than the other by a good two inches," he announced. "Honestly, the only reason I keep it around is because it's spot-on for predicting the weather," he ended with a low chuckle, his blue eyes sparkling. I smiled back at him, and we went inside Anderson's Mercantile to stock up on supplies.

Despite its relatively small size, the store fortunately carried most of the items on Mrs. Griffin's long list. If the store clerks were in the least bit hesitant to assist us Union folks in our efforts, we honestly saw no sign of it. *Money talks*, I reasoned. While we waited to get a final tally for our purchases in order to pay the bill, Fred nudged me and pointed to the café across the dirt road.

"I am fairly certain that if we were to enter the fine dining establishment known only by the elegant and easy to remember moniker 'EATS,' that we could sample some of the finest cuisine known to man. But since we are in a hurry, can I interest you in a piece of beef jerky or perhaps a pickled egg?" he said, referring to the glass jars on the counter. I was feeling queasy, uncertain whether it was the excitement of being off the ship or the rushing around. I fanned my face, feeling quite nauseous at the thought of either.

"Not for me, thank you, but you go right ahead. The only thing that sounds palatable is perhaps some butterscotch," I said, pointing to the glass display of brightly colored candies. "Or maybe peppermint?" Fred looked at me, his face registering his concern.

"You are looking quite pale, Kate. Why don't you step outside for a breath of air? It's very stuffy in here. I'll finish up and bring you some candy. How does that sound?" I nodded my assent, feeling too weak to speak, and stumbled out the door. I collapsed on the ancient rocking chair and took slow, deep breaths, trying to keep myself from getting sick right there on the porch. I felt my forehead and instantly registered that my skin was clammy and felt hot to the touch. What I had attributed to the excitement of an outing alone with Fred was the beginning of the flu. I put my head down toward my knees, desperate to avoid vomiting up whatever was in my stomach. I'd had a cup of corn chowder for lunch, and the memory of the thick and creamy soup made me feel even worse. *Oh no!* I tried to slow my breaths—in through the nose and out through the mouth.

Mr. Cronin and Patches came into view, and the carriage stopped right in front of the store. Fred came hurrying out, followed by the two clerks, who were each carrying bags of flour and cornmeal as well as boxes crammed with molasses, tea, and more. They started to load the wagon, and I struggled to stand as Fred thrust a paper sack of candy into my hands.

"We must be certain to thank our donors for this—" He stopped as he caught sight of me. "Oh, Kate, I hoped the air would do you some good, but you look . . ."

I never heard how I looked to him, as I fainted dead away.

I came to when I felt raindrops pelting my face as we raced in a horse-drawn carriage toward the river. It took me a minute to realize I was lying on the bench seat where a half hour earlier I had been sandwiched in between the men. I sat up slowly and saw Mr. Cronin riding Patches and doing his best to make it back to the boat. I looked backward to see Fred sitting between the bags and boxes of supplies on the open bed, trying to hold down a tarp to keep everything from being ruined. Oh, what a mess. I was still burning up, feverish even with the icy rain and the cold wind from the north. I looked back when I heard Fred calling my name. He was pointing at something, and I saw the most beautiful rainbow just as the rain stopped and we arrived back at the boat.

"It's the most beautiful thing I've ever seen," I mumbled, barely coherent, as I was carried off the wagon and onto the boat.

"Yes, beautiful," Fred echoed, and for a split second our eyes met and held. To this very day, I clearly remember exactly how happy I felt at that exact moment. Feverish, nauseous, weak, and exhausted, but deliriously happy as well.

CHAPTER 26

Thanks to a couple of well-placed signs, I found Connors' Cottages on the outskirts of the small, charming town of Dover, New Hampshire. My Newport neighbors, the Dolans, had recommended it, although for the life of me I could not recall what had prompted their trip to these parts. It was definitely off the beaten track, and I imagined that was part of the appeal of the place. Tonight's accommodations appeared to be rustic yet comfortable, and I felt they suited my needs completely. Surely, I could enjoy a solid eight hours of sleep in this quiet oasis.

I pulled in front of the small building marked "office" and got out of the car, not surprised that my legs felt leaden, causing me to limp slowly toward a door with a huge "WELCOME" sign. The main office and the dozen small cottages that dotted the grounds all featured stone facades, thatched roofs, and brick pathways. The overall effect was about as English country cottage as one might ever hope to find on this side of the pond. The large and small gardens were lush and the plantings dense, a perfect blend of what appeared to be both edible and ornamental varieties. The hedges that bordered the largest of the gardens were groomed perfectly. I promised myself a closer inspection once I'd had a nap.

"Welcome to Connors' Cottages," the young man behind the reception desk called out as I entered. Taking in my bedraggled appearance, he came around to help me with my bag. "Looks like you got caught in this afternoon's rainstorm," he said. "As long as you're Miss Katharine Wormeley, I can get you settled into your cottage immediately and bring you a pot of hot tea to warm you up."

"That sounds delightful, and yes, I am Miss Wormeley. Thank you, young man." He handed me a pen and motioned for me to sign the guest log. As I did, he asked me what had brought me to Dover, and I told him about my plans to move and a quick recap of my trip so far. "I've been fortunate to have enjoyed lovely weather on this trip. Today's rain was unexpected, to say the least."

"Well, I'm sure you know what Mark Twain had to say about the weather. If you don't like the weather in New England . . ." he began.

"Just wait a few minutes," we said in unison, both breaking into wide smiles.

"Let me take your bag, and I'll walk you to your room. Then, if you like, I will deliver your car and park it out in front of your cottage. How does that sound?"

"That would be grand," I assured him, and we left the office, turned left, and walked towards the cluster of cottages.

"We're full up tonight, thanks to all the leaf-peekers," Brian told me. "But we reserved this cottage just for you." We stopped in front of a small structure marked as number seven, and he inserted the key into the lock, opened the door, and followed me over the threshold. He pointed out the location of the lights and the en suite bathroom, placing my bag on a bench and handing me my key. "Shall I bring your car around before or after I make you a pot of tea?"

As much as the tea sounded wonderful, so did the idea of wrapping myself up in the handmade patchwork quilt on the bed and indulging in a quick nap before dinner. "No tea for me right now," I told him. "But perhaps later?"

"Of course." He took off at a run, and a couple of minutes later I watched as he expertly steered the vehicle to a space directly in front of my cottage. He hopped out and crossed the wide expanse of lawn, making his way toward me.

"The grounds are so well maintained. This is all so lovely. Is it in your family?" I asked.

"Why, yes, ma'am, it is," he said as he extended his hand. "I'm Brian Connors, and my folks run the place. It's been in our family for years. I just help on weekends and when I can," he added with a shrug.

We chatted for a couple more minutes, standing in the open doorway of my cottage. I was just about to thank him and go inside when he spoke up.

"That's probably the nicest car I have ever seen and definitely the best I've ever driven," he said. "When I get out of school, I hope to have a good job to afford something just like it."

I had a sudden idea that would benefit both myself and this quite charming and well-spoken young man. "Would your folks mind if you took the time to do an errand for me? It shouldn't take too long," I assured him.

He nodded enthusiastically. "That won't be a problem, Miss Wormeley. You were the last guest to check in. Just tell me what you need."

"If you could lower the top of my car and secure it for me, that would be grand. It doesn't look like it will rain tomorrow, and I much prefer to drive with it down. As far as the back seat, I seem to have tracked in a good amount of mud. Perhaps you could wipe down the upholstery? And then there's a bit more, if it's no trouble." Brian was nodding, seeming eager to help. "Would you be willing to drive it into town, fill it with gas, check the air in the tires and the fluids as well?" I had done all that just a few hours earlier, but the young man was so enthusiastic, and it seemed the errand would be a high point in his day. His eyes grew wide with excitement.

"Why, yes, ma'am," he said. "I'll go right now if it suits you."

"Yes, that would be fine. I've been driving all day on very little sleep. I believe I may lie down for a bit." I handed him several dollar bills for the gas and whatever else the car might require. "If the car were back, say about dinnertime, that would be perfect." As it was only half past three, Brian was less than successful at hiding his joy.

"You bet. Of course, ma'am. I mean, yes, ma'am. I'll have her back in one piece with gas and all. Don't you worry about a thing. You can trust me," he added.

"I believe I can, Brian. Please let your family know where you are headed so that they don't worry about you." He promised he would and, with a wave, approached the car and studied it from all sides, probably deciding the best way to lower the top.

I watched through the curtains as he slowly and methodically lowered, folded, and secured the canvas top. Longer arms made all the difference, I noted. Then he hopped behind the wheel, started it up and took off, slowly traveling over the dirt lot. He stopped at the main office, ran in, and was back out in less than a minute. *He'll probably go like the clappers as soon as he gets to the main road,* I thought with a chuckle. The worst-case scenario would be the disappearance of my car, but the more likely one? My lovely car would be given the opportunity to be driven the way it was intended by an adventurous and able-bodied young man, not a timid old lady like me. Either way, I had a good feeling about young Mr. Connors. My instincts had rarely failed me over the years, and I couldn't imagine why they would today.

I crossed the room, which felt much larger than the tiny exterior would suggest. I approved of the elegant Victorian touches: the four-poster bed, the floral wallpaper, and the velvet settee. I undressed down to my chemise and hung my damp clothes in the armoire so they would be ready for me in the morning. I had two days left of driving and was running quite low on clean stockings. After rinsing out the pair I had worn today and hanging them over the tub, I washed up in the lilac-scented bathroom and decided I would bathe later this evening or possibly in the morning. Right now, the only thing I knew I needed was to close my eyes and rest for a bit. Perhaps when Brian returned with my car, he could recommend a nearby place for a light dinner. I pulled down the quilt and slipped in between the crisp linen sheets. It had been a long week, and, in the words of "noted" Anglophile Edward Talbot, I was positively knackered.

•   •   •

I had fallen asleep in the middle of the afternoon when it was still light enough that I had not needed to light the gas lamp. But when I awoke many hours later, the room was pitch-dark. I had not been blessed with excellent night vision like my dear friend Sarah, who had had the eyes of a jungle cat, never stumbling and bumbling around as I was at the moment. I found my wristwatch on the dresser where I recalled leaving it, but it was too dark to see the time. I turned, stubbed my toe on the leg of the bed, and let out a string of expletives that would have made my navy admiral father proud. The adage "swears like a sailor" is quite true from my experience. I lit the gas lamp near the door and stole a peek at my watch. It was nearly midnight. Much too late for dinner and many hours too early for breakfast. *Damn.* I found a slip of paper that had been shoved under my door.

Miss Wormeley,

   Thank you for trusting me with your car. She is a beauty. I returned at 6:05 p.m. and knocked, but you must not have heard me. I left your change at the front desk.

   Thank you again, and enjoy the rest of your trip.

Brian Connors
P.S. You really need to purchase a spare tire before you go much farther.

I was hungry enough to unearth an apple that I remembered seeing in the bottom of my carpetbag a couple of days ago. I removed the lint that had found a home on the brownish skin and rinsed it quickly in my tiny sink. It was fairly mealy, and I ate around the dark bruised sections. All in all, it was a dreadful repast, and I vowed to make it up to myself in the morning with a breakfast fit for a queen. A gallon of hot black coffee, a stack of toast—no, pancakes, buttermilk pancakes with maple syrup, a couple of sunny side-up eggs, and a rasher of bacon. Or sausage. Possibly both.

Soon I fell back to sleep, visions of coffee cups and big fluffy pancakes dancing in my head. *Heavenly.*

CHAPTER 27

Dover, New Hampshire
Monday, October 7, 1907
Despite missing a meal, I slept soundly and woke feeling quite refreshed. After washing up and changing into clean undergarments and stockings and yesterday's dress, I walked outside into a crisp fall day, cooler than it had been these past few days. I noticed my car was in the same space across the lawn, and yes, it appeared that the young man had taken quite good care of it. I looked closer, noting with appreciation that it had been freshly washed and waxed. *Good on you, Brian,* I thought gratefully.

"Good morning," called out a man, possibly in his mid-fifties, from behind the desk as I entered the office. "Miss Wormeley? It is my pleasure to make your acquaintance. My son has talked about you nonstop. I'm Brian Connors, Senior."

Yes, he was definitely a more mature version of the young man so enthralled with my car. "And good morning to you, sir. Your son is quite an admirable young man. You must be very proud of him."

"I am indeed. He left this morning to return to his classes for Monday. He's studying at Dartmouth," he added. "He asked me to say goodbye and to thank you again." Dartmouth? *Hmmm.* Perhaps even more admirable than I had previously thought.

Continuing across the lobby, I was quite surprised to see a closed sign when I approached the breakfast room. Confused, I turned back to Mr. Connors.

"Excuse me, sir," I began. "I was told that there would be a full breakfast included with my lodging, and yet . . ."

"I'm so sorry for the confusion, Miss Wormeley," he said apologetically, but our meal service ends promptly at 9:00 a.m., and it's now—"

"Ten fifteen," I mumbled, looking at the grandfather clock next to the desk. *Oh my!* I could not recall ever sleeping so late. My schedule would be . . . Well, that was neither here nor there. There was a much more important matter to settle: Namely, where would my next meal come from? Back when I was serving on the hospital ship, and later running a hospital, a skipped meal was a daily occurrence. Either there was literally not enough food on board or there was simply not enough time to prepare a meal and eat it. But in the following years, I had found I felt much better when I ate light meals at fairly regular intervals. For now . . .

"I understand and apologize for my tardiness. Will you be offering meal service again soon?" I asked and was told that breakfast was the only meal they provided.

"I'm so sorry," he said, looking at me with a hangdog expression. "I might be able to scare up a tomato-and-cheese sandwich, but I'm afraid that's all I can offer you. The other guests about cleaned us out." With no viable alternative, I decided to return to my cottage, gather my belongings, and check out.

"I understand. The early bird and all that. Would you be willing to hold on to my bag for a short while so that I may venture out for a bit?" I asked, and he nodded.

"Brennan's Café is only a short distance down the main road, and they serve meals throughout the day. If you like, I'll call over to them and let them know you're coming." I thanked him, and he added, "The party checking into your cottage will be a late arrival. Your bags will be secure there while you enjoy your meal."

A couple of minutes later, I was greeted by name and led to a lovely window table in the warm and friendly Brennan's Café. It was a bustling place with a dozen tables, all of them occupied. The air was fragrant with the appetizing scents of freshly baked bread, cinnamon, and best of all, brewed coffee. The hostess had handed me a menu, and after taking a sip of water from the glass in front of me, I gave it a quick glance, found what I had been wanting, and smiled when a pretty young waitress approached with a steaming pot of coffee.

"Good morning, Miss Wormeley," she sang out. "I understand this is your first visit to Brennan's. Can I get you started with some coffee?" Tongue-tied with anticipation, I nodded mutely, watching her pour me a cup. I breathed in the fragrant steam and took a fortifying gulp. *Heavenly.* "Someone sure likes her coffee," the waitress with a nametag identifying her as Betty said in her singsong voice. "Shall I leave you to peruse the menu? No rush, take all the time you need." Swallowing my second satisfying mouthful, I gestured to the menu.

"I realize it's nearly lunchtime, but would it be possible to get an order of pancakes?" I asked hopefully.

"Buttermilk or Swedish? Banana or blueberries?" came her quick reply.

"Buttermilk, blueberries," I told her and watched in delight as Betty filled my cup for the second time in as many minutes. She told me she'd have my order in a jiffy and left me to enjoy my drink. While I sipped, I listened to the clamor around me and watched my fellow diners. I am a devoted people watcher, given the large amounts of time I've spent traveling, frequently on my own. I find human behavior fascinating; people are full of surprises, and there are, in my humble opinion, many more good people than not. At the table to the right sat a young couple sharing an enormous platter of eggs, toast, and sausage patties. They spoke in low voices, smiling shyly at each other. When they both attempted to stab the same chunk of sausage, there was a volley of "No, it's yours," and "Please, you had it first." So sweet. They were definitely in the early stages of their relationship. It would be years before they sat silently across from each other or, worse, arguing.

There were a few solo diners like me, and I recalled how a bistro in Paris had reserved their largest table for diners who were alone. One time, I had ended up at the table eating *croque monsieur*, a tarted-up name for a toasted ham-and-cheese sandwich, seated between an Italian opera singer and a physician from Hungary. Across from us had been a Scottish woman who was recently widowed and a young man who was, in his words, a world traveler. I believe he would be called a gypsy today, but labels had not been important among our little collection of souls. Perhaps it had been the delight of sharing a simple meal with others or the knowledge that it was highly unlikely any of us would ever cross paths again, but the conversation had been lively and deeply satisfying. I wish that practice would take hold here in the States, but honestly? I knew my traveling days were drawing to an end. And that was fine, just fine. I had seen most everything I had wanted to see in my time on this earth. Except Central Park, I thought. I must—

A sudden noise at the young couple's table startled me out of my reverie. The young man's hands were clasped around his neck, and his face was panicked and flushed red. His companion was jumping up and down, waving her hands wildly.

She managed to call out, "Help him, please! He's choking! Somebody, please!" I looked around and saw that most of the other diners were staring wide-eyed at the man, no doubt feeling as helpless as they looked.

I might have been the oldest patron in Brennan's that day, and quite possibly the only one with any first-aid related experience, but something had to be done or this young man would stop breathing completely. I pushed back my chair, stood, and limped to the table to my right. He was slumped over in his chair and no longer breathing, so I turned quickly to his friend. "What's his name?" I asked.

"Andy," she said, her eyes wild and searching, looking as if she was about to cry. "Please, ma'am, help him."

I said I would and got to work. One of the cooks had emerged from the kitchen by then, a large, dark-haired man wearing a white apron stained with food. In very broken English, he asked me, "How to help you?" Through a brief series of gestures and pantomime, we got Andy lying flat on the floor. First, I checked to see if his airway was open. A blockage would most likely cause his failure to breathe. I tilted his head back and lifted his chin. I opened his mouth wide and immediately saw a piece of meat, a fairly large one, lodged at the top of his windpipe. Acting quickly, I reached my small hand into his mouth and tugged on the chunk until I could pull it free. As soon as I did, he sputtered a bit, his renewed breaths coming in ragged gasps. He opened his eyes, saw me, a total stranger straddling him, and panicked. At nearly twice my size, I feared he would throw me off of him if he didn't calm down. I spoke slowly and calmly, hoping that if my words didn't comfort him, perhaps my soothing tone might.

"Andy, I am a former nurse, and I would like to help you if you'll let me. I need you to stay still, please, and try to slow your breathing." Taking slow, deep breaths, I mimicked what I wanted him to do, and soon he was breathing normally and his color was much improved. I gestured for the cook to help me lift him, and we got him settled back in his chair.

"Thank you, ma'am," Andy said, looking as good as new. "Don't cry, Maggie," he told the young woman, who was now draped over him, sobbing dramatically. She wiped at her tearstained face with her napkin and turned to thank me as well.

I've still got it, I thought, and there was a round of applause from the other patrons as I walked through the dining room in search of the ladies' room, where I scrubbed my hands clean and patted my face with a towel. I returned to my table, and seconds later a steaming platter of pancakes dotted with plump and juicy berries was placed in front of me, and I watched as my cup was filled to the brim with the dark, steaming brew.

"Bless you," I murmured gratefully, but Betty looked concerned, watching me with her hands on her hips. "What is wrong?" I asked, and she let out a low, throaty chuckle.

"I just don't know what we are going to do with you, Miss Wormeley," she said in mock severity.

"Whatever do you mean?" I asked, eying my plate. I had no clue what her issue might be and hoped that, whatever it was, it would not interfere with the consumption of my breakfast.

"When they called over from the hotel, they said there had been a miscommunication of some sort and that they would pay for your meal today. Maybe a missed wake-up call?" I started to explain, but she continued. "And now you saved the life of one of our customers. That would certainly entitle you to a free meal, but your meal is already free, so maybe you'd like to stay longer and we'll rustle you up a nice dinner. Free, naturally."

I told Betty that it had been my pleasure and that no thanks or additional meals were necessary. Finally, she reminded me to let her know if there was anything else I needed and I assured her I would. I tucked into my stack of still warm and quite fluffy pancakes after dousing them with nearly half of a pitcher of maple syrup. Had food ever tasted that good? If it did, I certainly could not remember when. I'd had no reason to believe that my life-saving skills would ever be utilized twice in the same week, but clearly Andy had needed me today. Perhaps my random meanderings were meant to serve a real purpose, after all. No, that was ridiculous. It had just been nothing more than a fortunate coincidence that had put us in the same place and time today. Unless . . .

CHAPTER 28

Despite my resolve to partake of light meals on my trip, I polished off the entire platter of pancakes along with copious amounts of coffee. Betty hugged me goodbye, the remaining customers called out their best wishes, and the hostess called out her thanks as I left the café, feeling full and satisfied. I would need to get on the road shortly, I realized, after glancing at the time. My lay-in, on top of my assisting Andy, had put me way behind my planned departure. I requested that Mr. Connors call ahead to that evening's accommodations up in Ossipee to let them know I would arrive a bit later than I had predicted. There was a very special someone who was expecting me, after all. I collected my bag and asked that the change from last evening be given to his son, with my thanks, and soon I was back in my spick-and-span car, heading north.

I calculated that I had been averaging approximately ten miles an hour of actual driving time for the past several days. Assuming I maintained the same speed and encountered no significant delays today, I would be arriving at the Inn at Lake Ossipee in time for dinner. I had every reason to believe that the evening ahead would be a lovely one, and I didn't want to miss a single moment.

It was a pretty drive, and the foliage was certainly as lovely as I had ever seen in all of my years of visiting New Hampshire. A breathtaking display of colorful leaves formed a sort of overhead canopy, and I greedily breathed in the crisp mountain air. Unfortunately, cars full of the folks that young Brian Connors had affectionately called "leaf peekers" were out in full force to enjoy nature in all of its glory this afternoon. The steady line of traffic didn't exactly slow down my driving time, but I certainly felt myself more on guard, watching for the odd driver who might choose to stop suddenly to catch sight of yet another stunning maple tree or the one who decided at the last moment to pull over on the shoulder of the narrow winding road. Thankfully, the other drivers were on their best behavior that day, and the miles passed without incident. The more relaxed I became, the more my mind began to wander.

I had learned at an early age to always look for the beauty in life, to seek out the positives in even the most dire of situations. This was, of course, quite easy to do when life was bountiful and joyful, as mine most frequently was. I can't claim to have lived a charmed life *per se*, but I was generally healthy, relatively affluent, and had the good fortune to have been born into a wonderful family and know the joy of lifelong friendships. If there is more to aspire to in this life, I honestly do not know what it is. My tendency to always try to focus on the positive has held me in good stead over the years and has assisted me in finding the silver lining in the occasional dark clouds I've encountered. The more life threw at me, the more I learned to roll with the punches, to adapt and find a way to flourish or, at the very least, survive. I prayed that my outlook would not change too drastically as my physical condition began to deteriorate.

I vowed to come clean with S on my health concerns this evening or possibly in the morning before I left. It would be a relief to put into words what I had been carrying around for the past week or so. And once I arrived home tomorrow and settled in, I would talk to Hilma. As my housekeeper and constant companion in Jackson, I would be counting on her to help me to navigate the bumpy path ahead of me. She would, of course, tell her husband, and Arba, well, it was unlikely he would ever speak a word to me about my failing health. But I knew that he would begin watching me more closely and assisting me in dozens of different ways over the coming months. The scarcity of words coming from Arba would be made up for in spades once I told Ariana what I had learned. I was toying with the idea of waiting until she was back home in Italy before springing my bad news on her. After I confessed to her that my drive had been nearly as foolhardy as she had pronounced it to be, I would never hear the end of it. If she were still here in the States, knowing my sister, she would hire a car and driver and show up in Jackson in less than twenty-four hours. No, it was probably better that I wait.

I decided to focus on the evening ahead of me, and I smiled as I continued my drive north. I had love in my heart, and life was good.

CHAPTER 29

The Inn at Ossipee Lake was as lovely as I remembered from my previous visits over the years. Originally the country estate of a wealthy gentleman whose hobbies had included fishing, hiking, and farming, it had been restored as an upscale inn offering services and cuisine that would rival those offered by a much larger hotel. Sprawled across sixty-five acres with private hiking trails and a well-stocked trout pond, the grounds provided the perfect setting for the rambling white clapboard dwelling with dark green shutters nestled into the hillside. A baker's dozen of guest rooms, each with private bathrooms, all boasted expansive lake views. Because, of course, the real showstopper was the pristine Ossipee Lake itself. If I remembered correctly, it is more than three miles in length and one of the larger lakes in the state. It was certainly one of the most picturesque.

I ask you, is there anything as lovely as a lake, especially one in New England in the autumn? Please don't get me wrong, I absolutely adore the ocean. My earliest and happiest childhood memories include the long walks we took as a family on the lovely beaches in Suffolk County. Collecting sea glass, shells, and rocks worn smooth from centuries of crashing waves— what a joy! As I got older, having lived in the "Ocean State," as Rhode Island is called for as long as I had, I held a deep and abiding love for the ocean: the roar of the waves crashing onto a rocky beach, the sea breezes, the endless miles of sand, and the salty tang of the air. Day or night, calm or stormy, oceans are a thing of beauty and awe. And I suppose rivers can be quite special as well. All the biggest cities boast a river running through them—Paris, London, New York, Boston, Chicago. The ancient Greek philosopher Heraclitus believed that "no man ever steps in the same river twice, for it's not the same river and he's not the same man." Based on my time in a floating hospital on the Potomac River, I must agree. My time there changed me in ways that I am still discovering even today. I wouldn't wish the atrocities we witnessed back then on my worst enemy, but I was forever grateful for the lessons I learned and the people I met on the river.

Yes, I love the ocean and I value rivers, but for my money? Give me a lake! I smiled, recalling how Sarah and I had come across a rustic wooden plaque on one of our sightseeing jaunts up this way. It proclaimed, "If you're lucky enough to live at the lake, you're lucky enough." We'd had a good laugh, and Sarah had wanted to buy it for me.

"But I don't live on a lake," I had protested.

"Well, you can save it for someday when you do," she had responded crisply as she reached for her coin purse. I wondered what had become of the silly souvenir, as I couldn't recall the last time I had seen it. Between all of my moves, somehow it must have gotten misplaced.

I adored Ossipee Lake, but my favorite was Newfound Lake here in New Hampshire in the heart of what is commonly known as the Lakes Region. Six miles long, and with eight subterranean springs refilling the lake twice a year, it was as clear and clean as any you'd find. The fishing was unrivaled, with an abundance of rainbow trout, Atlantic salmon, and both large and smallmouth bass. I had never been fond of fishing, a hobby that took far too much time and produced too few results for me to consider it a worthwhile pastime, with one notable exception. If I were invited on a camping trip (in my earlier years certainly, as the very idea of sleeping on the ground today would cause my senile skeleton to scream bloody murder) and that night's dinner required some pan-fried lake trout or, even better, rainbow trout, you would find me casting off any available pier to catch my share. I was not certain why everything tasted better when one is sitting around a campfire, but it did. I wondered what tonight's dinner special might be in the inn's elegant dining room. Now I had two reasons to be looking forward to the night ahead.

After I parked my car in the lot reserved for overnight guests, I slowly made my way up the walkway to the wide, weathered veranda. I stood for a moment, albeit to catch my breath. From my lofty perch, I could clearly make out young children building castles on the sandy beach and dozens of canoes and sailboats enjoying the calm waters and gentle breeze. The water glistened in the late afternoon sun, and I truly couldn't imagine a place more peaceful and idyllic than this. I snapped back to attention when a crisply uniformed attendant greeted me.

"Welcome to the Inn at Ossipee Lake," he said. "Would you care to register, or are you perhaps waiting for someone?"

"Yes, I would like to register. I reserved a room for this evening," I assured him. "I'm just remembering all the times I've visited this lake and how lovely it looks today."

"So you have stayed with us before?" he asked, but before I had a chance to reply, a baritone voice called out.

"Oh yes, Miss Wormeley is one of our most distinguished guests." A tall, quite formidable gray-haired gentleman in his sixties came into view. His large hands outstretched, he gripped mine and gently pulled me close. Before I knew it, he had enveloped me in a bear hug, and I relaxed against him, inhaling his fresh, clean scent as well as the horehound drops he kept close by whenever he was trying to curtail his tobacco usage. From what I could detect, it would seem that he was winning that battle. He relaxed his hold on me and held me just far enough away from him that I could see his dear face quite clearly.

"Katie," he said with a smile, and just like that, the years dropped away and I recalled the very first time I had laid eyes on this lovely man.

"Stephen," I responded, tears welling in my eyes. "How wonderful to see you, my dear friend."

"How long has it been, Katie?" he asked with a grin, his eyes bright and inquisitive. "And for the record, 'too long' is not an acceptable response."

"Since we've seen each other or since we first met?" The last couple of times I had been on my way to Jackson, I had been traveling by train or by car with friends and we had not needed to spend the night here on the lake, nor had we the free time required for a detour. And besides, Stephen was all mine. I had no desire to share him with anyone else. Why, Sarah had only made his acquaintance a handful of times over the years. Knowing Stephen as well as I did, I was fairly certain he would have been aware of my "other" trips to New Hampshire.

Stephen was waggling a finger at me. "Don't think I don't know when you've been nearby, Katie. Whenever you so much as crossover into the Granite State, a loud alarm goes off in my head, alerting me to the possibility of your imminent arrival. But do you get off the road to see your old friend Stephen Harrison? No, no, you do not." He hung his head in mock despair. "And here I thought you were my dearest friend." I punched him gently on the shoulder. A gesture I imagined would be quite common among a big sister and a little brother.

"Don't try to make me feel even an ounce of guilt," I warned him with a grin. "You know as well as I that there would have been no room at the inn for me if I'd reached out to you at the eleventh hour. This fine establishment has been booked solid every evening since you took over. Renovated it within an inch of its life, as I recall."

"You were there when we had our grand opening," Stephen reminded me. "More than fifteen years ago. And I have barely seen or heard from you since," he complained. That deserved an additional punch. "Ow, all right, you win." He snapped his fingers and announced, "It was two years ago in the spring. You and Sarah were heading back to Rhode Island and . . ." He stopped suddenly when he saw my stricken face. "Oh, darling, I wasn't thinking. So thoughtless of me. I almost forgot that your dear Sarah had left us." Stephen ran a hand through his thick and wavy gray hair, a nervous gesture of his I had witnessed dozens of times.

"Don't worry, my dear. I have felt especially close to Sarah this week. Her name has come up a number of times. Did I tell you I was spending the night at her home on this trip? You remember her husband, Edward, don't you?" At his nod, I continued. "I spent the first night at their home in Taunton. It was only this past Wednesday. How can it be that this week has positively flown by, but at the same time so much has filled my days? Both of memories past and new ones in the making. Old friends and a couple of new ones, I daresay."

Stephen smiled indulgently at me. "I hope to hear all about your recent adventures. That is why I have cleared my calendar for the balance of the day and evening, as well as whatever time you can spare me in the morning. I know you're positively champing at the bit to get home to . . ."

"Brookmead," we said at the same time and smiled.

"Let's get you settled in, shall we? Then we'll have time for a drink or a cup of tea, followed by a sumptuous meal, some wine, possibly a walk around the grounds. I've installed a number of new plantings and widened ever so slightly that creek that flows into the lake. Why, the damn thing gets as much attention as the miles of lake, I tell you. And don't even get me started on the trout pond." He shook his head in amazement. I had heard him threaten to fill it in any number of times, but children staying at the inn with their families absolutely loved it. "But first, any headlines from the week that you wish to share? Give me something to ponder while you get yourself straightened away, won't you? Any romantic interludes or scandalous encounters you wish to share with this lonely old bach? I wish to live vicariously through you, my dear. Break any hearts, perhaps?"

Well, actually . . .

"As a matter of fact, after a lovely dinner and a glass of port, the next morning over breakfast Edward proposed. Marriage," I added, certain that if my news elicited the same kind of response that I'd received from my sister, I would punch him yet again, this time with added force. But Stephen's eyes grew wide with delight, and he leaned in close.

"Do tell, and don't spare any of the juicy details."

It was my turn to wag a finger in his face. "Where are your manners, Mr. Harrison? I'm an old woman who has been traveling for hours. Shouldn't you show me to my room and offer me some sort of liquid refreshment prior to grilling me senseless about my love life?" I asked, trying and failing to adopt a tone of severity. "And you call yourself an innkeeper!"

"A woman of mystery," Stephen exclaimed, clearly disappointed that any further discussion of my romantic life would be delayed until his hosting duties were complete. "Well, you certainly have my attention, you spoilsport." He hoisted my bag and took my arm. "Let's get you settled in, darling girl." The limp that had impacted his gait for as long as I had known him seemed more pronounced than the last time that I had seen him. But then, we were all getting older. Even my darling Stephen.

He insisted on personally showing me to "my" room, one I had stayed in a number of times over the years. Fresh flowers adorned virtually every surface in the large and well-appointed space, the walls had been recently wallpapered ,and the furnishings were new as well. It was exquisite.

"Stephen, this is as lovely as I recall," I told him. "Lovelier even, if that is possible." He looked around, beaming with pride but attempting to exude an air of indifference.

"Hmmm, yes, I suppose I've spruced things up just a bit since you were here last. But for now, I'll leave you to get settled, and then please come and find me. We'll have a glass of sherry or a spot of tea, whatever your stubborn little heart desires, and you can tell me all about how you seduced poor old Edward. And this had better be worth waiting for," he added. "And promise you won't leave out a single detail. Then we will enjoy a fabulous dinner. Our chef has outdone himself," he said, once again sounding proud. "*À bientôt*, my dear. Don't keep me waiting too long," he warned and, after kissing my cheek, strode across the room and through the door.

"I'll be with you in a flash," I called to him as he started down the stairs. Hanging my meager wardrobe in the mahogany armoire, I smiled to myself, grateful for his hospitality. Stephen was a wonderful man and a trusted friend, and I could count on his discretion regarding Edward Talbot and his ill-fated proposal of marriage. The last thing I wanted was for news to get around among our circle of friends and for either of us to become the butt of jokes. I knew he would keep a confidence for me, as I had done for him for over forty years.

CHAPTER 30

I freshened up in the well-appointed bathroom and briefly considered a soak in the gleaming clawfoot tub, quickly nixing the idea as it would keep Stephen waiting for an unnecessarily long time. And I knew that if I indulged in a relaxing bath, I would not be able to keep my eyes open through dinner. I also knew that, tonight of all nights, I wanted to be wide awake. I ran a comb through my hair and tried unsuccessfully to twist it into the sort of stylish chignon Pris had fashioned for me the other evening. I finally gave up after a few tries and pulled it back into my usual bun. I didn't own any of the cosmetics that she had used on me; so much for my attempts to primp this evening. I pinched my cheeks and was pleased to see a flattering flush cross my face. My eyes were bright with anticipation. I was going to spend the evening with Stephen!

The story about Edward and me wasn't all that much of a story, I realized as I descended the long flight of stairs to the lobby. More of a postscript, an "oh, by the way." I was about to ask the desk clerk to ring for Mr. Harrison when he appeared next to me.

"Well, hello there," he said in a most seductive tone. "Do you come here often?" He waggled his eyebrows at me, which always made me laugh. He was just the most irrepressible flirt. One of the dozens of qualities that made me love him as much as I did. Before

I could respond, he took my arm and led me toward the lounge off of the lobby.

Unlike the decor in the guest rooms and other common areas, which I believed could be described as a modern take on French country with a touch of Victorian charm, the lounge area was styled after an authentic Irish pub. It offered a casual, friendly atmosphere one would hope to find in a neighborhood saloon, with hearty food and drink, beer on tap, and a glossy, hand-finished mahogany bar. It was dimly lit, with stained-glass windows and real leather banquettes. I knew from previous visits that *Joe's* was a popular watering hole for locals and tourists alike. Patrons stood two deep at the bar, and the bartenders were working quickly and efficiently, doing their best to keep the wait times reasonable and the glasses full.

"No live music tonight, I'm afraid," Stephen said. "Only on the weekends."

"You'll just have to sing to me, then," I told him. "After all, I've come all this way."

He smiled at me, one of the nicest smiles I have ever witnessed. How I had missed that smile. He led me over to a small booth for two in the corner, perfect for a private conversation between old friends.

"Sherry?" he asked, although he already knew the answer, and I nodded. After a brief absence, which I spent people-watching, he returned from the bar with two glasses. He set them down, leaned forward, and spoke just one word. "Converse!" Not wanting to keep the poor man in suspense any longer, I quickly recounted the details of Edward's awkward proposal. Stephen was not impressed, to say the least.

"How romantic," he said dryly. "Why, that's exactly the sort of proposal most women dream of. But not in the least bit suitable for the very desirable likes of you, my dear."

Naturally, I defended Edward. I have always had a real soft spot for the underdog in most situations. "Don't judge poor Edward. He meant well, and besides, I've had enough romance to last me a lifetime." Which was a good thing, as I imagined that there would be precious little coming my way in my remaining years. No new lovers were likely to cross *my* path.

Stephen leaned forward and grasped my hands in his. Such warm, strong hands. I felt . . . "Why are you so quick to give up on romance?" he asked me, all signs of joking gone from his handsome face.

I scoffed at that. "My darling, take a good hard look at the person right in front of you. What is it about me that would inspire romance?"

"Aww, Katie. What has happened to that girl I fell in love with all those years ago?" His voice was tender, but his eyes were bright with mischief. I pulled my hands away and took a sip of my drink.

"Anywho, romance aside, it's been an interesting trip so far. I've met new people and have enjoyed the most interesting conversations. I wouldn't have missed any of it for the world."

Stephen wanted to know more, so I told him about Billy Sullivan, Addie Kelliher, Hannah, Penny, Kate, Brian, and Andy. I concluded by remarking how totally random all of it had been. "No rhyme or reason. Merely happenstance, really."

But Stephen was shaking his head. "You're missing the big picture," he said. "Think about it. You prevented a little girl from losing her father and rescued a man from choking. You provided companionship to a veteran who needed someone to share a meal with. You gave sound advice to a young woman in crisis and offered encouragement to others. Your whole life has been leading up to this. Your time serving on the ship, running the hospital, opening a school, writing, and making stories available to others. Treasuring your family and friends. Don't you see, Katie? Your life has been . . . remarkable."

A lump had formed in my throat, and I found myself unable to respond. *But it's almost over,* I wanted to tell him. *I am running out of time.* I realized that Stephen was still speaking to me, and I willed my words to come. "I'm sorry, dear. Where were we exactly?"

He gave a low chuckle in response. "Well, I was right here enjoying a catch-up with an old friend, and suddenly she was off somewhere far, far away. Where did you go, dear one?"

I pooh-poohed his question and look of concern. "My mind tends to wander these days, Stephen. Maybe my sister and my friends were right. I should never have embarked on this trip on my own. I'm far too old."

He leaned forward, his voice low, his tone urgent. "You are the most capable woman I have ever known, my dear. I marvel at your energy and ability to cover so much ground and handle so many responsibilities. You're perfectly perfect. Please don't let the naysayers allow you to doubt yourself. You should be proud of all you have accomplished." He sat back and smiled at me. "All you require is a delicious dinner prepared by an award-winning half-French chef. You'll be right as rain, dear one."

I agreed with him. I always agreed with him.

CHAPTER 31

I had first met Stephen in 1862, when I served as lady superintendent at the Lovell General Hospital in Rhode Island. He had been a patient of ours, a soldier who had been hit by shrapnel during an artillery barrage and was subsequently being treated for pneumonia. Stephen's bed had been the one closest to the door off the main hallway, and I'd passed his room many times a day, rushing to meetings and such. One day I'd stopped in front of the open doorway to tie my bootlace, which had come undone. When I'd stood, I'd seen that he was watching me closely. What I'd noticed first were his bright green eyes. He had appeared both intelligent and alert, in direct contrast to many of the patients whose pain levels caused us to keep them medicated into a near stupor at times.

"You had the brightest green eyes I had ever seen," I mused half to myself, now studying him closely in the dim light of the pub.

"You were the fastest woman on the whole floor," he said with a smile. "I had to know 'Where is that woman always rushing off to?'"

"I introduced myself," I reminded him. "Clearly, I was not in that much of a hurry that I couldn't stop and have a chat with you."

"Yes, I remember. You said, 'Good afternoon, I am Lady Superintendent Katharine Wormeley. But you can call me Kate.'"

We both laughed at the memory, and I recalled how mortified I'd been. Even our surgeons and doctors hadn't called me by my nickname. His eyes now twinkled with merriment. "And I said, 'It is nice to meet you, Miss Lady Superintendent. Please call me Stephen.'"

"And then you proceeded to tease me quite mercilessly, if I recall."

"I was bored to tears lying in that bed day after day, and you were the first person I'd hoped to actually have a conversation with. I merely wanted to know what a lady superintendent did and what caused you to rush back and forth down the hallway so many times a day."

"And then you asked the whereabouts of the 'gentleman' superintendent, and what, pray tell, were *his* official duties?"

Stephen laughed aloud at the memory. "You were so embarrassed. I swear I had never seen anyone blush like that in my life. Like an English rose," he added, and I was certain I was now blushing again. I had tried to explain that there *was* no gentleman, and for the life of me I'd had no explanation for the assignment of gender to my title.

"I told you I didn't know why I was not referred to simply as superintendent."

"And I said, 'Well, let me be the first to refer to you by the more appropriate and less restrictive title of superintendent,'" he added.

I beamed at him, still recalling the pride I had felt hearing his pronouncement. It had quickly become part of my routine to stop by and chat with Stephen. At first, it had been a couple of times a week but had quickly increased to nearly every day. I had looked forward to seeing him and always felt a sense of disappointment when I saw that his bed was empty during my treks up and down the main hallway. I had known that he was probably being examined by one of the doctors on staff or that one of the nurses might have escorted him outside for a breath of fresh air. The fresh air was certainly a good thing for patient care and had definitely been in short supply. No matter how hard we had tried to keep the wards smelling pleasantly, the odors of rotting flesh combined with male sweat, disease, and hospital food had hung in the air. Now I took an appreciative sniff of ale, tobacco, and the crackling wood fire. *Heavenly!*

"I always enjoyed talking with you, my friend. It was one of the high points of my entire day," I said. My job had been a stressful one, most of my time spent desperately trying to stretch our limited resources to care for our wounded veterans. Talking to Stephen had been a welcome break and it had soothed my soul.

"Then one day you just stopped coming. I thought maybe you were ill. I asked one of the nurses, and she told me she had seen you earlier that day. I couldn't figure out why you didn't stop in any longer," he said, looking confused. "What happened back then, Katie?"

Oh my. I knew that I had to explain my behavior to this dear man, all these many years later. When I had been told that Stephen would be discharged the following week, I had been concerned. Who would monitor him at home, make sure that his wounds healed? How would he be able to receive ongoing treatments and checkups? When the chief surgeon had responded to my many questions, by asking, "Why is the treatment of a single patient any of your concern, Lady Superintendent?" I had been shocked. Just who did this doctor think he was, addressing me in this manner? As the official head of the hospital, it was my responsibility to ensure that—

That was when it had come to me. Like a slap in the face or a dousing with a bucket of ice-cold water. I had suddenly and uncomfortably been faced with the painful truth. I had developed personal feelings for this man, ten years my junior *and* a patient in my care. I was the inappropriate one, I'd realized. The doctor had apologized for his brashness and I'd waved him off. I had broken a rule critical to being an effective nurse and caregiver. Developing a crush on a patient was *verboten*, everyone knew that. How had I been so foolish not to see what had been happening? During whatever time he remained under our care, I would need to cease all contact with patient #4357, Corporal Stephen Harrison. I had avoided the hallway as much as possible over the next several days. When I had no choice but to pass his room, I would link arms with a nurse heading in the same direction or engage in a most serious conversation with one of the doctors. I couldn't stop and chat when I was already having a discussion with someone else, now could I? I had cut him off completely, and now I needed to explain myself.

"I realized I had fallen in love with you, Stephen," I said, meeting his gaze directly. "It was totally inappropriate, and I couldn't trust myself around you." I looked away, still feeling ashamed by my unprofessional behavior back then, but he pulled me into his arms and held me. I took several deep, shuddering breaths to steady myself, recalling how I had finally paid him a visit shortly before he was to be discharged. I had told myself I was being ridiculous and that any imaginary feelings I had for him were groundless and certainly not reciprocated. They had resulted from too much stress, long hours, and draining work, both physically and mentally. I had accumulated a significant amount of time off, and I would need to take it soon in order to rid myself of ridiculous thoughts like the ones I had been having. I had decided I needed to say a proper goodbye. I owed him that much.

"Did you know?" I asked him now, and he nodded slowly.

"It came to me later the next day, after I was back home and getting settled. I found myself replaying our conversation over in my head, and I just knew." He squeezed my hand, and I leaned back into his embrace. I had told him I wanted to say goodbye and to wish him the best in his recovery. He'd told me he'd hoped to have the chance to see me again and shared how much he'd enjoyed our talks over the past month.

Stephen pulled back to study me closely. "You asked me if my mother or wife would be overseeing my care at home," he said, and I remembered it all so clearly. We had never talked too much about

Stephen's family situation. He didn't wear a ring, but many married men did not.

"You said that you weren't married and that you weren't on speaking terms with your parents. You assured me that your roommate, Joe, would look after you." But I had been curious; his words had surprised me. I wanted to know what on earth could possibly cause his parents to stop speaking with him. Stephen was an honorable young man, wounded while fighting for his country. I had asked him how his parents could not be extremely proud of their son? "That's when you told me," I said sadly.

"It is because of me, because of who I am," he had said. "Joe and I are together. We love each other deeply, you see. I am happy to be going home to him. My parents are disgusted with me. They feel I am bringing shame to our family." He had shaken his head sadly. "The only relative who will have anything to do with me is an uncle up in New Hampshire."

Even now, more than forty years later, recalling how he had been disowned by his parents still hurt my friend deeply. His eyes were cloudy, and the lines on his face appeared more pronounced. This dear man had suffered so much, all for choosing to be his own authentic self. I recalled my own response to his admission. I had been flooded with feelings: surprise, as I hadn't known any homosexuals, not since my wild days in Paris years earlier, disappointment that he was yet another man who was unavailable to me, and mostly rage at his parents for caring more about societal norms and less about their own flesh and blood.

Suddenly, Stephen let out a long, deep chuckle. I looked at him in surprise.

"What's so funny?" I asked him.

"You asked me to come home with you," he said, still grinning widely.

"That's not exactly what happened," I corrected him. "I invited you and Joe to come and stay with me in Newport." I had plenty of room, and Newport offered sandy beaches and all the charm one could want in a quaint and historic seaside town. I would explain the situation to Mother, and I'd felt confident that she would have no problem welcoming two male guests who would no doubt share a bed in our home.

"And I said yes," Stephen reminded me with a smile.

Stephen and Joe, a lovely young man of Irish descent with a shy smile and a formidable wit, did join Mother and me in Newport a couple of months later. We had a positively smashing time showing "the boys," as Mother called them, all around the island, going clamming and sailing around Narragansett Bay with friends. Their visit extended to two weeks, and they promised to return again soon. This started a tradition of regular visits which lasted for nearly twenty years, long after my mother passed. When Joe succumbed to tuberculosis at the age of forty-six, Stephen had moved in with me for a time before announcing one day that his uncle had passed away and had left him an inn on Ossipee Lake that had been in the family for years. He'd planned to renovate it and run it himself. I'd promised I would be his first guest, not to mention his favorite one, and had kept my word. Over the years, I'd stayed at the inn at least a dozen times and always recommended it to others.

Now I looked across the table and saw traces of the young man I had developed feelings for while he was under my care. Those mischievous green eyes, that lazy grin. Oh, how I still loved this man.

"I truly fancied myself falling for you back then," I said sadly. "Thinking that we might have, oh, I don't know, something. Of course, that was before I found out that you were not interested in me or any woman."

"Katie-did," he said, once again calling me by the nickname he had bestowed upon me decades earlier, "we did have something, and by God, I believe we still do." I nodded, grateful I had not offended him, nor had he found the whole thing ludicrous. If he had laughed, I don't think I could have borne it, even after all these years. I leaned into him, and he wrapped me in a warm and wonderful embrace. "How about we order dinner, go up to my suite, light the fire, eat and drink, and have ourselves a real *tête-à-tête*? What do you think?"

I told him I thought it all sounded marvelous and, arm in arm, we left the tavern.

CHAPTER 32

The fresh rainbow trout with *beurre blanc* sauce was simply delightful. I smiled as I mopped the remnants of sauce from my plate with a chunk of still warm homemade sourdough bread. "What an excellent meal," I said to Stephen, who minutes earlier had polished off his own dinner of grilled lamb chops, fragrant with sprigs of fresh rosemary. "You must pay your head chef a small fortune. Henri, isn't it?"

Stephen nodded as he poured himself a snifter of brandy. "Yes, Henry Allen Taylor or, as he prefers, Henri Alain, is extremely well paid and worth every penny. Let me assure you the lodging industry is very competitive here on the lake, and the clientele we attract is quite discerning. They expect only the best, and if one establishment doesn't deliver, another will. But the overhead is astounding. I'm not sure whose idea it was to operate a fine-dining restaurant and an Irish pub under the same roof," he said glumly. "Well, of course I know. It was mine, but honestly, it's the profits from the pub that keep us afloat. No matter how much I raise the prices of the entrees in the main dining room, we can barely remain in the black." He stopped suddenly, noticing my expression of pure amusement. He raised his hands in defeat. "I know. I shouldn't complain. I love this place, and I have no plans to change a thing."

I had to laugh at that. "Oh yes, except for possibly the carpets or the wall sconces or the Adirondack chairs on the porch or the—"

"Okay, well, maybe a few tweaks here or there," he agreed. "Now, can I change your mind about joining me in an *après* dinner libation, my dearest?"

"No, thank you, Stephen. Everything was delicious, and I'm so full I might bust." Alcohol would clearly dull my senses, and we were planning an evening of cards and conversation. My dinner companion was a real card shark, and while I was not all that competitive by nature, I did not want him to completely annihilate me.

"Too bad, because Chef Henri told me he was preparing a German chocolate torte this evening, and I ordered two servings to be sent up in about a half hour." Stephen knew as well as anyone just how much I adored a rich, decadent chocolate dessert.

"Sounds wonderful, but only two portions?" I asked. "Why didn't you get something for yourself?"

"That's what I love about you. Well, one of many things, that is," Stephen told me. "The level of enthusiasm you muster when it comes to even the most humdrum of occurrences."

"Are you saying that I'm easy to please or that I'm simple-minded?" I asked, feigning offense. "Let's see what you have to say about my enthusiasm after I've beaten you soundly."

"Game on," said Stephen with a grin as he started dealing the cards.

•   •   •

Two hours later, the dessert had long since been eaten and I sat back, defeated, having lost three straight games of pinochle to my host. Combined with my losses to Edward from the other evening, I would need to step up my game considerably going forward if I were to reclaim my reputation as a formidable games woman.

"One more game for old time's sake?" he asked with a twinkle in his eyes. He shuffled the deck of cards, ready for another victory. "You look like you could use a win."

"I give up," I told him. "I hate to sound like a road-weary old woman, but I am indeed one."

Stephen shook his head. "You promised a proper catch-up my friend, and I'm going to hold you to it. Why, we still haven't talked about the upcoming winter and how often you'll allow me to come up to visit." He continued, telling me snippets about friends we had in common and promising more details were forthcoming. I had nearly forgotten how much Stephen loved gossip and reminiscing, often in equal measure. I listened to him prattle on, sharing stories about various hotel guests over the years—never naming names, but telling me about some things he'd witnessed and the conversations he'd overheard.

"I could not miss telling you this one," he said with a deep chuckle. "Last week, a young woman checking in on her own had requested a double room, insisting her 'friend' would show up soon. I decided to see if there was anything she might need to be more comfortable. The phone was in use, so I climbed the stairs and headed to her room. I knocked once, and she threw open the door, launching herself at me, stark naked."

My eyes widened at the image that came to me, totally unbidden. *Oh my!*

"As soon as she realized her mistake, she pulled back from me, shaking her head. 'I'm sorry, but I prefer younger men,' she told me with a frown on her pretty face. 'So do I,' I told her. I hightailed it down to the desk and ordered a bottle of our best champagne to be delivered to her room as soon as her guest arrived and not a minute before. I couldn't, in good conscience, risk sending a member of my staff into the line of fire like that." He shuddered dramatically.

"Was she your first? Naked woman, I mean," I asked, emboldened by the wine and the crackling fire, and Stephen shook his head.

"Not exactly. There were a couple of women I wanted to get to know better in my early courting years. But nothing that kept me from knowing who I was and how I was. No details now. You know I never kiss and tell," he reminded me with a wink.

"I know no such thing," I replied. "I have heard more about the state of your love life than almost any other topic from you. At one time, I knew who, when, and where. You shared entirely too many intimate details with me, and I don't even know your middle name."

"It's Mitchell," he said. "What else can I tell you to balance all of your supposed knowledge of my nonexistent love life?"

Hmmm. What facets of information was I missing when it came to my lovely friend?

"Favorite ice-cream?"

He scoffed. "Butter pecan, of course. What are we playing at here? True confessions? Surely, a man of mystery such as myself has to have deep, dark hidden secrets of a juicier nature than this. Let's see, I prefer showers over baths, steak more than chicken, beer, not wine, and I voted for Parker in the last election, not Roosevelt. Is that all you've got?"

The words were out of my mouth before I had the chance to consider them. "Well, what about first loves? Surely, I've told you about my scandalous liaison with the illustrious author William Thackeray at the tender age of eighteen."

Stephen's face darkened briefly. "That old scallywag," he said. "Deflowering an innocent young maiden such as you. The audacity!" he added vehemently.

I chuckled at that. "It was a most confusing time back then in Paris. Turbulent even. Why, the night we met, William was waiting for the reviews to arrive for his latest novel. He was an absolute wreck, hoping the critics would recognize the genius of *Vanity Fair*. And they did."

Stephen gave me a quizzical look. "*Au contraire*, my confused girl. I recall you telling me you'd met the scoundrel years earlier," he said. "Wasn't it when you attended Napoleon's second funeral?"

I gasped aloud at his excellent memory. "How on earth did you recall that?" I asked in amazement. I had indeed attended the second of French Emperor Napoleon Bonaparte's funerals when I was only ten years old. His first grave had been unmarked, and nineteen years later his remains had been moved as part of a most ornate military ceremony befitting the celebrated, if controversial, leader. I heard years later it had been the social event of the season in Paris. As a young girl, it had been a confusing blur of speeches, pomp and circumstance, as well as a dizzying array of flowers, wines, and pastries. Papa had allowed me to sip from his glass of champagne, and I had nearly made myself sick gorging on macarons and *pain au chocolat.*

Stephen chuckled at my look of astonishment. "You told me that your sister Eliza had been taken up with a dashing young playwright she met that evening at the reception."

I smiled happily at the memory. It was coming back to me now. "Yes, and James and I teased her mercilessly," I recalled. "She was quite enamored of Mr. Thackeray, but he failed to call on her the next day, and we left Paris soon after."

"And not eight years later, you returned to the City of Light, and this time it was you who caught his wandering eye . . . and other body parts, from what I understand. The image of that lecherous—"

I swatted at him playfully. "Leave it to you to dwell on the tawdry elements. Let us not forget that he wrote a wonderful book about the occasion. The funeral, that is, certainly not his time with me," I added quickly.

"Yes, and such an original title," Stephen added dryly. "*The Second Funeral of Napoleon*, wasn't it? How very inspired."

"He was perfectly lovely," I said. "I was not looking for a suitor to court me, now mind," I told him. Perhaps knowing from a very early age that I had no interest in marrying anyone was the reason that I had picked, repeatedly, less than suitable lovers. It's not like I wanted to marry him, I had told myself when assessing whatever man that I was seeing at that moment in time.

"So if Thackeray was not the love of your life, then who was?"

I almost gasped in surprise, but waved him off. "And you?" I asked. "Who was the lucky swain who . . . ?"

"Joseph," he said with just a hint of a smile. "That is despite the quite enthusiastic efforts of the older sister of my best friend when I was a shy and quite confused lad of only fourteen," he added with a groan.

"Do tell," I said, leaning forward, and that was how we passed the evening, well into the wee hours, swapping stories, sharing confidences, and occasionally drifting off to catch a few winks until one of us began again with, "and did I ever tell you about . . ."

CHAPTER 33

Tuesday October 8, 1907
Ossippee, New Hampshire

I believe it was nearly dawn when I finally fell asleep, my head in Stephen's lap and him gently stroking my hair. The fire had been reduced to smoldering embers, and he had pulled a cashmere throw over my shoulders. I woke a couple of hours later to find the two of us sprawled on the Persian rug in front of the fireplace, long since gone cold. I dragged myself into a seated position, all the while studying my friend. He lay on his back, his arms stretched out, looking as if he had not a care in the world. With his beautiful face exposed and vulnerable, I could clearly imagine the young man he had been, younger even than when I had met him at the army hospital.

I rotated my head slowly to relieve my sore neck and stretched my left hand, which had fallen asleep, trying to shake out the pins and needles. How long had it been since I had slept anywhere but in a fine bed with linen sheets and a down comforter? Still and all, it had been lovely.

As I glanced back at Stephen, I saw he was now awake, grinning widely at me.

"Darling," he drawled. "Staying out all night with a man of my reputation? What would your sister have to say about that?"

I feigned concern, my face in my hands. "Forget about my sister. Whatever will your staff think of me? My bed not slept in and us together all night long?"

"Trust me," he said. "Your reputation will remain unsullied. My own precedes yours, so never fear, darling girl. Now please join me for coffee, won't you, and whatever it is they should be delivering," he looked at his watch, "right about now." As if on cue, there was a knock on the door.

Before Stephen could speak, I shushed him. "At least allow me a modicum of dignity, if you would. Help me up, please, and I'll hide in the bathroom until they've gone." Stephen did as I asked, all the while shaking his head at my ill-placed modesty, and less than a minute later I heard him open the door to the waiter delivering our breakfast. I waited just a bit before joining him again.

"Smells divine," I said as I approached him, noting with pleasure that there were several mouth-watering choices on the banquet-sized table on wheels, all piping hot in individual sterling silver chafing dishes. "What is all this?"

"We have eggs benedict, French toast, sausage patties, fresh fruit, orange juice, and your personal favorite, a large carafe of freshly brewed coffee. What is your pleasure?"

"A little of everything, please," I said, handing him an empty plate. "I'll pour us both some coffee." So we sipped, and we ate, and we continued our conversation from earlier as if a couple of hours spent sleeping on the floor hadn't interrupted us one bit. At one point, Stephen put down his coffee cup and, placing a finger underneath my chin, lifted my face up to his and looked directly into my eyes. Before I could speak, he held up a hand to stop me.

"You mentioned ever so briefly meeting Mary Olmsted the other evening. We talked about nearly everyone we have ever known last night, all but one that is. He's been gone for several years now if I am correct. When are you going to tell me whatever happened between you and Fred Olmsted? You two were friends, good friends, as I recall. What caused the rift between you, exactly?"

I patted my already dry lips with a napkin, anything to buy some time. "Did I ever tell you about the types of cakes they served at Napoleon's second funeral?" I asked innocently.

Stephen rolled his eyes at me. "You're stalling, my darling," he said in his gentlest voice, and I nodded. Yes, I was. I hadn't told the whole story to anyone, not Sarah, not Ariana. But I could trust Stephen. I already knew that to be true.

So I told him. Everything.

• • •

"Are you quite certain you can't stay an additional night?" Stephen asked me later that morning as he stowed my bag on the back seat of my car. "We were having such a wonderful time before you decided it was time to go."

"I thought you said there were no vacancies this evening?" I countered as I adjusted my headscarf.

"Well, yes, but I thought we might share my room again," he said, that grin of his making its way across his face. I studied him closely in the bright midmorning sun, his firm jaw, piercing green eyes, that patrician nose. That utterly handsome, dearly familiar face I loved so much. I could swear that he hadn't aged a day in years. Unless my eyesight was failing faster than I had thought.

"I'm an old woman," I told him. "You plied me with liquor and fine food and kept me up all hours. Why, another night in the company of a scoundrel such as yourself and I would be done for indeed." My tone softened as I saw him nod slowly. "Do tell me you will come and visit me once all the fall foliage enthusiasts have gone back to their homes in Hartford and Worcester. How about Thanksgiving? Don't you usually close that week? Please say you'll join me. Hilma can put on a holiday spread nearly as fine as your Henri, but maybe you could bring a couple of his pies? Her crust leaves something to be desired. Oh, Stephen, please say yes." I took his hands in mine and felt my heart lift as he nodded his assent.

"I'll be there with bells on," he told me. "Why don't I phone you the week before, and you can let me know what I can have Henry prepare for us before he leaves to go back home?"

"To Paris?" I asked.

"Poughkeepsie," he said with a touch of cheek. "You be on your way now, my dear girl. I don't want to hear any further complaints about how I kept you up all night or delayed your arrival to your precious Brookmead." After one of his bear hugs, he helped me get settled behind the wheel and kissed my cheek right before I adjusted my goggles. "Please drive carefully. No speeding around those hairpin turns your White Mountains are so famous for."

I chuckled at the image of me driving at any speed even close to the posted limit and assured him I would take every precaution. "I will look forward to seeing you next month," I managed to say, despite the lump growing in my throat. "Be well, my friend." As I headed down the winding driveway, I beeped my horn and gave a quick wave. I heard him call out to me but couldn't make out the exact words. But I was fairly certain of what he had said.

"I love you more," I whispered back.

CHAPTER 34

I have not been completely honest in my recollections of the relationship I had with Fred Olmsted, and after sharing the unvarnished truth with Stephen this morning, I must admit I felt lighter, unburdened somehow.

From the moment I met him on that hospital ship on the Potomac River in Virginia back in 1862, I knew that Frederick Law Olmsted would have a significant impact on the rest of my life. I did not know how, and honestly, at times I'm still not sure exactly, but I knew beyond the shadow of a doubt his presence would be one I felt strongly and permanently. Despite my days as a young, single woman in Paris and London, I was, at the time, a thirty-two-year-old spinster living with my widowed mother in Rhode Island. We spent our days working on charitable endeavors and civic-minded causes and our evenings reading or playing cards. Volunteering as a nurse on a hospital ship was the most adventurous thing I had done in years.

Right away, I felt seen by Fred. Valued, somehow. Not merely as a quick study for the myriad of duties on my plate, nor as simply a good-natured helper always willing to pitch in and do the scut work no one else wanted to do. I am certain that he saw those traits in me—everyone did—but it was much more than that. I felt he understood me in a way that few others ever have. It was as if he'd somehow been allowed a sneak peek into my inner thoughts, hopes, and dreams, and what he had seen was intriguing, even, dare I say, fascinating? He saw the real Kate and found me to be someone worthy of knowing even better. At first, it was more of a sense I had, a feeling I got during a routine conversation of ours or in the middle of one of our impromptu staff meetings. He would say something, perhaps fill us in on a new procedure or make an announcement, and I would respond with a comment or just a nod, and a look would pass between us. We were simpatico, of a common mind, in total agreement right from the start. I quickly grew to trust those feelings and to trust the man himself.

Fred was well-bred, self-taught, and of the highest moral character. A plain-speaking man who could be counted on to support his staff members and always act in the best interests of the enlisted men we were there to serve. I admired him greatly; we all did. He was our leader, and his selfless manner and creative insights inspired us daily. When I looked upon him, I did not see a lame, balding gentleman who never seemed to need much sleep or sustenance like us mere mortals. As I have said, in my eyes he was larger than life, a *mensch*, my Jewish friends would have said. He never once disappointed me in all the years I knew him. Except at the end, when he broke my heart. But I am getting ahead of myself.

I came to learn that when he saw me, I was not merely a mousy worker bee scuttling around in my drab uniform, which was frequently covered with remnants of dried oatmeal and blood. He saw me as a woman: vital, important, and unique. My thoughts and opinions were heard, and they were valid, and that made all the difference. When someone sees your true self and doesn't find you lacking, it inspires a feeling of confidence. I first understood my value, my self-worth, from my parents, but somehow along the way during the detours and missteps of my youth, I lost something. A few of the pieces that made up the puzzle that was me had gone missing. During my time working for Fred, I found them and they once again became a part of me, and they were strengthened over and over again through our regular exchange of letters, our occasional phone calls and infrequent meetings.

Before I go on, and believe me, I don't mean to sound like a gushing schoolgirl with a crush, I need to make something perfectly clear. Mary Olmsted was spot-on when it came to categorizing the hard and fast truths about the relationship her husband and I shared: he did love me, I certainly did love him, and finally, there was nothing inappropriate between us. Fred was an honorable man dedicated to both his family and his work. He saw me as a colleague, a trusted associate, and a valued member of his tight-knit circle of friends.

Did I wish for more from our relationship? If I am being honest, then yes, I occasionally found myself wishing that he was free to be with me. That I might be someone worthy of being on his arm in public and by his side at a home we shared. I never spoke these thoughts or wishes aloud, not once, because, after all, who could I tell? Certainly not Fred himself. I wouldn't have dared suggest something so impossible, so reckless. We were faithful allies, staunch supporters of the other, and never the object of idle gossip or speculation.

I had always known that I could count on Fred's honest opinions and answers to my questions and concerns over the years. At my request, he weighed in on my personal and professional decisions, my plans for travel, and the future of my various charitable commitments. I did not always take his advice, but discussing things through with him was essential. For the most part, I believe I was, in turn, a good friend to Fred. I listened when he shared pieces of his life and his work with me. I celebrated, at least in spirit, his many successes over the years, sending cards and telegrams marking his accomplishments. I tried to be a support to him when his beloved stepson Owen died and when his stepdaughter Charlotte became incapacitated. But the balance shifted over the years as my dependence on him became, perhaps, unwieldy.

I never realized just how much I had come to rely on him until it was too late. It began innocently enough, I suppose, this knowledge of mine that I was possibly taking advantage of a married man, a devoted father and grandfather with a business to run and a full life that did not include me. It was an offhand comment from a mutual friend of ours who was visiting me in Newport at the time. I had shared with him that Fred and his sons had been asked to work on a local project, Easton's Beach, one of Newport's most popular spots. He had said something along the lines of how that would make two local projects for Fred, the first being me! I asked him what he had meant, and he laughed it off, stating that he knew how much I counted on Fred for support and advice. I let the subject drop but wondered if Fred had complained about me and the time he invested in our relationship. I began to draw back a bit, sending fewer letters and cards, and our weekly phone calls became monthly ones and only then if I initiated them. Then, during an annual checkup, my doctor, a family physician who had treated me for years, asked me about my mental state, inquiring if I had been experiencing delusions or feelings of despair lately. Nothing of the kind, I told him indignantly. I asked him where he had gotten such ideas, and he shared with me that a trusted medical doctor had inquired as to any symptoms that I might have shared with him. I later found that it was a friend of Fred's, a Dr. Jacobi, who had reached out to my doctor. She felt that the behaviors of mine that Fred had shared with her were clear signs of hysteria—concerning, but not entirely uncommon in women of a certain age. Needless to say, I was heartbroken and furious.

Outraged, I called Fred immediately. He was in the middle of a family celebration of some sort, but he took the time to listen to me. Between my tears and the anger bubbling up inside me, I managed to convey my outrage that he had taken it upon himself to expose me in this manner. If he'd had concerns, why had he not spoken to me directly? After seventeen years of friendship, surely I deserved better. I felt betrayed and humiliated. Spent after my emotional outburst, I listened as he told me he could not speak on this matter at the time and that when I was of a clearer mind, perhaps we could discuss it further. Until then, he wished me the best, and he ended the call.

The following days blurred into weeks, during which time I experienced the worst feelings of loss I had ever known. My charitable work suffered, and phone calls, letters, and invitations went unanswered. I couldn't tell Ariana or even Sarah just how much the loss of contact with "Mr. Olmsted" pained me. Realizing I would be unable to hide in my house in the center of town, I booked passage on a ship traveling from New York to Liverpool. The time away and the change of scenery helped me to gain perspective and after a few days spent wandering the lovely public gardens and parks, I departed Liverpool and returned home, determined to rejoin the life I'd built for myself.

Sorting through the stacks of mail that had accumulated in the time I'd been gone, I found a letter from Fred, immediately recognizing his elegant, familiar penmanship. I tucked the letter in the pocket of my housedress to read later. Twenty minutes later, to be exact, I could be found hunched over in the pantry off the kitchen. Although I was alone in the home, it was not uncommon for friends and neighbors to stop by, and I wanted, needed privacy.

My Dear Miss Wormeley, he began, and as I scanned the words for something more, I quickly realized that this was a standard letter from an old friend, asking after me and sharing snippets of work that he was involved in. I didn't know what I had been expecting, an apology, perhaps, a declaration of . . . I honestly didn't know. But there was a postscript, an unusual addition to a letter from Fred.

Whatever comes in life, nothing can ever make me lose my perfect confidence in you. FLO

I read those words over and over, and they provided me with a feeling of peace, closure even. He valued me, my intellect, and my friendship. The romantic overtones that I'd occasionally allowed to color my judgment were fleeting, idle fantasies of a sometimes-lonely woman with an overactive imagination. Fred had been worried about me and had talked to a professional in confidence about his concerns. His behavior was absent any malice or ill-will. Perhaps the issues with his daughter had left him on high alert, sensitive for anthing that seemed amiss. He was a concerned friend, and I decided that I could make peace with that.

A few weeks later, I sent him a birthday greeting, and he followed up with one to me. And our friendship continued, minus the drama I'd unwittingly introduced. Years later, when I learned Fred had been confined to an asylum, suffering from exhaustion and senility, I experienced a fleeting sadness for this brilliant man and his loving family. But I'd felt no sense of loss, as he'd been lost to me years earlier. And honestly? He had never been mine to lose.

I have never told all of this to a single soul, but I had told Stephen this morning. I had held off sharing my health concerns with him, as there would be plenty of time for that over Thanksgiving next month. But I'd answered his question, revealing to him the identity of the one true love of my life.

"It was you Stephen," I had said. "It was always you." And he had held me close.

CHAPTER 35

October 8, 1907
Jackson, New Hampshire
If you have ever had the good fortune to drive through the White Mountains during the peak of the foliage season and experience the magical burst of colors that extends as far as the eye can see, you can imagine how I felt during the last leg of my journey. The brilliant explosion of autumn dazzles the mind and awakens the senses. I recalled the first time I had visited the region nearly twenty years ago. I was in awe of the rugged and challenging terrain, as well as the sight of the magnificent snow-topped Mount Washington, at over six thousand feet in elevation, which literally took my breath away. The second time I was here was in the fall, and I fell in love with the region, a love that has lasted to this very day.

Why on earth had it taken me so long to decide that this was home, the place I wanted to live out my days? I had known that I needed to be here now, in order to experience all of this lush beauty. I have often suggested to anyone who would listen, usually my long-suffering housekeeper, Hilma, that these magnificent mountains should be called the Rainbow Range with their annual display of red, yellow, purple, bronze, and orange leaves mixed with the green of the pine trees. It is a never-ending source of delight for me.

But apparently, the range was first sighted from shipboard, and the highest peaks would often be snow-capped, appearing white. An alternate theory is that the mica-laden granite of the summits looked white. Either way, the name White Mountains stuck, and besides, no one had asked for my opinion. Gorgeous colors aside, at any time of the year the beauty of this magical place can be enjoyed. "I'm back," I said aloud as I caught sight of the Old Man of the Mountain, a formation of granite that strongly resembles the profile of a man's face. "The old woman of the mountain is back, and I'm here to stay."

My heart continued to soar as I entered Jackson, nestled among the mountains, a picture-perfect small town that has attracted artists, outdoor enthusiasts, and odd ducks like me for decades. We were a vibrant community of sculptors, painters, photographers, and writers year-round, and it was a sportsman's paradise every season as well. Hikers, mountain climbers, cyclists, and skiers were often here for a week or possibly the whole season, adding an interesting and welcome diversity to the natives and full-time residents. *Like me,* I thought with a smile. A full-timer at last.

I drove slowly through the town, noting with delight the homes sporting a fresh coat of paint and the bustling small businesses that I loved to frequent. I passed by the White Mountain Café, which boasted they served the best cup of coffee in the region. It was a close second to Hilma's rich brew in my mind, but their cherry pie was outstanding. Murphy's Hardware was next door—a place where my handyman could spend hours checking out the odds and ends and visiting with the proprietor, Danny Murphy. Ford's Pharmacy now sold gasoline, I noted, which would make filling up quick and convenient. Then I saw the price: twenty-two cents a gallon. *Outrageous.* I was certain that I could save money by making the short trek to North Conway, but perhaps in a pinch . . .

I drove out of the town center and turned left onto Thorn Hill Road. I was almost home. The five acres of land on which Brookmead rested gave the place a grand feel and additional privacy. I felt I had the best of both worlds, a quiet and nurturing home conveniently near to the town center. I turned right onto my property and followed the well-worn path to the house. And there it was, in all of its glory, the late afternoon sun causing it to glow, seemingly from within. I pulled on the emergency brake and sat there for a moment, wanting to take it all in. A sweeping gambrel roof and wide, generous verandas on two sides. Black shutters stood out against the whitewashed exterior and, while quite ordinary by comparison to some of the grander homes owned by friends and acquaintances, to me it was nothing short of sheer perfection.

I released the brake and continued along the driveway, driving to the side of the house and stopping in front of the stairs leading into the keeping room. As I set the brake again and flipped the magneto switch, my faithful groundskeeper, handyman, and friend Arba ambled over from behind the house.

Years earlier, I had offered the couple the opportunity to own the home when I died. They had gladly accepted, and I had begun to put in reserve a small portion of their wages each week in order to make that happen. They were certainly quite grateful for the house, but no matter how many times I offered whatever vehicle I owned to Arba to drive, he refused. Hilma confided that he didn't cotton to "those newfangled motorized ve-hickles" and believed that his horse-drawn buggy, in all of its ancient and honorable glory, was a much better way to get from point A to point B. Despite her husband's misgivings, I knew Hilma treasured the drives we took together as much as I did. After a couple of days to rest up after my journey, she and I would head off on another road trip, ideally armed with the delicious sandwiches that Hilma always packed, along with a couple slices of her famous Swedish crumb cake, apples, or some other fruit we were unlikely to eat, and a flask of coffee, hot and strong. My mouth was already watering.

Arba was a tall man with a gruff manner, given to lengthy diatribes about the current state of the union. Despite Hilma's claims that he was a real softie at heart, I found him to be mostly grumpy and stubborn, and I loved him dearly anyway. As I stepped down from the running board, he doffed his hat briefly. That would be the extent of my greeting, of that I was certain.

"How's she runnin'?" he asked.

"Well, I'm doing fairly well here, thank you for asking. And how are you on this fine day?" I responded gaily.

"She give you any trouble?" he persisted. I studied him closely, believing with all of my heart that he wanted me to let loose with a litany of complaints about the car and life in general. Well, I could toss him a bone, I decided charitably, so I told him how I had overheated that morning between Boston and Lawrence, Massachusetts. He nodded his understanding. "These durn ve-hickles are unreliable as . . ." He had a few choice comments to make about the times we lived in and how we were likely well on our way to going to "hell in a handbasket," as he liked to say, but I was in a wonderful mood and didn't want to listen. Not today. I smiled and turned as I made my way toward the house. Just as I reached the third step leading up to the porch, he called out. "What happened to your spare tire, Miss? Are you telling me you drove this entire way without so much as a single spare tire?"

Whoops. "Can you take care of that for me, Ar?" I asked sweetly, and he responded by grumbling, which I took as his assent. He emptied the car of all of my belongings and headed toward the house, arms full. "Oh, and one more thing? I recall asking you to fix this step last spring. Do you remember? The third one from the bottom. I said it was loose. Can you please take a look?" Again, I received a barely decipherable response. *Grumpy old cuss*, I thought just as Hilma burst through the door. Her round face glowed with pleasure as she pulled me in for a hug. She was as short and stout as her husband was long and lean, and she smelled of cinnamon and apples. I settled into her embrace and breathed in deeply. *What a delight!*

"You made it. And all in one piece, I see," she said. "And you just missed it. Miss Lucy had her litter this morning. Seven of the tiniest little mites you have ever seen. Would you like to meet them before or after I fix you a snack?"

"Let's go now," I said.

"Wait until you see the little darlings," she replied and followed me back outside, across the driveway, and into the barn. There in the corner in a large box lined with towels, I found Miss Lucy, my orange tabby, surrounded by seven little balls of fluff in a variety of hues. Little darlings indeed.

Hilma beamed with pride as we watched the kittens jockeying for position around their mother. "Any ideas for names?" she asked me. "You always come up with the best ones."

"The two little orange ones, let's call them Addie and Penny," I said recalling the two red-haired girls I had met on my trip. "As far as the others, let me give it some thought," I replied to buy myself some time. Names and faces were swirling about in my head. Kate, Hannah, Babs, Elizabeth, Louis, Billy, Andy, Brian . . . so many possibilities. I patted Miss Lucy gently on the head before briefly chucking her chin. "Well done, Missy," I told her. "Well done."

CHAPTER 36

"You look like you could use a pick-me-up. Let's get you settled with a cup of tea and some fresh baked coffee cake and you can tell me everything," said Hilma as we walked back to the house.

"Make it coffee instead, and you've got yourself a deal. Will your curmudgeon of a husband be joining us?"

Hilma winked at me and shook her head. "Let's let him check out your durn ve-hickle for any scrapes and dents first. He's been so worried about you, you know." I chuckled at the idea of the quiet, stoic farmer losing any sleep worrying about me.

"He's annoyed with me because I got a flat and forgot to buy a spare tire along the way," I reported, shaking my head. I had clearly added more fuel to the fire that was Arba's general discontent.

"Oh, he'll get over it; you know him," Hilma said with a smile. *Yes, indeed, he would.*

While I freshened up, Hilma brewed a pot of coffee and filled a tray with squares of coffee cake, cups, forks, and napkins. I settled myself in my favorite settee in the parlor and loosened my boots. *What a relief.* I vowed to spend the bulk of my time in stockinged feet for the foreseeable future. Hilma came bustling in, and despite my protests that I could serve myself, she poured me a cup and handed me a plate of cake. *Delightful.*

"Any other issues along the way on your joy ride? Any mishaps or delays?" Hilma asked before splashing a dollop of cream in her own cup. "Was it boring out there on your own?"

I smiled at that. *Boring?* No, not one bit. And honestly, this past week I had generally never felt less alone.

I thought of dear Edward and how I needed to call him and, assuming it was still on the table, turn down his proposal. I recalled my conversation with Billy Sullivan at his gas station and hoped that time would help to dissipate the fog of grief in which he had surrounded himself. I longed for my old friend Priscilla to be content in her lovely home with her prickly husband and that they would grow old together.

I reflected on the advice I had bestowed on young Hannah regarding her marriage and hoped I had not been too blunt with her. After all, who was I, a spinster nearing eighty, offering advice on marriage and motherhood? But I had felt it was sound at the time, and I was, if nothing else, a practical woman with good common sense, despite a couple of less than stellar decisions along the way. I trusted that Mary Olmsted had made it safely to her home in Deer Isle, Maine, and that she remained sprightly and clever for a good long time.

I would continue to pray for the Kellihers and their standing in the close-knit community on the hill. I needed to set up a system to send regular payments to the doctor and vowed to contact my bank in the morning. I hoped that Penny's wish to vote and receive rights equal to her male counterparts would come to fruition and soon. Perhaps I would still be alive to see that happen. *That* would be something to celebrate.

I smiled, thinking of the ambitious Mr. Mayer and his goal of becoming a kingpin in the entertainment industry and of dear Kate and her dreams of travel. I pictured her sweet face glowing with delight as she opened the boxes of books that would soon be winding their way to her. And of Brian Connor's academic pursuits and his goal of owning a car like mine. I hoped he wouldn't settle for a mere automobile in his quest for success.

My heart was full as I recalled just how wonderful it had been to spend a long overdue night with Stephen, and I knew I would see him at my holiday table even if I had to drag him here myself. I wondered if my neighbor Jed Stickley would want to join us. He was a lovely man, a lifelong bachelor. He and I were close friends, but there had never been any sort of romantic spark between us. Maybe?

"Boring?" I responded with a chuckle. "No, my friend, it was actually anything but. In fact . . ." I paused as the telephone started to ring.

"That will be your sister. It's the third time she's called today," Hilma said, a note of disapproval in her voice. "Let me get it." She stood and picked up the phone receiver. "Hello, Wormeley residence, this is Hilma speaking. Yes, yes, Mrs. Curtis. Your sister has arrived. Safe and sound, I might add. There's nothing to . . . Well, surely you will give her the opportunity to hang up her coat for goodness . . . Well, let me check." Hilma covered the earpiece with her hand and asked me in a loud stage whisper, "Can you talk to your sister, Miss Kate?"

I nodded and crossed the room to where she stood and motioned for her to hand me the phone. "Thank you, Hilma. That will be all," I said with a wink. I watched as she nodded and headed toward the kitchen. I cleared my throat and spoke into the phone.

"I'm home, my dear. As I told you, there was nothing to be concerned about," I announced gaily.

My sister gave an audible sigh of relief. "That is good to hear. I've been worried all day. I'm sorry about how Daniel and I responded to your news. The proposal, I mean. It was rude and thoughtless. We never should have . . . Katie, are you still there? Are you listening to a word I've said?" I was looking around and taking in the delightful scent of fresh flowers, lemon wood polish, and freshly mowed grass. I was home, home at last.

"Yes, A, I'm here. And thank you for saying that. It just hurt my feelings to think that my getting married was a big joke to the two of you."

"What are you saying? Are you seriously considering marrying Edward?"

I laughed at that. "No, dear, never gave it a second thought, and nor should you. It's been a long week, and right now I'm looking forward to some of Hilma's cake and a cup of hot coffee. So if you'll excuse me . . ."

"I understand, of course. But I just want to know . . . how was it? How was your road trip?"

I smiled, leaning back against the settee, recalling the sights and sounds, the cities and towns, the mountains and the long stretches of dusty road, the lives of the people I'd met, old friends and new, those who had departed and those who remained. My trip?

"Oh, Ariana," I replied. "It was remarkable."

THE END

AUTHOR'S NOTES

Katharine's Remarkable Road Trip is a work of fiction. Although I have attempted to be historically accurate, and I conducted a great deal of research into the life of Katharine Prescott Wormeley (KPW), her road trip is something I created as a way to explore and reveal her character and many accomplishments. I was first introduced to her when doing research for *Landscape of a Marriage*. I regularly came across references to this woman—a scholar, translator, author, volunteer nurse, hospital administrator, philanthropist, vocational school founder, and trusted friend and advisor to Frederick Law Olmsted (FLO), and I wanted to know more. When I read that she had owned homes in Newport, Rhode Island, and Jackson, New Hampshire, both relatively near to my home in Massachusetts, my first thought was . . . road trip!!!

I traveled to her former home in Newport, and although it is not open to the public, the house at 2 Red Cross Avenue is on the National Register of Historic Places. It is an elegant home with crisp white trim and eight bedrooms. A visit to New Hampshire revealed that there is a lovely country inn where her beloved Brookmead once stood. Both locales are stunning!

The more I learned about KPW, the more I knew I wanted her to be the focus of my next novel. Building a timeline of her life was relatively straightforward as there is an abundance of information written about her family, background, and accomplishments. But coming to a true understanding of the woman herself proved to be more of a challenge.

On her volunteer work as a nurse on a hospital ship during the Civil War, here is what Katharine had to say:

We all know in our hearts that it is thorough enjoyment to be here. It is life, in short, and we wouldn't be anywhere else for anything in the world.

They say that a lady must put aside all delicacy and refinement for this work. Nothing could be more false. It is not too much to say that delicacy and refinement and the fact of being a gentlewoman could never tell more than they do here.

The moment the pressure is off, we all turn to be as funny as we can. I am astonished at the cheerful devotion of the surgeon and the medical students. They toil all day at the severest work . . . then turn in whenever a mattress is handy . . . and come out of it full of fun—in which we all join until the next work comes, and we are fresh to work in cheerful concert together.

Clearly dedicated to her volunteer efforts during the Civil War, KPW has been described as "lively, fashionable, and full of fun" and conversely as "high-minded, homely, and humorless." Other accounts refer to her as energetic, persuasive, manipulative, and articulate. Was she an intellectual with a touch of daring or, according to her friend Georgy, a "fascinating wreck"? Based upon the letters she wrote to her family and close friends, I would say all of the above! There is no doubt in my mind that she was a complicated woman, a free-thinking pioneer, a devoted daughter, and a generous friend.

Hers was indeed "a life well lived."

What drove Katharine to accomplish all that she did was her firmly held belief in the importance of helping others, as well as a yearning for the freedom to live her life as she saw fit. Considering the constraints that society placed upon women during her lifetime, I am certain that she viewed spending time on a hospital ship during wartime as exciting and possibly even romantic. The opportunity to function with authority in positions generally held by men, combined with an absence of societal restrictions and demands would have been very enticing to her. After the war, she continued in her philanthropic endeavors, and when an opportunity presented itself to translate the work of the French writers she adored, I believe it was an ideal way for her to stay connected to the outside world while retreating into the quiet life of an academic.

But the most puzzling aspect of all was her relationship with FLO. Clearly, theirs was a long, close, and complex friendship. FLO admired her "excellent and cultivated mind" and agreed with her claim to be "one of the only ones who rightly understood and appreciated him." He referred to her as his "fetching friend," and described her as high-strung and of the highest breeding. For her part, she clearly revered him, possibly even to the point of worship, and characterized their relationship as both "ardent and confidential." She has said of FLO, "Every day I have understood and valued and trusted him more and more. There is perfect accord between us. We worked together under the deepest feelings." It is unclear whether theirs was a platonic intimacy or something more. Although I created the character of Stephen Harrison as the love of her life, she referred to FLO as "one of the two men I had loved best in life outside my own family." Who was the other man? I have not been able to find an answer to that question.

On the subject of fictional characters, I took liberties with creating friends, neighbors, and associates as well as those she met during her time on the road. As far as the historical figures that I refer to, here is what I know to be true: She did spend time with William Makepeace Thackeray in Paris, but I do not know the extent of their relationship. Louis B. Mayer did open his first theater in Haverhill, Masachusetts, before becoming the founder of MGM, Metro-Goldwyn-Mayer, but there is no evidence that he and Kate ever crossed paths. References made to her acquaintance with Mark Twain/Samuel Clemens, Georgeanna Woolsey, Clara Barton, Louisa May Alcott, and Stanford White are historically accurate, to the best of my knowledge.

Kate spent her final years living in her beloved Brookmead. After her death in the late summer of 1908, Arba and Hilma Pittman took ownership of the home and ran it as an inn for many years.

I hope you enjoyed learning about Katharine and joining her on her remarkable road trip!

GWO

REFERENCES

Library of Congress Research Guides: Civil War Men & Women (2018)

Notable American Women, A Biographical Dictionary: 1607-1950; Harvard University Press (1971)

The Encyclopedia Americana (1920)

A GREAT BIG THANK YOU TO:

My family and friends for their support and unconditional love. I recently came across an addendum to Emerson's claim that "It's not the destination, it's the journey," and it goes like this: "It's not the journey, it's the companions." I could not agree more. Time spent with each of you is an adventure for which I will be forever grateful.

My early readers: **Kerry Chaput, Barbara Wurtzel,** and **Jeanie Roberts** for their valuable insights and feedback, and my editor, the fabulous **Jenny 'Q' Quinlan** for her skills and expertise.

Rhode Island author and educator **Fred Zilian,** the **Newport, Rhode Island Historical Society,** and **Warren & Leslie Schomaker** from the **Jackson, New Hampshire Historical Society** for the encouragement, resources, and support they provided.

My friend **Susan Smith Briody,** for her talents in researching and creating the vision for the lovely book cover of which I am so proud.

Reagan Rothe and the **Black Rose Writing** crew and my fellow authors for their inspiration, support, and friendship. I won't say, "It takes a village," but I guess I just did.

Thanks for everything!
GWO

ABOUT THE AUTHOR

Gail Ward Olmsted was a marketing executive and a college professor before she began writing fiction on a full-time basis. A trip to Sedona, AZ inspired her first novel *Jeep Tour*. Three more novels followed before she began *Landscape of a Marriage*, a biographical work of fiction featuring landscape architect Frederick Law Olmsted, a distant cousin of her husband's, and his wife Mary. After penning a pair of contemporary novels featuring a disgraced attorney seeking a career comeback (**Miranda Writes, Miranda Nights**) she is back to writing historical fiction featuring an incredible woman with an amazing story.

For more information, please visit her on Facebook and at
gwolmstedauthor.carrd.co

OTHER TITLES BY
GAIL WARD OLMSTED

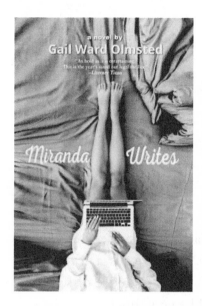

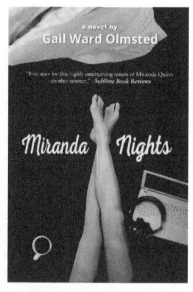

NOTE FROM GAIL WARD OLMSTED

Word-of-mouth is crucial for any author to succeed. If you enjoyed *Katharine's Remarkable Road Trip*, please leave a review online— anywhere you are able. Even if it's just a sentence or two. It would make all the difference and would be very much appreciated.

Thank you,
Gail O

We hope you enjoyed reading this title from:

BLACK❀ROSE
writing™

www.blackrosewriting.com

Subscribe to our mailing list – *The Rosevine* – and receive **FREE** books, daily deals, and stay current with news about upcoming releases and our hottest authors.
Scan the QR code below to sign up.

Already a subscriber? Please accept a sincere thank you for being a fan of Black Rose Writing authors.

View other Black Rose Writing titles at
www.blackrosewriting.com/books and use promo code
PRINT to receive a **20% discount** when purchasing.

Made in the USA
Middletown, DE
03 August 2024

58437889R00138